Jackson Loring

Book One

WWII Homefront Series

Nancy Dane

Jackson Loring

Book One

WWII Homefront Series

by
Nancy Dane

NDB PUBLISHING
Russellville, Arkansas

Books by Nancy Dane

Tattered Glory

Where the Road Begins

A Difference of Opinion

A Long Way to Go

An Enduring Union

A Reasonable Doubt

Jackson Loring

Books for Children

Sarah Campbell,
Tale of a Civil War Orphan

William's Story

A Boy Named David

To the memory of

Ruth Higgins

A Brave and Determined Woman

Acknowledgments

On a wintery night many years ago, our good friend Ken Higgins stopped by our mountain home to go coon hunting with my husband. While they sat near the woodstove waiting for dark, Ken began telling stories of his childhood.

Although at that time I'd never had a book published, the heart of a writer beat in my chest, and it soon became apparent that the heart of a storyteller beat in his. I quickly grabbed a tablet and began scribbling notes. And so this story was born. Most of this book is fiction, merely based on an idea I gleaned from Ken's real life.

For my readers who hate spoilers, I've inserted the real story on the next page. Don't read it until you finish the book.

Thank you, Ken, for sharing the tale and for giving me the idea for such a great story. I am delighted to finally be sharing it with everyone. A huge disclaimer: *Ken's family was not in the moonshine business!*

A big thank you to artist Callie Self for the fabulous cover. I also want to thank my grandson Matthew Garrett for posing for the cover art. I see a lot of Matthew in Jackson or vice versa. ☺

The Real Story

As stated in the acknowledgements, most of this story is fiction, merely based on an idea I gleaned from Ken Higgins's real story. Ken's daddy, Bud, did go off to fight in WWII, leaving behind a large family. While Bud was gone, Ken's mother, Ruth, refused to cash a single army allotment check. Ruth, like my Janie, slaved to keep her big family fed and clothed, denying herself the easy way out, determined to use the army pay to lift them out of poverty. And she did. When Bud returned, she had saved enough to buy a farm, a tractor, and even a pickup truck. This woman was truly a heroine.

Chapter 1

"Daddy's leaving!" I whispered. The dreadful thought knotted my stomach. Last night he'd said I was the man of the house now, but at fourteen, I didn't feel much like a man. I gave up trying to sleep, turned over, and groped in my thoughts for a way to change Daddy's mind. It was useless. Mama had already tried.

As night died a whippoorwill sitting in the yard gave one last mournful call and flew away. I stared out the window as the far black ridges lightened with morning and sun crested the hill to send golden shafts into the bedroom. But this day held no brightness for me.

I threw back the sheet and slipped from the lumpy cotton mattress, trying not to wake Sammy, my younger brother, whose sprawling arms and legs now pirated much more than his half of the bed. Climbing into overalls, I hooked the galluses, and on bare feet tiptoed across the rough board floor into the empty kitchen where the smell of fried meat and baked bread lingered. My breakfast warmed on the wood stove, and Daddy's and Mama's dirty plates sat on the table.

We usually ate together, talking and sharing the early morning. I hated missing this last time together. In spite of the lump in my throat, I choked down a little of the side-meat, biscuits, and gravy.

Sammy, scratching and yawning, came into the room.

"What's for breakfast? I'm hungry," he said.

"Same as always," I said and pushed back my plate, grabbed the milk bucket, and headed for the barn. Although the fire-red sun had just risen, heat had already wrapped around the morning like one of Mama's heavy quilts. There wasn't a speck of dew in the dead grass bordering the path. I wondered if this drought would ever end.

Just over the garden fence a brown rabbit watched me with scared eyes before bolting from the pea patch, its puffed tail zigzagging past the wilted vines as it hunted and finally found a scoot-under where the woven wire had come loose from a locust post. It disappeared quickly into the pasture beyond. I looked around for the cur, but he was nowhere to be seen. On a hot morning like this, he was probably lazing somewhere in the shade. I made a mental note to fix the fence. From now on such things would be my responsibility.

Bossy, the red-mottled Guernsey, waited in the lot at the log barn and greeted me with an impatient moo. I dipped feed from a large barrel inside the feed stall and then opened the gate. The cow almost trampled my bare feet while trying to get at the grain in her feedbox. Feed was scarce, so I had poured in just enough to keep her still while I milked. When she pushed her head into the stanchion, I pushed a notched board that latched her in place. Then I sat down on the three-legged stool and brushed off her udder. Soon streams of milk drummed a tattoo against the bottom of the pail. As the bucket filled, the rhythm became a gentle swish, swish, swish. The sound fetched a long-tailed, gray mama cat from the dusky interior of the barn. She sat down nearby, grooming herself with a pink tongue and waiting for some of the warm, foamy milk. I stopped milking for a minute and rubbed her furry head right between the slanting gray-green eyes. Then I rubbed my own eyes, fighting the salty sting of tears. In spite of being pressed tightly together, my lips began to quiver. I was fourteen. Men did not cry; nonetheless, a trail of tears wet my face and dripped onto my overall bib.

Bossy began moving her feet and quivering the skin on her back where the flies pestered. She raised a hoof and almost upset the bucket. I was actually glad for the diversion. Just in time, I jerked it away. She was prone to kick, but in my distress this morning, I had forgotten to use the kickers, a contraption made of chains that held a cow's back feet together. They hung nearby on the wall, so I rose to get them, fastened them around her hocks, and began milking again.

My mind was as unsettled as the froth now nearing the top of the bucket. I tried to imagine life without Daddy, life without his quiet, steady presence. I wondered how Mama could ever manage without him...how could any of us? The cow caught me off guard with the bushy end of her burr-filled tail. While I rubbed smarting eyes, she arched her back and raised her tail, getting ready to pee. I fell backwards trying to save the milk, this time with little success. Milk flew everywhere.

I eyed the cow vengefully and then I eyed the pitchfork. Daddy had said not to fork her because she was just being a cow. I knew better. She was a demon from the pits of hell intent on making my life miserable. I let her be, but the look in my eyes warned that she had better watch out when Daddy was gone. When Daddy was gone...the thought made my eyes smart and my lips quiver again. I could barely see the path back to the house.

I went in the back door and set the not-so-full bucket of milk on the bench inside the kitchen. Daddy stood in the front room doorway. He did that a lot lately, stood and stared outside, not saying a word. I couldn't figure out why. There was nothing out there worth seeing. I went to stand beside him.

There was nothing but the dusty road that wound past our house, crossed Little Piney Creek, and then snaked up the hill to Grandpa's—nothing but the sagging barbed wire fence separating the pasture from our yard where the grass was dead now, and off to the right, a tall catalpa tree with drooping leaves.

I had to admit those far-off hills were sort of pretty. I had never been anywhere else, but I'd heard traveling folks say Arkansas was a pretty place. I stared a while. Finally, I looked up into Daddy's long, slender face, into eyes dark brown like my own, and he reached to squeeze my shoulder.

"Daddy, do you have to go?"

He didn't answer right away, but I already knew. Not much else had been discussed around our house lately. He and Mama had argued over it for weeks—although Mama did most of the arguing. Daddy never said much. But each evening after supper, she would start in again. I would grab my beat-up guitar and head for the creek, not coming back until the house was dark and quiet.

In spite of anything Mama said, I knew Daddy would do as he thought best. I was miserable. I couldn't face losing him. He was my best friend. I wanted to tell him—to beg him not to go. But like Daddy, I never talked much about my feelings. Instead, I watched the sun climb higher above the hills.

"I forgot to turn out the chickens." I turned to go, but his hand stopped me.

"Son."

"Yes, sir?"

His face was drawn. "I want you to understand why I'm going." A muscle twitched as his jaw tightened. I had the horrible thought that Daddy might cry.

"There's no easy way to keep evil from the world. Jackson, I was a good soldier."

I had seen his sharpshooter medals. They were put away in a black case in Mama's trunk.

He went on, "It's mighty peaceful lookin' out this screen door. I want to keep it that way."

I nodded. I knew about Hitler trying to gobble up Europe—I knew about Pearl Harbor too.

"Can you understand?"

I hung my head. "Yes, sir, I guess so."

When he put both hands on my shoulders, I felt them tremble. "I wish I didn't have to go, son. But I do."

"Yes, sir, I understand," I said. Really, I didn't, but I wanted to go before the tears I batted back poured down my face. "I'd better let out the chickens."

He patted my back and nodded. My shoulders sagged as I walked toward the back door. I got the egg basket from the bench. Before going outside, I glanced back. Daddy still stood in the doorway, staring outside.

My thoughts on Daddy, I did the chore automatically. I unlatched the chicken house door, propped it open with a rock, gathered the few early eggs from the straw-filled boxes lining one wall of the small shed, then propped open the gate of the chicken wire pen so the hens could return later to lay. As usual, Enoch, a feisty bantam rooster, was the first one out. Other speckled bantams and big white leghorns stopped to scratch inside the pen before following him outside. Enoch had already bolted for the pasture and was gobbling up a fat, brown grasshopper.

I didn't want to miss a second of being with Daddy, yet I lagged going back to the house, dreading the goodbyes. When I stepped through the backdoor, they were arguing again, their voices plain through the closed bedroom door. The lump in my throat got bigger, hearing them go at it. Mama raised her voice.

"Duty! You're leavin' me here with four kids, and you've got the nerve to call it duty! Keith Loring, a man takes care of his own. That's duty! I wish to God you'd never read any of those newspapers and gotten all stirred up about the war. You've done your part!"

"And I can be a bigger help because of it," Daddy shot back. Then his tone softened. "Honey, we've been all through this," he pleaded. "I know it'll be hard, on both of us. But, Janie, it's something I have to do."

"No!" she bit out. "It's something you want to do."

"I've never wanted anything less."

"Keith, you could still get out of it. You could talk to the colonel." Mama began to talk fast. "We could move back to Pine Bluff. Roy says because of the war the cottonseed mill is booming again. If you went back to work there, you could get a critical-worker deferment. This time I just know we could save enough to buy a farm."

For years Mama had dreamed of having a real farm and a big herd of beef cattle. We could barely grow a garden on this little patch of land that belonged to Grandpa.

"No, Janie." It was quiet for a bit. Finally he spoke again, "At least you won't have to worry about money. The army allotment is twice what I've been making working for Roy."

Mama's voice was sharp. "You could make lots more working overtime at the mill."

The door squeaked and Daddy came out, leaving the door open. I had never before seen him slump-shouldered and defeated looking.

Mama stayed put, her back stiff and her jaw stubborn. But her eyes showed hurt. I figured she actually wanted to run to him. When things went wrong, Daddy had a real comforting way of putting his arms around her, telling her that everything would be all right.

In spite of August heat turning our tin-roofed shack into an oven, she shivered and rubbed at gooseflesh peppering her arms. She finally took notice of my baby brother Timmy tugging on her skirt. Mama set him on her hip, drew a deep breath, and quickly plopped him onto the bed and grabbed a dry diaper.

Timmy lay plucking at tiny specks floating in the sunlight streaming through the cracked bedroom window. When he tried to roll over, she swatted him. After that he lay still, sucking his thumb and pulling at loose thread on the faded quilt.

"How am I supposed to keep you dry—wash, sew, cook for all of us—and do a man's work too?" Mama muttered around the pins. When Timmy, solemn eyed, stared back, her tone softened.

"Timmy, honey, it's not your fault." Smoothing back his fair curls, she kissed him, hugging him tightly to her chest. "Nobody's fault but your daddy's!" She spoke loud, wanting Daddy to hear. She gazed into the other room at his tall frame and her eyes narrowed. "No one's forcing him to go!"

Daddy leaned against the open front door, tugging at a khaki collar and staring out through a shimmer of heat. He spoke without turning. "Man works like a dog for seventeen years, and what's to show, a measly patch of ground I don't even own."

Swallowing back tears, I bolted outside. But I hunkered on the back steps to peek back inside.

Mama approached and he faced her. "At least try to see my side. Sure, I could have waited, maybe had a few more months here, but sooner or later they'd have called me back." He searched for words as his fingers dropped to trace the two stripes proclaiming him a corporal in the US Army.

"This war's no cakewalk. I lie awake nights sweatin' over what if we lose. I have to do my part to make sure we don't."

"But you're thirty-four years old; there's younger men—" she began.

"Yeah, and not nearly enough. Paper said a month ago most of the 1-As have already been drafted."

"Sometimes," she faltered, looking past him out the door, "sometimes a man is runnin' from, not going to."

Wide-eyed, he grabbed her shoulders, giving her a little shake. Hurt colored his voice. "Get that fool notion out of your head! I never wanted to be any place but here with you and the children."

She pulled away. "Getting yourself killed isn't going to make a heap of difference in who wins the war, but what about me strugglin' to raise these kids alone?" Her chin quivered and she turned away. Then, white-faced, she quickly turned back.

"And what about her!" she asked, pointing outside.

I looked through the back door screen, straight through the house, and out the front to see my older sister, Rita May, wearing a bright red flowered dress. There was a goldenrod flower tucked behind her ear. She was twirling across the yard, dancing with an invisible partner.

"You know she's ripe for trouble," pleaded Mama. "If you're here you can talk sense to her, tell her to keep away from that no-account Lucas boy."

"At her age, talkin' won't do any good," vowed Daddy. "Don't fret. Rita May's smart. She'll be fine."

"Don't be surprised if we all go to blazes!" snapped Mama. "A family needs a man around!"

"They're good kids. And you'll manage fine, Janie. You're that kind of woman."

When Mama shot him a hard look, he sucked in a deep breath and dropped his head. In the stillness the pendulum clock on the mantle struck seven times. As the last chime died, Daddy gently took her arm. "Please, let's not part like this!"

My fists clenched as I willed her to give over. Clearly she was torn, but Rita May called from the yard.

"Time to go, Daddy?"

Daddy stared at Mama, waiting. Each tick of the clock was a hammer to my heart.

Mama turned her back.

Daddy frowned. "Yeah," he answered. "It's time. Get your brothers."

Rita rounded the house and spied me on the back steps.

"Jackson, go get Sammy. Hurry. Daddy's leaving."

I didn't like being bossed by her, but I wanted away—away from the house, away from Daddy's hurt eyes, and away from Mama—so I bolted across the yard and headed for the creek. I figured that was where Sammy would be since he spent every spare minute playing in the water. When I got to the end of the ridge, I yelled, hearing my words trumpet across the creek and echo, shrill and tinny, down the hollow. When he didn't answer, I headed on.

Going about a hundred yards, I rounded a bend to find him kneeling on a slab of cracked, dried mud beside one of the last holes of water that remained in the creek. He cocked his head, tossing back a fall of shaggy, straw-colored hair. Glowering, he rocked back from muddied knees onto bare heels.

"Sammy, you heard me! How come you never answered?"

He stood slowly, swatted a mosquito on his neck, and wiped its remains down a ragged leg of overall. "I made this raft and was just now gonna see if it'd float!" He pointed to a small contraption made of sticks and vines lying at the water's edge where water bugs skated and dragonflies hovered low over the warm water.

I remembered being eight, so I was sympathetic. "You can try it later. Right now we have to go. Daddy's leavin'. If we don't hurry he'll sic Rita May on us." Mud squished between my toes as I turned from the slime-covered pool.

Sammy hid the raft by pushing it under a tangle of honeysuckle. When he looked back to inspect the hiding place, I gave him a shove and he hurried on.

"Come on, Laddie," he spoke to the dog resting, head on paws, on the shady bank and wagging his long tail. I wasn't surprised to see the yellow cur there. He was Sammy's shadow.

Puffs of dust exploded from each step as we ran from the hollow. Stirred by gusts of hot wind, the fine powder stung our eyes and filled our noses before settling on limp sumac growing beside the path. At the top of the ridge, Sammy slowed to hopscotch across stripes of sun slanting through the trees.

"Hurry up!" I barked. "We ain't got time for lollygagging."

He frowned but quickly crawled through the fence while I held the barbed strands apart, and we entered a brown pasture where drought had sucked life from every green blade. Even the usually hardy clumps of foxtail grass lay dry and brittle.

Bossy spied us and lowed hungrily. She craned her neck and reached a long tongue to grab a low-hanging persimmon branch and began to chew. She watched us with doleful eyes as we scurried past.

Sweating and panting, we reached the back porch where Rita May waited in the doorway. She scowled, stopping Sammy with a hand to the shoulder before he could climb the three rickety steps.

"You've been out in the woods again. Most likely down at that stinking creek. You know seed ticks are awful in August. I bet you're covered with them!" She pointed an accusing finger. "There they are crawlin' up your foot! Both of you wait right here till I get a kerosene rag."

We took the rag and rubbed the smelly stuff across ankles and down pant legs, killing the tiny critters before they could burrow into skin.

"Hurry up!" She held open the patched screen door.

I liked my sister fine except for when she tried to boss me. "Hey, bossy!" I spit out, "I'll be glad when you go back to your old waitress job!" I hurried past, barely dodging her swift hand.

Daddy smiled at me. And his eyes softened as he tousled Sammy's hair.

"Howdy, Hop-along."

"Ah, I ain't no cowboy," vowed Sammy.

"No? What are you today?"

"I'm a sailor."

When I snickered, Sammy whirled.

"Hey, smarty-pants! Don't make fun of me! I seen you yesterday down at the creek playing like you was some big music star, bowing to a crowd."

I flushed. Lately I tried hard to act manly. It rankled that Sammy had caught me in a lapse and tattled.

"Son, we've all got dreams. It doesn't hurt to pretend a little. I'll be doing a lot of that soon—pretending I'm back home with all of you." Daddy was trying to make me feel better, but it was the wrong thing to say in front of Mama.

"Pretend!" she exclaimed. "Lucky if you ever come back. Those bombs at Pearl were real enough." When Daddy frowned and shook his head, she hushed and picked up Timmy. He had started crying when she sat him on the floor.

Sammy's eyes clouded. He raised his voice over Timmy's wails. "Daddy, you're gonna be all right, ain't you?"

"Sure," Daddy began but stopped short. He glanced at Mama, then hunkered down and gathered Sammy close. When I came near, he slipped an arm around me too.

"Boys, I don't know what's ahead...." He bent and stared at the floor, his face tense and pale. "One thing I do know—every minute I'm gone, I'll be hoping to get back here as quick as I can."

My brave front crumbled. "You've just gotta come back, Daddy!" Tears spilled down my cheeks as I grabbed him around the neck.

Sammy's voice trembled, "Ain't you just going to Little Rock again?"

"For a bit. But then I'll be going somewhere else for a while."

There was a ball of ice in my stomach growing bigger and bigger. Mama looked as though she had one too. She watched in frozen silence as he laid his hand on my shoulder. I was wishing this were a bad dream. I wanted to waken and find Daddy on his way to the cottonseed mill, not on his way to war.

"Jackson, like I said, while I'm gone you're the man here." He looked me in the eye and there was pity in the gaze. "Every man has battles to fight. You'll have plenty right here. And they won't be easy." He stood, keeping his hand on my shoulder. "Always remember, a wise man fights best with his wits. I've taught you how to think for yourself, and you know right from wrong."

"Yes, sir." I pulled myself tall and rubbed away tears.

"Good. I'm counting on you." He squeezed my shoulder. "Shoulder's almost thick as mine."

I managed a wobbly smile.

He turned to Sammy. "I'm going to ask a big thing of you too. It may go against the grain, but I'm asking you to mind your big brother just like he was me. Of course your mama has the final say on everything."

"Yes, Daddy."

Daddy turned to Rita May. She had taken Timmy from Mama and now held him on one slender, cocked hip. Mama looked on with a frown. Lately, Mama seemed mighty worried about my sister, ever since Rita May had quit school, taken a job at the café in town, and moved into a boardinghouse.

Rita May was seventeen. Folks were always going on about how pretty she was, about her high cheekbones and her sparkly green eyes. She got those from Mama. But Mama's hair was light, almost the color of corn silks. Rita May's reminded me of the golden-brown caramels that I loved but rarely got from Rawlings' store. She was named after one of my grandmas way back yonder, the one who got killed in a flash flood on Piney Creek. Her son Jim was my great—I don't know how many greats back yonder— grandpa. Daddy had told me stories of him and how he sided

Union in the Civil War and then got hanged at Fort Smith for spying. I never got tired of that story.

"Rita May," Daddy spoke. Mama looked hopeful. But she frowned when he merely said, "I expect you to help out all you can."

Rita May agreed, but fidgeting, kept her eyes on the clock. "If we don't hurry, we're going to be late," she said.

Daddy nodded and reached to take Timmy from her hip and held him close. When Timmy withdrew a wet fist crammed into his mouth and grabbed at Daddy's face, Daddy buried his face against the baby's neck.

"Daddy," Rita May urged softly, "I have to be at work in less than an hour. If we don't leave right now, we'll miss our ride. John will leave for Clarksville without us. You'll miss the train and have to hitchhike all the way to Camp Robinson."

Daddy raised his head, and for the first time in my life, I saw tears glisten in his eyes. Inside I froze even more.

After one last tender kiss for Timmy, Daddy handed the baby back to Rita May and reached to hug Sammy and me before turning to Mama. Slowly, he tilted her chin, and without a word, let his fingers trace her high cheekbones and then drop to her lips.

"Oh! Keith," she grabbed the front of his uniform, "please don't go!"

When she swayed toward him with a moan, he gathered her close and pushed a wave of hair from her forehead. He stroked it, then tipped up her tear-streaked face and kissed her.

"I'll come back." Then he spoke low, almost whispering. "You're still the prettiest girl in the world. I love you, Janie, always have, always will."

He stepped back and pulled a flat garrison cap from his belt, put it on, and then grabbed up the duffel bag.

"Let's go, Rita."

She nodded, and after kissing Timmy, set him on the floor.

With one regretful look back, Daddy strode through the door and down the steps. Before passing from sight in the last dusty curve of the road, he paused and looked back at our forlorn little group huddled in the doorway.

I saw his image wavering through my tears as he raised a hand. We waved back. Then he was gone.

Chapter 2

Long after Daddy had vanished, we stood desolate, still, and silent. Sammy sniffed and wiped his nose with the back of his hand while I tried to swallow the huge lump in my throat. Timmy alone was happy. He gurgled, glad to be perched once again on Mama's hip.

Mama groaned. She thrust Timmy to me, turned abruptly, entered the tiny bedroom she had shared with Daddy for the past four years, and shut the door.

"Gosh," said Sammy as he stared owl-eyed at the bedroom door. "Mama sounded just like old Laddie when he got caught in Daddy's coon trap. She must be hurtin' awful."

Totally at a loss, Sammy and I sat down at the kitchen table and stared at each other, while Timmy played happily on the bench beside me. I had never known of Mama going back to bed in the daytime, except for when my brothers were born.

"I wonder if Mama's gonna cry the whole time," I worried, remembering the last few days and her red-rimmed eyes. Mama usually didn't cry. Lately, she didn't smile much either. I could remember when she did, when there were little happy lines around her mouth and her eyes sparkled. That was when we lived in Pine Bluff, before Daddy got laid off at the cottonseed mill.

After that Daddy managed to get some odd jobs, but not enough to keep us going. He said someone forgot to tell Arkansas that the Depression had ended. He wanted to move back to

Johnson County so he could work for Uncle Roy, but Mama refused. She said there was no money to be made working for Roy. She kept hoping the mill would call him back. First she used our savings, the money intended for buying a farm. Then she sold our stuff, little at a time, to buy groceries and pay rent. When there was nothing left to sell, we moved back to Johnson County—back to Little Piney Creek and the tiny house where I was born. Mama hated the clapboard shack propped up on rocks. It was quite a step-down from the nice white house in Pine Bluff with its neat picket fence. But most of all, I think she hated being beholden to Grandpa.

"How long you reckon she's gonna stay in there?" asked Sammy.

I was scared but tried not to show it. "Doesn't matter," I answered as I looked around and felt the weight of responsibility settle. "No need for us to sit here idle when there's work to be done."

"Daddy's gone. Daddy's gone." My thoughts echoed like the ticking clock as I stood and began scraping and stacking the mismatched plates. In spite of being preoccupied, I handled them carefully, for I hated having to use syrup bucket lids for plates as we had done before Daddy recently bought these plates in a box of junk at the auction sale.

"Sammy, throw the scraps out to Laddie," I ordered, doing my best to imitate Daddy's deep voice. "And get right back in here and keep Timmy quiet while I wash the dishes."

"But, Mama always washes the—"

I silenced him with a glare that I hoped was like Daddy's *don't give me any sass* look. Daddy never tolerated sass, and I didn't intend to either. Meekly Sammy took the plate and went outside.

I stood at the kitchen window and watched as he trudged past the hens taking a dust bath. Then he gave a wistful look toward the shady creek, but after a look back at the house, he bent to rake the greasy remains of breakfast into Laddie's chipped dish.

From the corner of my eye came a flash of black and gray, a flurry of feathers. Sammy whirled, but too late. Enoch, the rooster, had flogged him again, sinking sharp spurs deep into the flesh of Sammy's bare back between the overall galluses.

Sammy swore and hurled the plate. In horror, I watched it fly past the bird to shatter against a rock. Sammy balled his fist and shook it at Enoch.

The rooster looked to be gloating as he stood preening beside the outhouse. Enoch never bothered anyone else, but just let Sammy turn his back and the bird was all spurs and six-guns.

"You ornery varmint, I'll get you someday! Just see if I don't!" yelled Sammy. With lagging steps he entered the house with the broken plate, its shattered pieces a crooked pile in his hands.

"It was that ornery Enoch!" he cried. Sammy sneezed and wiped his nose with the back of his hand.

"Mama thought that was the prettiest one," I said. It was the one with yellow roses all twirled around with ivy.

His face fell. I eyed him with disappointment, then took the pieces and threw them into the trash.

"It was old Enoch's fault. He flew right up and knocked it out of my hand." Sammy glanced up to the ceiling, looking sort of scared, like he hoped God was busy elsewhere, and I figured his fingers were crossed behind his back.

I gave a hard stare. "I was watching out the window, Sammy." When he flushed, I added, "Can't be helped now, but be more careful," I scolded. "I have to draw water. You stay here with Timmy. Watch him close. You know how he tries to put everything into his mouth."

I grabbed the pail and went outside, going the few paces to the well. Wiping sweat, I studied the sky and wished for thunderheads. The well was deep, but the spring in the springhouse was getting low. Although the distant hills were hazy, not a puff of cloud softened the brassy sky.

After sliding aside the wooden lid covering the well, I unhooked the chain that attached an old wooden bucket to the pulley. The chain slid through my hands, and as the pulley creaked, the bucket slowly entered the dark hole. Finally it splashed. I lowered it a bit more, making certain it was full, and then with a scowl I pulled fast, hand over hand.

"Dang bucket leaks like a sieve with water a'pourin' back out the bottom," I complained. When I swung the bucket and dumped a gush into the pail, some of the precious water splashed onto the ground.

"Just like I thought!" I muttered, lugging the pail inside. "Only half full. We gotta get a new bucket with that allotment check!"

A heap of gray ash was all that was left of the breakfast fire, so I raked the leavings into the ash-hopper and began building another fire. First I pushed a wadded newspaper into the firebox and then lay kindling of pine shavings on top before adding sticks and striking a match. The tongue of flame flickered, caught, and quickly licked up the paper and the shavings. Soon more heat filled the already stifling room.

Sammy sat Indian-style on the floor and called to Timmy while he dangled the baby's favorite toy, an empty thread-spool attached to a piece of red yarn.

"Come get your car, Timmy. Come on. Come on."

He dragged the spool slowly, and when Timmy reached his dimpled fist, Sammy jerked the spool high and laughed. Timmy puckered and let out a howl.

"Give him the toy, Sammy," I demanded after a glance at the bedroom door. "And keep him quiet, or I'll tend him and make you wash these dishes."

While water heated in the teakettle, I shaved long curls from a bar of lye soap into the metal dishpan. Uncertain of how much Mama used, I decided to add a little more for good measure. It was too much. When I finished washing the plates, the hot water left in the kettle failed to rinse them. It meant another trip to the well.

This time as I drew water, my thoughts were on Daddy. I wondered where he was by now. Probably not even to town, although it seemed to me that he had been gone for hours. How could I already miss him so much?

I finished the dishes and carried the soapy water far behind the house and slung it into the brush. I was tempted to just toss it out the back door like some folks did, but that drew flies, and Mama would skin me alive. She was forever saying, "We might be poor, but we're not trash."

After hanging the dishtowel to dry, I carried the rinse water out the back door to divide between the climbing rosebush on the garden fence and the wilting tomato plants. Mama had tried to save them by making a shade from tow sacks. I especially hoped the rosebush survived. Mama set great store by the showy red flowers, and when they bloomed, although I would admit it to no one, I enjoyed them too.

It didn't take long to sweep the floor. Most of the dirt sifted down through the cracks. The house was small, only four rooms—one main room running the length of the house, two bedrooms on the south, and a little room Daddy had tacked onto the back porch for Rita May. I looked around. Things looked as good as usual, which wasn't too good. Whitewashed walls, rough board floors, and broken down furniture couldn't look too good. I frowned, remembering the other house filled with nice things.

"Hey, Jackson, let's go to the store and spend the nickels Daddy gave us. I'll get a pop. You get some candy and we can share," Sammy suggested.

I glanced at the bedroom door. I had never before gone to the store without permission, but Daddy had left me in charge. I slowly nodded.

"Hot dog!" Sammy jumped up and headed for the door, barely slowing when I reminded him to wash up first. "Oh, I ain't dirty."

I picked up Timmy, and after another look at Mama's door, I followed, lugging him on my hip. In spite of the heat, it felt good to be in the sunshine and away from the lonely house. In no hurry to return, I ambled along, stepping gingerly in the sunny spots, slowing where the shade was cooler on hot, bare feet. A terrapin inched across the road. When I nudged it with my toe, it ducked its head and legs inside its yellow-speckled, green dome. Timmy took his thumb from his mouth long enough to point and laugh. I decided if the terrapin was still around on our way home, I'd get it for him.

Birdsong filled the trees. They must have enjoyed the shade as much as I did. A gray squirrel chattered in the dusty oak above me. I pointed my finger and plugged him right behind the ear. I wondered when Mama would ever trust me with a real gun. Maybe with Daddy gone she would give over, but knowing Mama I doubted it would be anytime soon.

As I neared the store, my steps quickened. Sammy had promised to share, but being left alone too long with a frosty strawberry Nehi could be tempting.

I glanced at the posters in Rawlings' window. Mama didn't need urging to "Can All You Can." She always canned every bite we didn't eat fresh. And she didn't need to be told to save empty pickle and mayonnaise jars for canning. She had been saving glass jars long before the war conservation program.

Laddie lay panting on the porch steps of the gray, weathered store. Sammy was on the porch, with the lid lifted and his head poked inside the large, square icebox full of colas. A loud laugh covered the sound of the bell above the door as I stepped inside and sat Timmy on the floor. Wade Lucas was leaning on the counter talking to Mr. Rawlings' nephew, Rudy Hayes, a skinny teenager who clerked part-time at the store.

"Yeah, Rudy, that Rita May has curves in all the right places. And she ain't a bit shy about showing 'em off—nor them pretty, long legs either."

Rudy hee-hawed again. My fists balled and my face burned. I took a step closer. "Shut your dirty mouth, Wade."

He turned, and his mouth slit into a nasty grin. "Who's gonna make me?"

"How about me?" Mr. Rawlings stepped from behind the curtain covering the storeroom. He stood, legs apart, with his big hands tucked into arms crossed over his chest. "Lucas, you ought to be ashamed, big fellow like you baiting a boy." Mr. Rawlings gave an even harder stare. "And there won't be any more vile talk in my store about a nice little lady like Rita May."

Wade was tall, close to six foot, but he was average in build. Mr. Rawlings was a muscled mountain. Wade shrugged and gave a half-hearted laugh. "Keep your shirt on, Rawlings. I was just funnin' him." He rose lazily and headed for the door. As he passed, he looked at me. "Tell your sister I'll see her Saturday night."

I shot an ugly scowl and silently cussed him with some choice words I had learned from Ben. I clenched my fists tighter and wished Ben were here. Ben wasn't as tall as Wade, nor as big, but he was salty. He would beat Wade to a pulp for saying anything bad about Rita May. Ben was Rita's boyfriend—at least he had been before he joined the Navy. Now he was a boatswain's mate second class.

Mr. Rawlings spoke. "Get on home, Rudy. You're through for the day." The sour look he gave his nephew made me think he disliked him almost as much as I did.

As Rudy flung the screen door open, Mrs. Johnson came in and asked for 3 pounds of flour. While Mr. Rawlings weighed it, I sat on a wooden crate, taking deep breaths and willing my temper to cool. I thought about Wade's bright blue eyes and his coal-black hair and hoped Rita May hadn't thrown Ben over for him. I frowned, wishing Ben wasn't somewhere in the Pacific.

"My, how Timmy is growing." Mrs. Johnson patted his head and then went to poke around in the bolts of cloth stacked on a table against the far wall. She was a tiny woman with a pleasant face tanned brown as an acorn.

"It broke my heart to see your daddy walk past the house today. Zearl told me he was leaving permanent for the Army. Be sure to tell your mama I'll be praying for him, right along with my boys. Prayer is such a comfort, especially in war time."

I had to take her word for it. We Lorings weren't big on religion—although I had heard some of our kin were. And my Grandma Matthers had been. But she had died before I was born.

"How's your mama holding up?" asked Mrs. Johnson.

"Just fine, ma'am." We Lorings weren't much on sharing family business either.

The Johnsons were our nearest neighbors and our distant kin. I wasn't sure just how. Since I had cousins from both sides all over the county, I never could keep it all straight. The Johnsons had five sons, three gone to war. Since Zearl was short-handed with the boys gone, Daddy had worked some for him on the farm this past year. Even Mrs. Johnson had worked in the fields right alongside the men.

Sammy came inside. "Think maybe I should try orange or cola this time?" he asked.

"You know you're gonna pick strawberry. You always do," I answered.

He grinned and went back outside. While Mrs. Johnson chattered away, my gaze drifted past the pigeonhole mailboxes where Mr. Rawlings sorted the mail, past the glass-fronted counter filled with cuff links and hatpins and bold-faced pocket watches. Then it riveted on the wall just beyond. Suspended above the counter was the most beautiful thing I had ever seen. I jumped off the box and went toward it, my mouth hanging open. It was a guitar made of dark red wood, almost black, hanging by a strap on Mr. Rawlings' back wall.

Mr. Rawlings saw me. "Want to try it?"

"Really!" My voice squeaked with excitement. More than anything, I wanted to be a guitar player and be a big star like Roy Acuff on the Opry.

"I don't reckon you'd hurt it." Grinning, he turned and took the guitar from the wall.

Carefully, as if it were made of glass, I cradled the guitar, propping my foot on a chair used by the checker-playing crowd on Saturday nights. I tuned it, then placed my fingers for "C" chord and strummed the strings. Goosebumps covered my body.

"How about a little 'Under the Double Eagle'?"

I smiled sheepishly. "Don't reckon I'm quite up to that. But Ben taught me 'Get Along Home Cindy, Cindy'."

"That'll do."

He cocked his head and listened while I cut loose playing and singing. When I finished, Mrs. Johnson smiled and clapped. Mr. Rawlings looked serious. "Boy, you've got talent. You have a good voice and rhythm. You've got a natural feel for that guitar too. If you keep it up, you'll go places." He pointed to the guitar. "That's a Gibson. It's what the professionals play. I took it in trade for eats, gas, and some cash for a traveling fellow down on his luck. That was right before the war. I kept it in the storeroom until now. Figured he'd come back for it, but he never did. Maybe he got drafted."

"Thirty dollars." I read the price tag aloud, working up nerve to ask if he'd come down any. We would be getting the allotment checks—and Daddy had practically promised me a new guitar for Christmas—but thirty dollars was a powerful lot of money.

"Yeah. That's way too pricey for most folks, but that's what I've got to have. But I could check around and see if there's another used one for sale," offered Mr. Rawlings.

"Thanks, but I already have an old one."

My empty arms ached when he took the Gibson and hung it back on the wall. I chose a Hershey bar and paid for it along with the strawberry Nehi in Sammy's hand. I was surprised when he pulled another nickel from his overall pocket and dropped it into the jar on the counter that held donations for the cigarette drive.

"Where did you get that?" I asked.

"From Uncle Roy. He told me to put it in the jar for him next time I came to the store. He wants to help buy smokes for the soldiers."

"Daddy doesn't smoke," I pointed out.

"No, but there's lots that do. Uncle Roy says there ain't nothing worse than wanting a smoke and not having one."

I wondered if Uncle Roy used to smoke. I had never known of it. But maybe that was why he was forever chewing on a twig.

On our way out the door, Sammy spied something he wanted, a set of toy punch-out airplanes and army tanks. It didn't faze him one bit when I pointed out that they were mighty flimsy being made of super thin wood, and Timmy would tear them up first thing. He pointed out that Timmy could ruin a guitar too. I took the hint and shut up. I reckoned he was entitled to his own dreams.

"Mind what I said about practicing," called Mr. Rawlings. "I'm not just blowing smoke, boy. You have real talent."

Ben had always said the same thing. I thanked Mr. Rawlings and with dragging steps followed Sammy outside. We sat on the bench on the porch and drank the pop and shared the chocolate bar. I drank slowly, saving the last for Sammy. He finished the bottle and went to sit on the steps beside Laddie.

"Wish I could have all the pop and candy I wanted every day," he said while pulling beggar lice and burrs from Laddie's coat. "Don't you?"

I grunted. But pop and candy were not what I wanted. A strawberry soda didn't satisfy the longing for that shiny Gibson guitar.

"Mama might be wondering about us. We better get home," I suggested.

Sammy nodded, but his face showed the same dread I felt. Things at home just weren't the same without Daddy.

———⌒⌒———

At home Mama was waiting in the front room, her face tired and pale.

"You all right?" I asked.

She nodded. "Where ya'll been?"

"Rawlings'."

As her brow crinkled, I hurried to add, "Daddy gave us nickels and..."

"And you couldn't wait to spend them," she muttered. "Where is Sammy?"

"I reckon he's down at the creek. He took off that direction."

She stepped to the doorway, twisting her heavy, long blonde hair into a tight rope and pinning it firmly at her neck. I had heard Daddy say he liked it down and free from hairpins—but Daddy was not here. She gave the last hairpin a push, and since Sammy was nowhere in sight, she stepped outside and called. He came running.

"Sammy, I want you to take care of Timmy while Jackson and I go to see your grandpa."

My eyebrows flew up. We never had much to do with Grandpa. I hadn't been to his house in months. "Why we going to Grandpa's?" I asked.

"I'm going to borrow his mule and dicker with him about a job of work."

Mama work for Grandpa! I was amazed.

I climbed through the barbed wire, and while I lifted the top strand high and put my bare foot on the next one to push it down, Mama followed. When we cut across the pasture bordering the yard, the short, brown grass crunched beneath our feet.

Old Bossy came from a nearby patch of woods and gave a loud moo in protest of a hungry belly. Hoping for a bucket of feed, she came trotting, but Mama ignored her and stalked on toward the woods. There was nothing left for Bossy to browse. The cow had eaten everything within reach.

"Unless it rains soon," Mama spoke, "I'll have to find more pasture for the cow. We can't get along without milk, cream, and butter."

"I'll have to ask Pa for one more favor," she fretted. "I'm sure he'll let Bossy graze in the big pasture down by the creek, but he'll want payment." Her jaw tightened. "More than likely, it'll be more chores than I've bargained on. It can't be helped. That cow is a skeleton."

Mama had a hankering to own good farmland. She often complained that unlike the fertile bottomland not far from here, this rocky ground was poor. Nothing but sage grass grew unless fertilized liberally, and my grandpa, Cole Matthers, was not a man to do anything liberally—except drink.

Bees darted in and out of a half-dozen of Grandpa's beehives that sat in a row near the fence where we climbed through again. I wondered what they were finding to work in the drought. Mama's determined steps slowed as we climbed the last incline leading up to a house much larger than ours, with peeling white paint and surrounded by a junk-filled yard. A rusty piece of screen wire curled back from what little screen remained of the screened-in front porch. It waved back and forth in the hot breeze fanning my face.

"Pa gets sorrier every year. He lives worse than a sharecropper," she said in an undertone, "but he doesn't have to. He'd have plenty if he didn't drink it all up. I guess it's a good thing Mama's dead. Living like this would have killed her anyway."

Grandma Matthers had died before I was born, but I had heard the story many times. Grandpa had been too drunk to fetch a doctor when Grandma took sick. It was her heart. By the time my Uncle Roy had fetched the doctor, it was too late.

The front door creaked open, and Grandpa stepped out to investigate the commotion raised by a pack of razor-thin hounds. He was a short, thick-chested man who would have been handsome except for what Daddy called a dissipated face. Daddy said it was the look of a heavy drinker. Today Grandpa had a stubble of red beard. Thick red hair mixed with gray curled from the rounded neck of a sleeveless undershirt stretched tautly across his barrel chest. When he spied Mama coming up the lane, he kicked one of the dogs from a cane-bottomed chair and took a seat in the middle of the piles of junk on the long, wooden porch.

Frowning, Mama stepped around a discarded set of sagging bedsprings and a white enameled chamber pot turned upside down, exposing a rusty hole in its bottom. At sight of Grandpa, she drew a deep breath and squared her shoulders.

"I'd rather take a beating," she muttered more to herself than to me, "but to make ends meet I have to have Pa's help."

I had no idea what she meant. When the allotment checks started coming, ends would be meeting just fine—better than ever.

Grandpa's old tomcat, Tiger, sidled up and began rubbing against my ankle. Not wanting to miss anything and keeping my eyes on Mama and Grandpa, I lifted a bare foot and rubbed Tiger's back with it.

Grandpa reached down beside the chair, picked up a large red can of Prince Albert tobacco and pried open the lid. With thick, brown-stained fingers, he sprinkled the dried tobacco onto a thin white paper and rolled tight the makings. After licking an edge, he sealed the cigarette, pinched shut one end, and put it in the corner of his mouth. Then he dug into a pants pocket for a match. I admired the way he struck it with his thick thumbnail. Finally, after taking a long drag, he squinted against the smoke, and for the first time looked directly at Mama. She had not climbed the rotting steps. Ignoring me, he looked at her.

"Figured you'd be over."

She gave him a sullen look.

He took another puff, and with narrowed eyes, went on, "Reckon you're figuring on a handout, with Keith runnin' off and leaving you with a house full of young'uns."

Her eyes snapped. "I'm not asking for a handout. I'll work for anything I get from you, always have."

"What'd you have in mind?" His look grew shrewd.

"I'll split the wood Keith cut for you if you'll let my cow graze with yours, and I'll do the washin' and mendin' and any sewing you need done. I'll want cash for that."

Grandpa was known as a shrewd bargainer. While he pondered, she rushed on.

"But I'll trade for any work the boys do. They'll do your milking and muck out the barn—and keep your corn hoed out next summer for the trade of the sugar we need. I know the government allows you extra coupons because of your honeybees. Figured you might have a little sugar to spare in spite of your other business," she stressed sarcastically.

"And," she said, "I'll plow for you come spring for the use of that big scoop shovel and your mule to pull it with."

"What in the world you want the slip scoop for?" Grandpa flipped ashes from the end of the cigarette.

"I'm going to build a cellar in back of the house. Fix it like a dugout so we can sleep without freezing to death this winter like we've done for the last four years. I'm sick to death of stuffing all those cracks with newspapers and the children still almost blowin' out of bed on a windy night."

I gave Mama a surprised look. She had been after Daddy to build a cellar. He had said he would when he got time, but he kept too busy trying to feed and clothe us.

The land was Grandpa's. He could forbid building the cellar. I wondered if he would. He might say no just to spite Mama. They hadn't gotten along for years. Maybe they never had. Mama didn't talk much about her childhood.

Grandpa chuckled.

"You ain't gonna have time to read no newspaper, may as well use it to stuff cracks. But, I'm tellin' you, there ain't no way you or him," he jerked a thumb at me, "can handle that slip. Hit's hard for a full-growed man. You best put that crazy notion out of yer head."

"That's my lookout. I'll manage," vowed Mama.

"Boy," he squinted at me through a cloud of smoke, "I'll expect you early."

"One thing," Mama added, "I don't want him in on any of your shenanigans. Not ever. You understand?"

Grandpa laughed hoarsely. "Why, I was hopin' to pass on my business to the boy someday." He stood, walked down the steps, and slapped my back. "Hit's mighty lucrative."

"Yeah, things sure look prosperous around here," she said while her eyes swept the clutter.

"Hit makes me plenty, and without much sweat on my brow, Miss Smarty! I ain't had to break my back at the sawmill like Keith and Roy do. They should've joined me years ago when I asked them."

She ignored the remark. "I mean it. Jackson's to have nothing to do with it." Her lips thinned. "Nothing!"

At his slight nod, her stance softened. "Can I take the mule and shovel now?"

I waited.

"Hit's a blame fool notion." Grandpa shook his head in disgust. "But since you're determined, I'll go hitch it up. I misdoubt you two can even do that."

Chapter 3

Mama opened the stove door and built a small breakfast fire while I sat rubbing sleep from my eyes and blinking at the light of the kerosene lamp.

"I'll make a pot of oatmeal for now. If you boys want something more, you can fry side-meat later," she spoke to me as I slipped into my overalls.

She had traded her own work dress for Daddy's old brown trousers and rolled them up at the bottom. They worked fine cinched at the waist with her belt. Before heading out the door, she roused Sammy. He would have to stay home and tend the baby.

If all went well, she intended to be digging by first light. I had paid close attention when unhitching and hoped the harness would go back together easily. I had promised to be at Grandpa's early.

The coming sunrise barely lit the path leading to the tin-roofed log shed that served as barn and storage building. To make certain there was no possum or coon hiding in the feed barrel, I struck a match before dipping up grain. I tried using my thumbnail like Grandpa, but it didn't work so I gave up and struck it on the side of the barrel. The raw-boned gray mule that Grandpa called Big Dan came trotting along with Bossy to the sound of grain shaking in the bucket. There was no grass left in the small lot where we kept them penned at night.

Hitching up went well, for I had watched Grandpa closely. The sun was just rising as we left the lot. Mama paused beside me to watch the land wake. Silent and still before us, in shades of gray, it looked like one of the colorless tintypes in Grandma's old picture album. A rooster's piercing crow ended the quietness. Deep shadows quickly disappeared from the hills, chased away by the top curve of a blood-red ball. Such a sun meant a scorching day. I dreaded the heat.

After milking, I unlatched the chickens. Tending the chickens was supposed to be Sammy's chore, but any time he came near them, he sneezed his head off, so we had swapped chores. Now he gathered the kindling and carried in the firewood.

I took the eggs and milk and headed for the house. When I passed Mama, she was hanging onto the handles of the scoop and struggling to turn Big Dan. Big Dan blew and shook his head, protesting the bit.

"You may not like it, old fellow, but there's work to be done." Mama slapped his rump, and as he started forward, she pushed down on handles attached to the two-foot wide shovel. The scoop raised just enough to slide over the rocky ground as she guided the mule back up the steep incline about thirty yards west of the house.

She urged him to the top and, at the right spot on the bank, raised up the shovel handles to tip the scoop down and make it bite into the dirt. Instead, the scoop bounced off the hard earth and jerked the handles from her hand. She yelled, "Whoa."

"Mama, let me try."

Although Daddy had been gone several days, she seemed in no better mood.

"Your daddy ought to be doing this, instead of running off to who knows where." She ignored my jutted jaw and went on, "Take the milk to the house and strain it, then feed the shoats. You have to get on to Grandpa's. Maybe you can help later."

I hung around to watch awhile longer. This time she held tighter and, although it barely reached the roots, a shallow slice of dirt and grass tufts slipped across the lip of the shovel.

I strained the milk and put it into the springhouse, fed the hogs, then stopped to watch Mama.

"How's it going?" I called.

"At this rate I might get a cellar built by next fall," she answered, and then spoke to the mule, "Get-up, Dan!"

She guided him down the bank and a few rods away before tipping the scoop and dumping the dirt, and then making a wide circle, she stopped for a breather. "This awkward contraption is hard to handle!" After one glance toward the house, she squared her shoulders, and after urging me on to Grandpa's, she started again.

I looked back once before passing from sight to see her hard at work again. Mama was strong, exceptionally so for a woman of her size. I reckoned she'd make out all right handling the scoop and Big Dan.

No one answered my knock at Grandpa's back door, so I stepped inside, glanced around, and shuddered. The bucket and empty milk jar looked clean, but they were the only clean things in the cluttered kitchen. And after stepping inside Grandpa's barn, I knew how I would be spending my morning—it didn't appear to have been mucked out in ages. I looked at my bare feet and decided not to use the stanchion. I'd snub the little Guernsey to a post outside to milk her. Pricilla never kicked, and her soft-brown eyes were gentle, unlike our Bossy's that flamed with the devil's own fire.

The tomcat showed up meowing for a taste, so I squirted some warm milk into his mouth. He sat licking his whiskers and begging for more. Returning to the house, I filled a cracked dish full for him and strained the rest of the foamy, warm milk through a square of cheesecloth and into a gallon jar. Small bits of cow hair and a couple of gnats filtered out. I was rinsing out the strainer when Grandpa came through the bedroom doorway and into the kitchen. His red hair was standing straight up on one side and plastered to his head on the other. He stretched and yawned.

"Got any coffee made, boy?"

"No, sir, but the cow's already milked."

He grunted and reached for the blackened pot on the stove. Without making a fire to warm it, he poured it into an unwashed cup on the counter.

"Grandpa, you got a pair of boots I could wear to muck out the barn?" He gave me a sour look when I added, "It sure is a mess in there."

He pointed to a pair of overshoes squatted in the corner. They were ten miles too big, but I didn't want to go all the way home. Besides that, I had only one pair of boots, and I didn't relish messing them up with all that muck.

"Thanks." I grabbed them and headed for the door.

"Hey, boy!"

I looked back, waiting.

Grandpa took a sip of cold coffee, then frowned and nodded toward the jar of milk. "Ain't you forgetting something?"

I got it and headed out the door, grateful to be outside again, even though the morning was already hot. As I put the milk in the springhouse, I thought it small wonder Mama never talked about her childhood. Of course, I supposed things had been different when Grandma was alive. Mama said she had been neat as a pin, hard-working, and thrifty. I stopped and looked back at the house. I wondered if Grandpa missed Grandma and her neat ways, or if he liked things fine just as they were.

It took three hours of hard shoveling and hauling in a wheelbarrow, but finally the manure was spread on the garden plot. I was replacing the shovel inside the tool shed when I spied a big radio battery on a dusty shelf. My heart began beating fast. Uncle Roy had given me an old radio and all the stuff to hook it up; however, the battery was ruined and he had already thrown it away. I had been dying to get one. Daddy had promised a new one when there was any extra money. Even with the allotment check, I figured that might still be a while. We had been living hand-to-mouth, and there were too many necessities to buy first.

I pulled off the boots and slowly headed for the house, trying to come up with the best way to approach Grandpa. I had not been around him much since we moved back, but I remembered how unpredictable he was. At times he was sunny and full of fun. In an instant, for no apparent reason, he would turn cold as winter and hard as ice. Finally I decided the worst he would do was say no.

When I returned at midmorning, Mama stopped. She must have known something unusual had happened when she spied me cutting across the pasture, and in spite of the scorching sun, breaking into a run while lugging something in my arms. I yelled excitedly, bounding across the brown grass.

"Look what I got! See what Grandpa gave me." In my hurry to slip through the fence, my overalls caught on the barbed wire and had to be carefully worked free.

"What is it?" Sammy ran to the fence. "Lemme see. What did he give ya?"

When I reached into the bag and pulled out a large battery, his face fell.

"Aw, I thought it was maybe some candy! Don't know why you're excited over that old thing."

"It's a radio batt'ry! We can listen to The Grand Ole Opry on Saturday nights! And *The Lone Ranger, Lum and Abner,* and *Amos and Andy...*"

Mama's eyes narrowed as she came around the mule. In a flat voice, she interrupted, "Your grandpa never just gave you that battery. What did he want for it?"

"Oh, it's a old one he hadn't got rid of. I asked if I could have it to run the radio that Uncle Roy gave me. Grandpa says it's no good, but Uncle Roy says you can lay a old batt'ry in the sun and it'll get good again, at least for a while."

Mama's mind was already on more practical matters.

"Sammy, wash Timmy's hands and face and give him a cup of milk and a piece of cornbread. When he's finished eating, wash him again and put him down for a nap. Jackson, do the dishes and sweep the floor. We'll have a can of pork and beans and some cold cornbread for dinner, so you won't have to make a cook fire."

Still excited over the battery, I nodded happily.

"Mama, can I lay this out on a rock in the sun first?"

"I suppose."

"What's got your goat?" I asked Sammy, who stood by frowning.

"It's been awful today. I begged to play in the creek, but Mama said not to take Timmy anywhere near the water. I was stuck here under the elm tree trying to keep rocks and sticks out of his mouth."

The muddy circle around Timmy's lips proved that sometimes Sammy had not been quick enough. Considering Timmy had taken his first steps only two weeks before, I knew he was amazingly hard to keep up with.

"Cheer up. Now we're gonna have lots of fun with the radio."

Whistling on my way to the house, I stopped to catch a big, fat June bug and tied its legs with a string fished from my pocket and gave it to Sammy. As it flew around his head, he laughed and ran up the hill toward Mama.

"See, it's a airplane, aflyin' over Japs and Germans droppin' bombs."

"Stop it, Sammy!" cried Mama. "Can't you play anything but war! War isn't a game. Folks are gettin' killed every time a bomb drops."

He hung his head.

Her tone softened, "Have fun with that bug a while longer and then turn him loose."

Mama kept digging until the sun stood directly overhead. I had dinner on the table when she came inside.

"The hole's not too big yet, but I am making progress. For the last hour, the scoop has been fuller every time."

"You must be getting the hang of it," I said.

"Reckon I am," she said, rubbing her hands, "in spite of the blisters."

Sammy and I had just finished eating and gone back outside when Laddie suddenly pointed his nose toward the road and barked. Sammy's mouth fell open.

"Would you look at that! I never!" A sleek gray Lincoln car came down the rutted lane. "It's Rita May riding in there!"

The car stopped in the front yard under the catalpa tree, and Rita May stepped out and waved good-bye. I glared at the dark-haired driver.

"Howdy boys. What you gaping at?" She laughed and went toward the house. I ran to catch her and stopped her with a hand to her arm.

"Ben wouldn't like you going around with Wade."

"Well, you're crazy if you think I'm going to sit home, twiddle my thumbs, and wait for Ben Tyler!" she exclaimed. But she would not meet my eyes.

"What's wrong?" Mama called from the doorway as she stepped outside.

"Nothing." Rita took Timmy off Mama's hip and kissed his neck, again and again, making him laugh. Then she explained, "There was a grease fire at the cafe, so we'll be closed for the rest of the day while Frank repaints. By the way, did I leave my purse here?"

"It's on your bed," said Mama. "Who's that brought you home?"

"Wade Lucas. That's his new car."

Mama's lips thinned, and even more so when she saw the car sway on up the hill toward Grandpa's.

"This isn't the first time I've seen Wade Lucas come by here, but always before it's been in the middle of the night in his old pickup with the headlights off. I can just guess how he's paying for that new rig." She gave Rita a troubled look. "You're playing with fire, Rita May."

"For gosh sakes, Mama! He just gave me a ride! Besides," she looked huffy, "he's been workin' in Little Rock for two years. I'm sure he's made oodles of money."

"Too bad he doesn't spend some of it on his mama—Nora Lucas goes as threadbare as me."

"Here, I brought you five dollars." Rita reached into a pocket and stuck out the money.

"I wasn't hinting..." began Mama.

Rita May interrupted, "I told Daddy I'd help out until his checks started coming." She went inside, letting the screen door slam. Shortly she returned with her brown purse, the strap on her shoulder. Without a word, she marched up the road to Grandpa's. Odd as it seemed to me, Rita May got on well with Grandpa.

I wondered if it might be a good time to ask Mama if I could move into Rita May's room. The way things were going between her and Mama, I doubted she would ever leave the boarding house to move back home.

Midafternoon while I unhitched Dan, Mama drew and heated water and had a hurried wash in the bedroom. When she came out, her hair was freshly brushed, twisted, and pinned to the back of her head. She had changed into her brown work dress.

Along with Sammy, I sat on the living room floor, turning knobs on the radio. I had hooked up all the stuff Uncle Roy had given me—just like he said—run the aerial wire, driven in the ground rod, screwed the lightning arrester under the window, and run the leads inside. But all was silent. Sammy banged on the side of the case.

"Hey, stop it!" I scolded, "You'll break..."

Mama interrupted. "Jackson, I need to tend to some business with your Uncle Roy. Peel some potatoes. I'll fry them when I get back. I shouldn't be gone long." Changing her mind, she turned back, "On second thought, you come along and drop the mule off in Pa's pasture."

"Yes, ma'am... Sammy! Don't touch it! I told you Uncle Roy said it took a long time. We'll have to put the batt'ry back in the sun and start over. We never left it long enough." I became doubtful about the battery myself and asked, "Mama, how much you reckon a new batt'ry costs?" I quickly added, "Daddy said I could get one with the allotment money."

"That allotment money isn't going to be spent on any such foolishness."

I frowned and gathered up the dead battery. "Daddy said." I muttered the words under my breath, and Mama pretended not to hear.

The loud whir of a saw drowned the sound of our arrival at an open shed sitting in the blazing sun, not shaded by the big oaks that grew just beyond. Short Uncle Roy, muscles sweat-soaked and bulging, pushed a plank toward the whirling blade, and my friend Jake, a gangly fellow, held it as the sharp teeth ripped it in two. Mama sidestepped a pile of sawdust and waited until he threw the two boards onto a pile and reached for another.

"Roy!" she called, waving a hand to catch his eye.

Startled, he looked up and pulled back the throttle, slowing but not stopping the saw, and the noise lessened.

"Howdy, Sis. What are you two doing out in this heat?" He flashed me a white-toothed grin.

"I came to talk business, Roy."

He drew a red bandana from an overall hip pocket and removed a blue-striped engineer's cap before wiping his brow. His hair, just a bit darker than Mama's, lay plastered to his head. His green eyes twinkled.

"Business—I can talk about that in one word—bad."

"I want to work for you, take Keith's place," she remarked abruptly.

Uncle Roy looked surprised and shifted the twig in the corner of his mouth from one side to the other.

"You know I only used Keith if I had a big order to fill. This mill usually doesn't hardly make enough to keep me and Sue in bacon."

Mama frowned and was quiet for a bit before she spoke.

"Okay. No cash unless you have a big order. For now I'll trade work with you. Pretty soon I'll need help walling and roofing a cellar. I'll need some timber for the roof too."

"I heard Keith left. You tackling the diggin' by yourself?"

"Yes. Is it a deal?"

"Janie, you always was one to take the bull by the horns." He grinned. "I reckon me and Jake could use some help." He jerked a thumb toward Jake who had taken the opportunity while Roy and Mama talked to plunge a dipper into the water bucket sitting on a nearby bench and take a long drink. I sidled over to talk. Although he was seventeen, Jake treated me as an equal. Sometimes we went hunting and fishing together.

As usual, he asked about Rita May. He wondered when she would be home. I told him she had just dropped by, but not for long. Jake was Mrs. Johnson's son and some kin to us, but it was pretty distant on the Matthers' side and so far back I don't think even Grandpa Cole was real sure of the exact connection.

Roy's voice drifted over. "I reckon I'll have some evenings free to help with the cellar."

"Good," she said. "By the way, I wanted to ask you about the cellar—just a little way down, I struck some shale. It sure made the digging easier, but do you think it'll be too unstable?"

"Naw. I don't think you'll have too much trouble with caving if you can get some rock walls laid up."

"That's what I'd hoped. I'll be here tomorrow morning." Mama started to leave and I followed. Then she turned back. "If you get a big order, could you use Jackson too?"

He took off his cap and, scratching his head, looked me up and down. He shook his head. "Naw, he's too runty." When Jake laughed, Uncle Roy winked at me and then turned to Mama. "What you been feeding this boy, Janie?" he asked. "He's almost big as me." He replaced his cap and grinned. "Sure, I'll be glad to have him."

I was surprised, but I quickly warmed to the idea. I loved the mill, the sight, the noise, the smell of it all—Uncle Roy yelling at the broad-chested, red mules dragging in timber, the powerful whirring blade that bit through tangy pine or spicy hardwood and made it into boards. I was even intrigued by the cranky old engine that had to be repaired almost daily.

As she walked away, Mama motioned for me and called back over her shoulder. "Thanks, Roy."

He turned to me. "That mama of yours always was a go-getter." He rolled the sassafras twig in his mouth, and chewing on it, he returned to work.

I made plans to meet Jake on Friday night and hurried after Mama. I was puzzled when rather than taking the dirt road the mile and a half back home, she went the opposite direction, toward town.

"Where you goin'?"

"Since Roy may not need us often, I'm going to ask Miss Hilda if she needs help with cleaning and laundry. After she sees how big you've grown, I'm hoping she'll hire you to do odd jobs."

I couldn't understand why Mama was in such a swivet to get work. It was true—we had little cash. And there weren't many canned goods this year because drought had burned up the garden, but the allotment checks would fix everything.

Not that I was dreading having jobs. Working for Miss Hilda might be exciting. Everyone said she was rich. I began planning how to spend all my money as my bare feet stepped carefully, avoiding rocks hot enough to brand hide. We walked in silence. The heat sapped any desire for conversation. A half mile farther we came to a two-story, gray rock house shaded by giant oaks and surrounded by a wrought iron fence. Miss Hilda's bulldog spied us. He lunged forward, barking and snarling, and then bared ugly yellow teeth and growled low in his throat.

"Put down that rock," hissed Mama. "Miss Hilda thinks more of that dog than some folks do their children." And her withering look made me think that at that moment, Mama didn't think much of me.

"Miss Hilda, are you home?" Mama called through the potracking sound the guineas made as the odd-looking fowl marched about in their black and gray checkered suits.

Stout Miss Hilda pushed open the front screen. Her iron-gray hair covered with a scarf, she held a feather duster. Miss Hilda was a widow and her last name was Krause, but we always called her Miss Hilda. I suppose it was an easier mouthful than Mrs. Krause.

"Fritz, hush!" she scolded. The bulldog paid little attention until Miss Hilda came down the walk and grabbed his collar. "Come in, come in—he won't bite with me standing here."

I took one look at Fritz straining against his collar, and asked Mama if I could wait outside the gate. She agreed.

In less than ten minutes she came back down the walk and scurried past the dog, going far around. In spite of Miss Hilda gripping his collar, I never felt safe until the metal gate clicked shut.

Not exactly smiling, but with a look of satisfaction, Mama strode briskly down the road. "I had hoped Roy would pay cash, but all in all, it's been a prosperous afternoon. Miss Hilda is going to hire me for washing and ironing. And she did agree to hire you for odd jobs."

I was glad to hear that. But I had to ask the question which had been nagging at me. "Last time you talked about taking in laundry, didn't Daddy say no?"

"That's my business," she snapped. But she was in a good mood and soon admitted with a smile, "Your daddy was right about one thing—I do have plenty of my own chores. Trouble is, they don't pay anything, and Hilda Krause pays well. She has all that money left to her by her dead husband."

"How did he get so rich?" I asked.

"He was a doctor in Saint Louis before moving here to retire."

I toyed with the idea of becoming a doctor. It would be nice having all that money. But I didn't imagine doctoring left much time for guitar picking. Besides, I should make lots of money playing music when I got to Nashville.

As we rounded a curve, Wade's car went past. He slowed to keep from dusting us. Rita May waved, but she looked at me instead of Mama.

"I wish that girl would straighten out," fretted Mama.

"Ben wouldn't like her going around with Wade," I muttered.

"Ben is no great catch either," said Mama.

"What you got against Ben?" I had high hopes that Rita and Ben would marry.

"Nothing really. He's just too rowdy for Rita May. She needs someone to settle her down—a husband that's steady like your daddy," she answered, "but I will admit I like Ben better than Wade."

I idolized Ben. He always took time to teach me new stuff on the guitar. Even when Rita May was around and tried to get rid of me, he never treated me like I was a bothersome kid.

By the time we got home, my stomach was bothering me worse than my worries about Rita May and Ben. I was as hungry as a bear. I was glad that Sammy had already peeled the potatoes. While they fried, Mama stirred up a batch of buttermilk biscuits. Soon the smell of them baking drifted from the oven. When they were done, I ate two of them, a mountain of crisp potatoes, and several slices of fried salt pork. After that, I had no trouble polishing off four more biscuits topped with melted butter and honey.

That evening Mama seemed almost happy. And I was doing fine myself, until right after supper. Then Daddy's favorite chair sure looked empty. I swallowed a lump in my throat, picked up my guitar, and headed for the creek.

There was a special place, high on a bluff perched over Little Piney. I often went there to play my guitar. I sat on a flat rock and stared down through the willows at the dark pool below. Tonight the mood of the creek matched my own, sober and still. I pulled the guitar close and strummed some mournful minor chords. I could say things with music that I never could with words.

"You're sad, ain't you, Jackson?"

I jumped when Charlie spoke right behind me. He could slip through the woods without stepping on a twig. I found that amazing for such a big man.

He dropped down beside me. "Why you sad?"

"Daddy's gone, Charlie, and I don't know when he's ever coming back. He's gone off to fight in the war. And he might even get killed."

When Charlie nodded, his too-long black hair fell forward. "Mama died. Sissy died. It made me sad."

I liked Charlie, in spite of the fact that he was Wade Lucas' kin and had the simple mind of a young child instead of a man. He often joined me on the bluff when he heard the guitar.

"Where'd you get the fish?" I pointed to a stringer full of rock bass, perch, and bream. "Creek's so low, didn't think there was any fish left."

"Oh, I know a hole that's real deep. Joel says it's got a spring. There's still lots of fish in it."

Even though Charlie wasn't bright, he was the best hunter and fisherman around. He found game when no one else could. Daddy vowed Charlie charmed them, like one of those snake charmers in India.

"Want me to show you?" he asked.

"Sure, but later. It's too late for fishing now. It'll be dark soon."

He pulled a tiny watch from his overall bib. It was set in a brooch, the kind women pin on their dress.

"Mama give me this watch."

I had heard that a million times—almost every time I saw him. He rubbed the watch face lovingly. His blue eyes were sad. "What time does it say, Jackson?"

"It's ten after eight."

"Yeah, I got to get home 'fore these fish dies." He lifted his huge bulk off the rock. "Joel won't eat no dead fish."

"Tell your brother howdy."

He looked down at me. "Don't be sad. Okay?"

"Okay."

Charlie might be Wade's cousin, but he was as different from him as night from day. I sat awhile longer and watched the evening fade into long shadows as night crept into the hollow along with the music of the crickets and katydids. Then I stood and went home.

The next evening, I lugged the battery indoors. Sammy hovered over me.

"Get out of the way, Sammy! I can't see what I'm doing."

"You reckon it's gonna work?"

"It's been in the sun for days," I answered. "It'll work now if it's ever going to." Before I fastened the last wire, I crossed my fingers for luck and then turned the knob. A mess of jumbled static suddenly jumped into the room. Sammy's eyes grew huge and I shouted.

He put his ear closer to the speaker. "Aw, this ain't no fun. You can't hear a word, just a bunch of noise."

"Just a minute." I reached for the other dial and turned. At first there was only sputtering and more static, and I was becoming disappointed myself. Suddenly I tuned in to a station where a voice blared out about the smooth shave from Shelby razor blades. I did a triumphant dance in a circle, patting my mouth making war whoops.

"It works, it works!" yelled Sammy. "Mama, come hear the radio!"

The back screen slammed and she came inside wiping soapsuds from her hands onto her apron. "Good! Jackson, see if you can find any news."

I was surprised, for Mama sounded as excited as I felt. Only two stations came in clearly, and I wasn't sure yet where they were from, but one was giving the news. We held our breath and sat with heads cocked near the radio. The gravelly voice told how thousands of Germans had been killed in the northernmost part of the Russian front, but everywhere else things were gloomy in Russia. However, there was good news from France. A bunch of Allied fighter planes had made a canopy shielding Allied troops on the ground and in the process had downed or damaged almost 300 enemy planes. I wondered if the enemy had any planes left. I had no idea how many planes either side had.

After that, the voice went on to say, "Now to the home front—married men under the age of 45 with dependents face the prospect of being called in the draft in the not too distant future."

"Daddy was right." I said and looked at Mama. Her lips were in a tight line as she stood up.

⁓

A week later, there was still no word from Daddy. No allotment check, either. Mama said not to worry, Daddy would write when he got settled, and the check would come soon. I stayed at home each day with Sammy and Timmy while Mama worked at the sawmill. I tried hard to make things easier for her. I straightened the house and even tried to cook supper, but I made some messes.

Mama came home each evening tired and sawdust-covered. Tonight she frowned when she started up the steps and saw a pile of burned biscuits on the ground.

"Jackson, you have to be more careful. When you're cooking, don't leave the stove for a minute. Flour and lard cost money."

"Yes, 'um." I was glum. She had not asked me to cook. I was trying to help. But there was not even a thank you for my efforts. Lately Mama did not cook big meals. Before Daddy left there had been plenty to choose from: meat, bread, gravy, vegetables, and always pie, cake, or cookies. Now, most of the time, there was only meat and bread, or beans and potatoes, and she never wasted sugar on dessert.

After supper I sat in the lamp-lit room on the floor listening to the radio. After several more hours in the sun, the battery was working for now, but barely.

"Did you hear that!" I asked, bug-eyed. "Oh, no!" I moaned when crackling static replaced the voice. Wiggling the antenna wire failed to help, so I franticly banged on the side of the radio. "It can't go dead now! Not right in the middle of the most important stuff of all!"

"What is it?" asked Mama.

Sammy and I both began to talk excitedly. Mama caught the phrase "spies" amid the hubbub.

"One at a time, boys! I can't understand a thing you're saying."

With silent agreement, I took charge. "The reporter says those eight spies on trial in Washington, D.C. are only a small part of the folks who are tryin' to give our military secrets away. 'Saboteurs,' he called them. They're usin' outlaw transmitters and secret antennas, hid out in trees or between the walls or floors of houses, to broadcast information to the enemy! We're supposed to be on the lookout for anything suspicious about our neighbors and report it to the local authorities."

Mama frowned. "Let the authorities do their own snooping. I don't want you boys snooping around at any of the neighbors, you hear?"

"Yes, 'um," I answered moodily.

"Our neighbors are all good people," she added, while folding the cloth on her lap. "There, I'm finished with Miss Hilda's tablecloth. You can take it over to her in the morning, Jackson. She's having company for supper on Friday, and she wants you to mow and rake her yard."

"Mama, can I keep the money Miss Hilda pays me?"

She hesitated, then slowly nodded and answered, "What she pays for the raking, but what she pays for the tablecloth, bring to me."

"Hot dog!" I jumped up. "I'm gonna buy a new batt'ry."

"Instead of spending every penny quick as you get it on foolishness, you ought to save up for important things."

"Daddy says fun is important."

She frowned. I had touched a sore spot. When Mama had wanted to save every penny, Daddy would tweak her nose and say, "Hey Scrooge, fun is important too." Daddy had always loved the

movies. He told me, when he was a boy, he would hitchhike into town to watch the old silent pictures.

We never went anymore, but I treasured the memory of Saturday afternoons in Pine Bluff at the show with him, gorging on buttery popcorn and ice-cold pop. I didn't say so. Mama might change her mind about letting me keep my money.

That night I lay in bed. Sleep was slow in coming. Not a breath of air made its way through the open window—but the gnats did. I lay in a pool of sweat, swatting bugs and wishing for winter.

"Jackson, get still!" hissed Sammy.

"You're scratching just as much as I am," I shot back. However, I tried to quit wiggling, and soon he breathed deep and steady while I stared at the dark ceiling.

I thought about Daddy. I wondered where he was and if he would be gone for a long, long time. I tried pushing the thought aside that he might never come back, but it kept edging its way back. I determined to think of something else.

The next week would be the opening of school. I dreaded having nothing better to wear than last year's patched overalls. I rolled over and sighed and wished the allotment check would come.

Chapter 4

The next morning, as soon as the chores were finished at Grandpa's, I rushed home to get the tablecloth that Mama had left lying on the table in a sack. I grabbed it and the dinner pail that sat beside it and rushed out the door. I yelled goodbye to Mama. Today she was working on the cellar. I waved to my brothers who were watching with great attention as the slip scoop filled with dirt, just as though it were the first time, rather than the hundredth time, they had seen it.

The morning was hot and still without a hint of fall, but sometime during the night after I went to sleep, there must have been a high wind, for now the ground was covered with dead leaves, big limbs, and sticks. My bare feet stepped over where they lay scattered across the dirt road.

In high spirits, I pursed my lips and began to whistle. It was a song I had heard for the first time last night while listening to the radio. I didn't care much for the words about three teenaged sisters who were all in love—one with a soldier, one with a sailor, and the other with a Marine. But I did like the tune.

I reached for a stick and began strumming on the make-believe guitar. There was nothing I wanted more than that Gibson guitar. But there was no way I could get that kind of money. It would take far too long to save up. I'd be lucky to get enough for a battery.

Just before arriving at Miss Hilda's, I stopped to fill my pockets with rocks. If Miss Hilda was outside, she would call off the bulldog, but, just in case, I was taking no chances.

Fritz began barking savagely even before I came in sight. I was relieved to see Miss Hilda in front of the shed, dragging the dog by his collar. Stiff legged, Fritz was determined to stay out of the shed, and I wondered if even stout Miss Hilda could force him. She finally leaned, puffing, against the outside of the latched door while Fritz howled and scratched on the inside.

"Come on in, Jackson," she called between pants. "I wasn't expecting you this early or I'd have put Fritz up sooner. You're here bright and early."

I unlatched the tall metal gate and walked down the flagstone walk to join her. There was a variety of tools leaning against the shed: a big wheeled mower, a rake, a hoe, a wheelbarrow, and a shiny spade. A pair of Jersey gloves lay across the handle of the wheelbarrow, proof that Miss Hilda had left nothing inside the shed that might be needed for yard work.

"How about a glass of lemonade before work?"

"Thank you kindly, ma'am."

Lemonade was a rare treat. Sugar was scarce at home—and lemons and ice even more so. Sometimes Daddy had bought a block from the iceman, and we would make crank freezer ice cream, but only on special occasions like the Fourth of July. Never before had I swirled ice around in a tall glass on a regular workday. I could hardly wait to tell Mama and Sammy. Wouldn't Sammy be green with envy?

I felt a twinge of guilt. Poor Sammy, stuck at home tending the baby, while I drank lemonade and made money to boot! Oh well, Sammy would enjoy listening to the radio when I bought a new battery.

"That sure was tasty, Miss Hilda." I replaced the empty glass onto the tray and rose from sitting on the porch steps, regretful of having gulped the frosty drink. But there was no time for sipping. I didn't want Miss Hilda to think me a slacker. She might not hire me again.

There was not much grass left but what little there was, I mowed, and then I attacked the raking with a vengeance, while thinking now that the sun was higher, it had turned mighty hot. The back of my shirt grew wet, and I wiped my brow often and pushed back the locks of damp brown hair that constantly fell over my eyes. By noon there were a half-dozen piles heaped high between the giant oaks in the big yard.

With the sun directly overhead, I sat down under a tree and opened my dinner pail. The delicious smell of fried chicken rose as I pulled out two drumsticks and a biscuit. Mama had done the cooking this morning. I ate slowly, enjoying each bite, while gazing up through limbs at puffy clouds drifting by.

Since Daddy wasn't around to do any hunting, meat was a rare and tasty treat. There had been few roosters for butchering in this year's hatches. Mama saved every female pullet for laying hens. I wondered if she would let me take Daddy's shotgun out by myself this fall. The promise of a mess of young squirrels just might persuade her. I intended to try. I tossed aside the chicken bones and wiped greasy hands down the legs of my overalls. I got up and began to rake again, but then I stopped and gazed at the shed. I reckoned it sure wouldn't hurt to make friends with that dog. Miss Hilda might not always be around to run interference.

The bones had landed nearby. I got them and cautiously approached the shed. All was quiet inside. I toyed with the idea of unlatching the door and barely opening it to toss the bones inside.

Somehow, the idea knotted my stomach. That was one strong dog. He might lunge out in spite of all precautions.

There was a small window in back. Rounding the building, I peered up at a window too high to reach from the ground, so I tipped over the wheelbarrow and climbed onto its metal bottom. The window, grime-covered and stuck tight, might be pried opened with a pocketknife. I fished out my knife and after several attempts finally pushed up the window. Fritz heard the efforts and went into a fit of barking.

"Nice dog, nice dog. Here I've got something for...." I stopped short. I had spied a strange looking contraption—a pole covered with wires. I hitched myself up higher on tiptoe and had a better look. It looked like some sort of antenna! I thought about the warning I had heard on the radio.

"Get down from there!" rang out Miss Hilda's sharp voice. "What are you doing!"

I stumbled in haste and tumbled to the ground. My heart pounded as I scooted on my rear back against the building and tried to explain.

"I was just tryin' to give Fritz these chicken bones." I pointed to the bones that had fallen to the ground. "I was hopin' we could make friends. I meant no harm."

"Oh, I see." Miss Hilda relaxed. "I'd rather you left the dog alone. I know you meant well, but I don't want him making up to anyone. My husband trained him to protect me. He can be vicious, and it's better if he stays in the shed whenever you're around."

She turned to leave. Then turning back, she crisply ordered, "Stay away from the shed. I don't want Fritz upset."

"Yes, 'um." I stood hastily and brushed off the seat of my britches, my mind whirling. Miss Hilda? But wasn't Krause a

German name? And Fritz? The more I thought about it the more clear it all became. Miss Hilda was a spy!

The hardest thing I had ever done was to rake the yard and act as though nothing had happened. I kept glancing at the house and several times caught Miss Hilda staring out the window. Each time I wondered if I would leave here alive. When I finished, the sun had dipped low in the west, and bare limbs left long shadows on the ground. I wanted to run home without speaking to Miss Hilda, but that was sure to arouse suspicion. She answered my knock immediately. I wondered if she had been watching me all the while. With a fixed smile, I told her the job was completed, the weeds pulled from the fence and the piles of leaves and sticks raked and hauled off.

She thanked me and said, "Wait right here."

I quaked. Was she going for a gun? Mama and Sammy would never know what happened to me! Should I run for it?

I was ready to bolt when she returned clutching a small black, beaded handbag. She withdrew a matching coin purse and drew out two crisp dollar bills.

"One for you and one for your mama. Tell her she did a nice job on the laundry and the tablecloth. You did a fine job too. I'm sure I'll have more work for you."

My eyes popped. It was big wages. I knew grown men who earned less for a day's work.

"Thank you, ma'am." I walked toward the gate, holding myself in check to keep from running. It looked as though I might leave here alive after all. I had just raised the latch on the heavy metal gate when she called after me.

"Oh, come back! I have something to send to your mama." I returned with lagging steps. Miss Hilda shortly came from the house with a bulky paper bag. "Careful with these. They're some drinking glasses I thought your mama could use. The way I use... well, they pile up, and I hate to throw them away."

"Thank you, ma'am." I could not imagine throwing away drinking glasses!

"Remember to stay away from Fritz."

"Yes, ma'am, I'll remember." I struggled to keep a tremor from my voice.

When the house disappeared behind the trees, I pounded down the road, my bare feet slapping the ground. At the crossroads, I paused. Uncle Roy lived in the opposite direction. He might know what to do.

Breathing hard, I hesitated. But would Uncle Roy take me serious? Maybe I should get more proof. I started for home at a slower pace. I wanted to tell someone—maybe I would tell Sammy. I hoped he could be counted on to keep his mouth shut.

"Come on, come on old feller." Sammy motioned to Enoch as he crouched and slowly approached the rooster with a bit of cornbread in his hand. "I ain't a'gonna hurt ya—much."

Enoch stood, with colorful tail feathers blowing in the breeze, his head held sideways in order to keep a cautious beady eye on Sammy. Enoch could not see the big stick held behind Sammy's back, but Enoch was a wily bird and suspicious of any friendly gestures, especially from Sammy. He had just had to run for his life, flapping madly, after giving Sammy the sharp point of spurs in the back of the leg.

Now Sammy was in hot pursuit with Enoch barely two steps ahead. "Sammy! Leave that poor bird alone!"

"Poor bird! I got black and blue marks up and down my legs from that poor bird!"

"Forget Enoch for now—I got somethin' important to tell you."

I drew him aside and hurriedly told my discovery.

"Jackson, Miss Hilda ain't no spy."

"Of course she's a spy! Aren't you listening?" Exasperated at his ignorance, I lashed out. "Like I told you—I saw a secret antenna! And I'll bet the outlaw transmitter is there too! I would have seen it too if old lady Krause hadn't caught me and almost scared the liver out of me. Good thing she bought my story about feeding Fritz, or you'd probably never have seen me again!"

Sammy's green eyes were scared. "We better tell Mama."

"Not on your life! War is men's business. You don't see women shootin' at Japs and Germans, do you?"

Sammy shook his head, not bothering to tell me that he had never seen men shooting at Japs or Germans, either.

My chest swelled. "You heard Daddy say I was man of the house while he's away. It's up to me to tend to this." I deflated suddenly. "Of course German spies are real dangerous, and I might need help with the capture."

"The authorities, like the radio said?"

"Well...maybe later," I hesitated, knowing how Mama was distrustful of anything government. "I thought maybe I'd ask Uncle Roy. He's smart."

He noticed the sack. "What's in there?"

I looked at the forgotten sack in my hand. "It's drinking glasses that Miss Hilda gave Mama."

"Lemme see." Sammy peeked inside. "Boy, we'll have plenty now." Until now the family had shared two glasses and a goblet.

"Why, theses are snuff glasses. Miss Hilda must use snuff!" I declared when Sammy drew one out.

"There's still some snuff in this un'." Sammy poked his finger inside and then licked off the dark powder.

"Gimme that! You shouldn't do that." I jerked the glass away.

"Why not? It's sorta good—kinda sweet like."

I glanced to make certain we were out of Mama's view before pulling out another glass and digging around its bottom to come away with a smattering of powder for myself. It was sweet—and tangy. We hurried around the corner and hunkered down in front of the house. Then I drew out each glass carefully, and we took turns removing the traces of tobacco. Some glasses held more than others, but we finally managed to have fairly equal quids pinched between bottom lip and gum.

With my tongue stuck out and a finger halfway to my lips, I suddenly stopped. "I just thought of something." I looked worriedly at the glass. "What if Miss Hilda knew I'd dip this snuff, so she put poison in with it—that'd fix me good and get me out of her hair quick."

Sammy looked at his own finger and then began to spit. "We better wash out our mouths."

We hurried to the water bucket and rushed back outside to gargle and spit again and again. Sammy was on the verge of crying.

"I think we ought to tell Mama. She might know a remedy."

"No!" I protested. "She'd just tan our hides for dippin'—and if it's poison we're goners anyway. All that'd happen if we tell is we'd get a whippin'—and then we'd die."

Sammy was stricken. He walked back inside, went to the table, sat down, and placed his head on his arms. He looked up shortly.

"How long you reckon it takes?"

"What?"

"Dyin' of poison."

I shrugged. "Guess it depends on which kind." Seeing his scared face, I tried to comfort. "With some kinds you just get sick and don't die a'tall."

"I hope that's the kind Miss Hilda uses."

"Me too."

Mama noticed that neither of us ate much supper. She looked closely at me, then at Sammy.

"I declare, you boys look peaked. Jackson, you're plumb green."

I rose quickly from the table and rushed outside to retch off the end of the porch. Mama followed with a wet cloth and worried aloud, "I guess it's something you ate. Here comes Sammy too!" She handed me the rag and returned inside.

"We're poisoned sure!" hissed Sammy. "I ain't never felt like this!"

My answer was a doleful look and a loud retch. Mama returned with a bottle of castor oil and a spoon. I wiped my mouth and moaned, "Please no, Mama!" My pleading had the usual effect—none a'tall.

"I hope it's not the well water," she worried. "I hate using the well for cold storage. It's too easy to contaminate the water." Since the spring had gone dry, we had put the milk and butter in a bucket and lowered them into the well. Not that there was much milk or butter these days. In spite of grazing in Grandpa's pasture, Bossy had almost gone dry.

A short time later we boys lay in bed arguing. I had the final say. "No use telling now. We're both gettin' better. I tell you, Sammy, that was the sickening, not the killin', kind of poison."

Sammy was not convinced, but he was too sleepy to argue.

Mama kept me busy the next day. It was almost as though she invented jobs to keep me home. I took down the stovepipe, cleaned out the soot, then put the pipe up again—mucked out the barn and the chicken house and filled the nests with fresh hay—finally, I split kindling and short wood for the cook stove. It was late when I finished milking Bossy.

"Sammy, you'll have to take care of the chickens tonight."

"No," he argued. "I sneezed all night the last time I did."

"You've got to," I pleaded. "It might be my only chance. Miss Hilda locks Fritz in the shed when she's gonna have company, and Mama said she's having company for supper. When I get done at Grandpa's, I aim to have one more look in that shed to see if I can find a transmitter. I want to tell Uncle Roy it's for sure there. He might not take it serious if all I saw was the antenna."

"Okay," he slowly agreed. "But be careful."

Priscilla was easily milked, her big teats almost squirting milk on their own. Grandpa was not home. I was glad, for lately he had taken a notion to be talkative. I did not to want to stand around jawing with him this evening. I hurried and put the milk into his springhouse. Instead of returning home, I circled around the pasture, going through the woods and coming out far down the road.

I ran. The sun was already low. When the rock house loomed near, I slowed and slipped from tree to tree, until I was directly behind the shed. I cocked my head to listen. Everything was quiet. Miss Hilda had already put Fritz into the shed as I had hoped. I looked at the fence, deciding the climb should be easy with bare feet. I could wrap my toes around the fancy curlicues. I tried to quiet the voice in my head telling me this was a crazy, foolish thing I was about to do.

I looked cautiously all around and took a deep breath, eyeing the distance from the fence to shed. Gathering courage, I dropped to my knees, crawled to the fence, and climbed up on the round balls decorating each upright rod. Quick as a flash, I scaled the top, squeezing between the points that topped each pole like sharp arrows aimed skyward.

Astride the top, I froze. Fritz's barking came loud and clear as I heard the shed door open.

"Hush your barking, Fritz. It'll do you no good. You have to stay inside tonight, but I'll let you out tomorrow. There now, be a good boy."

Fritz went wild. I wondered if he could smell me.

"What in the world has gotten into that dog?" Miss Hilda muttered to herself and sighed. "I may have to get rid of him. He's getting too hard to handle."

With plodding steps, she started down the flagstone walk toward the house. Each step echoed like a bullet. At any second, she was bound to see me perched on top of the tall fence. My mouth went powder dry, and at the same time, sweat popped out all over my body.

Somewhere from memory came Daddy's remark that a person could feel a stare. I squeezed shut my eyes and hoped Miss Hilda would not feel mine!

The steps kept going and then miraculously began to fade as she passed on. The front door opened and closed.

I threw my other leg over and jumped to the ground. Hunkering low, I reached the shed in a stumbling dash and ducked behind it, trembling and panting. I pulled the wheelbarrow to the window. Fritz began barking harder.

Yes! There was the odd looking antenna with wires all around—but what about the transmitter? It suddenly dawned on me that I had no idea what a transmitter looked like. Surely I would know one if I saw it. It might look sort of like a radio, but I wasn't sure.

All I saw were rakes, hoes, shovels, a shelf full of empty canning jars, and, in one corner, several pieces of furniture, including one old chair that leaned crazily because a leg was missing. There was nothing else suspicious in the shed.

After another long, hard look, I climbed down, disappointed. I gave a regretful glance toward the house, another toward the sun, and decided against any more snooping. I would have to hurry, or Sammy would be telling Mama where I was.

After replacing the wheelbarrow exactly as it had been, I jogged to the back fence and quickly climbed over and hurried down the road. At the crossroads, my breath came in ragged gasps and I had to slow.

Through the trees, I saw the sun had disappeared and a pink glow lit the horizon. With a sinking feeling I spied Mama marching down the road toward me. There was murder in her eyes. She was pushing up the sleeves of her dress as if preparing for a fight.

"Andrew Jackson Loring!" Still rods away, she began the tirade. "Sammy told me what you're up to...what in tarnation do you mean accusing a good woman like Miss Hilda of something ridiculous! I'm a good mind to have your Uncle Roy whip the daylights out of you!"

She arrived breathless and purple faced. "No. I have a better idea. I'll shame you good and put an end to all this foolishness!" She grabbed my arm and propelled me forward.

"Mama! You ain't going to Miss Hilda's!"

"I most certainly am! And so are you."

"Stop, Mama! We can't go there—you don't understand! She's a German spy!"

Mama lengthened her stride, pulling me even faster. "Of all the crazy notions."

"Mama, she'll lock us in the shed—or maybe shoot us! Can't you understand?" I was desperate.

"I understand you been snooping at the neighbors like I told you not to." She snorted, "Just like your daddy—letting those news reporters talk you into poking your nose where it doesn't belong instead of staying at home where you do!"

I racked my brain for a way to convince her to turn back. None came. It was like Daddy always said—with her mind made up, Mama was more stubborn than Old Dan.

With dragging steps I followed as slowly as possible. She shot me a look and jerked on my arm, and I began to pick up my feet. It flashed through my mind that I was too young to die. I thought about David O. Dodd, the boy hero of the Civil War. At school we had studied how, just like my Grandpa Jim, he was hanged for spying. But David O. Dodd had been hanged at Little Rock and for spying for the Confederacy. He had died with brave words on his lips. I knew that I would not. I was already about to wet my pants. The one consolation was how sorry Mama would be when the German shot me. I could imagine her begging my forgiveness as I drew my last breath.

Birds flitted to roost in the twilight as we approached the metal fence. I tried once more.

"Please, don't go in there, Mama! Please!"

She ignored me and pushed me ahead through the gate. It clanged shut and Fritz began to bark. Then it was too late. Mama knocked and the front door opened and Miss Hilda stood in a pool of light. Behind her a sparkling three-tiered chandelier lit the dining room where a table was covered with silver and crystal and a fancy white cloth.

"Janie! What's wrong?" She stepped onto the porch and closed the door.

"Miss Hilda, I'm awful sorry to interrupt you. I know you've got company coming. But I had to clear up a little misunderstanding."

Miss Hilda looked concerned. "What is it?" She glanced at me. "Is there a problem over what I paid for the work? I'll be glad to..."

"Oh no. It's nothin' about that," Mama quickly interrupted. "Well..." she hesitated before plunging on, "it seems Jackson's been listening to too many spy stories on the radio."

I quaked and looked at the ground. Daddy was right—I could feel Miss Hilda's stare.

"Yes?" she questioned, puzzled.

"He thinks you have a secret antenna and maybe a transmitter hidden in the shed and you're sending secrets over the air to the German government."

"Wherever did he get that idea?"

Miss Hilda sounded surprised and acted the picture of innocence. But I knew better! I bristled when Mama began to apologize.

Irate, I blurted out, "I saw the antenna with my own eyes! You can lie, but I saw it! And you talk funny too—like a foreigner."

"Don't you dare—" Mama began, but Miss Hilda cut in.

"It's evident the boy thinks he saw something suspicious. Let's go take a look and see what it was. Just a minute, I'll have to get Fritz's leash." She entered the house, and I began to plead.

"We gotta get out of here! I'll bet she's got a gun!"

The door opened and Miss Hilda returned with a flashlight in one hand and something clutched in the other, but I could not see what it was. She walked briskly toward the shed, asking us to stay back until Fritz was secured.

I was cold, but it had nothing to do with the night air. My stomach churned, and my heart leaped into my throat. Miss Hilda's hand was in her pocket. I could see her outline in the twilight.

Scared stiff, I eyed the gathering darkness, thinking of escape. I could run for it—but Mama! I could not leave her! With a sinking feeling, I stepped forward beside her. Just then Miss Hilda called. "I'll shine the light around and you tell me when you see what we're looking for."

Outside the bright beam of the flashlight, Fritz barked furiously and strained against the leash. The pool of light shined first on the cluttered assortment of yard tools, and then, as the beam came around, I saw Fritz tied short to the leg of an old bureau with a large oval mirror. The light reflected off the glass, blinding me until it moved on.

Now she was getting close to the antenna and I held my breath. Suddenly there it was in the wavering light, but Miss Hilda moved the light ahead without stopping. I could scarcely believe how she had ignored the evidence of her guilt.

"There it was!" My voice was a croak. "Mama, there's the antenna—just like I told you!"

Miss Hilda turned in surprise. "Where?"

My hand shook as I pointed to the right. The beam of light followed and shone boldly upon the wire-covered pole. There could be no denial now! But Miss Hilda burst out laughing. I spun back to face her. Miss Hilda was covering her red face with one hand and laughing a deep belly laugh that made the flashlight jiggle crazily. I was stunned. Miss Hilda looked past me at Mama. "Well, there's my spying equipment."

My own Mama was laughing!

"Don't feel bad," quickly added Miss Hilda. "It is a strange looking contraption. You were right to be suspicious."

I was red faced. "What in tarnation is it?" I asked Mama in a whisper.

"It's a clothesline for drying washing in the house—things like silk hose—things a woman doesn't dry outdoors."

My face blazed. I looked at the floor, feeling my ears go hot. Instead of being a hero I was a dumb kid!

Mama had sobered. "See, I told you. Now, young man, you apologize!"

I managed a mumbled apology and Miss Hilda graciously accepted. "You're a brave boy, Jackson—a patriot."

It was nice of Miss Hilda to say that. I wished Mama had felt the same. The house was hardly out of sight when she lit in.

"Since I can't trust you, you'll not be working for Miss Hilda."

"But—"

"No. Not another word. And you're not to leave the house, except to go to school and to Grandpa's until I say so. You've got to learn to mind!" She quickened her pace and muttered to herself, "Blasted government telling folks to spy on their neighbors."

I wanted to argue with her, but I was already in enough trouble so I stayed quiet. Heartsick, I trudged along, head down, and wondered how I would ever get a new battery now.

She stopped and faced me, putting her hands on her hips. "And another thing, what were you thinking, getting Sammy involved in something you thought was dangerous? What if it had been? I caught him sneaking out of the yard tonight because he was worried about you. You're supposed to look out for Sammy, not drag him into trouble. Remember what your daddy said? You're responsible for your little brothers. Are you listenin'?"

I mumbled, "Yes, 'um."

Chapter 5

School was a square, two-story, red brick building full of windows, about three miles from our house by way of the road, but Sammy and I cut through the woods as the crow flies and saved ourselves almost a mile. Laddie followed every step until we got to the edge of the woods, and then—just as he had done since Sammy's first day of school—the dog stopped. It was the strangest thing. He never went farther. Mama said he came back home every day, but he would be waiting here at the same spot for Sammy when school was over.

I had walked most of the way barefoot, slipping on my boots just before the building came into sight. I frowned at the brogans as I pulled them on over sockless feet.

Mama insisted that we wear shoes to school—like it was some sort of shame to go barefoot, but I was more ashamed of the cracked, worn leather boots almost coming out at the toe. Oh well, I consoled myself, when the allotment came, a new pair of boots was sure to be on Mama's list of necessities. And as there was an inch of ankle sticking out below my ragged overalls, I was sure to get a new pair of them too.

I didn't exactly hate school. Parts of it I actually liked. But I did hate feeling like a country bumpkin alongside the town boys—if a few houses, two stores, a cotton gin, and a couple of churches on a dirt road could be called a town. The real town, Clarksville, where Rita worked, was twelve miles away. I guess Hagarville, named after an old blacksmith, Mr. Hagar, was more what you'd call a community. But that didn't keep the boys who lived here from looking down their noses at kids who wore patched overalls and worn-out brogans. I put on my don't-care face and began to swagger, getting ready to face them. They'd never know that Jackson Loring cared one whit about his ragged clothes.

Sammy hung back, and when I looked around I noticed he looked worried. "You all right?" I asked.

"Yeah," he answered, but I could see his eyes were bugged and scared.

"You're lucky, Jackson, you got the same teacher again. I got a new one."

"Hey, Mrs. Zachary ain't Hitler. I hear tell she's real nice. You'll like her."

He nodded. "It's just been a long time since last year, and I'm sort of wondering if I remember anything. Reckon they'll put me back in first, if I can't get things right today?"

"Naw. Everybody has to do some brushing up. Even the teachers forget stuff." Although I wasn't sure about that, it sounded reassuring, and it must have worked, for Sammy's face brightened and he came up to walk beside me. He was just a little kid, but somehow having him there made me feel better as about fifty pairs of eyes raked us.

The bell rang and Sammy and I parted on the steps. He went into a room on the right for first, second, and third grades, and I went down the wide hall and past the room for seventh and eighth. I glanced toward where the eighth grade sat and felt somewhat superior as I climbed the stairs to the ninth grade room.

It was a big room with a wooden floor, high ceiling, and outside walls filled with windows that reached almost from top to bottom. Everything looked the same as it had on the last day of school, except neater. Instead of smelling like chalk and sweaty bodies, it smelled like soap and Bon Ami cleaner. Chalkboards filled the front wall, and large maps hung on either side. The worn black Bible and blue and white globe of the world sat on the scuffed top of Mr. Caruther's big desk, and in front of it, even rows of desks marched down the room.

Passing down to the last row, I picked a seat near the back and dropped into it. I stuffed my Big Chief tablet and my pencils underneath into the rack between the curved metal legs. Trying to look bored, I slouched over and rested my arm on the armrest and traced my finger along some initials carved into the old wooden top. They were crooked, but deep. J D J. I figured it was Jake Johnson's handiwork, because his middle name was Dean. I noticed another set near the top beside the old inkwell hole. R M L + B J T.

I grinned. Rita May Loring + Benjamin Jacob Tyler. Rita May was just as apt to have carved it as Ben. She loved making wildflower bouquets and carried a penknife in her purse to cut dogwood stems and such.

The town boys came inside in a group, and with a bunch of pushing and shoving, they picked seats on the other side of the room. I nodded howdy to Rusty Terry as he dropped into a nearby seat. Covered with freckles, he looked like a sure-enough country bumpkin, with shaggy bright red hair and buckteeth. His clothes were in worse shape than mine. At least my hair was nicely trimmed since last night, and Mama had sewn neat patches over the holes in my overalls. Rusty's bare knees stuck out of his. I liked Rusty. He could bat a ball better than anyone I ever saw, except Ben.

Ben was the best ballplayer in the county, maybe in the state. In spite of that, he had liked playing with us kids. When he graduated, I had sorely missed him at school. I think Rita May did too. Maybe that was why she never finished her last year.

I looked outside at our makeshift ball diamond and wondered if soldiers and sailors ever played baseball. If they did, Ben and Daddy could both show them a thing or two. Daddy was a good pitcher and outfielder, though not nearly as good as Ben.

Mr. Caruthers interrupted my daydream when he carried the large flag from the left front corner into the middle of the room. Mr. Caruthers seemed old to me, for he was bald in the front and wore glasses, but Daddy said they were the same age, thirty-four. He told us to stand and give the pledge. I gazed at the bold stars and stripes. A lump rose in my throat as I thought about Daddy fighting for that flag. I could hardly sing "America."

Mr. Caruthers said a few words about the greatness of America and the value of freedom, and after reading a Psalm from the dog-eared Bible, he said a prayer for all the fighting men. Thinking of Daddy, I felt proud.

Mr. Caruthers began writing on the big black chalkboard that covered the front of the room and school began. I was glad we'd be starting with arithmetic. I hated English class.

In spite of the open windows, by ten o'clock the room was stifling. Not a whisper of breeze stirred the drooping trees outside. Their branches looked too tired to hold up the leaves. I drooped too and squirmed more than I studied.

At recess I walked up behind Sammy, who was playing marbles with Carl Tyler, Ben's little cousin. I nudged him with the toe of my boot.

"How's it going? You gettin' busted back to first?" I teased.

"Naw. I did good. And Jackson, you were right, Mrs. Zachary is real nice."

I ambled on over to a group of fellows playing mumbly-peg. Out of a dozen pocketknives scattered on the ground, only two were standing up. Reaching into my pocket, I drew out mine and pried it open. I gripped the backside of the blade between thumb and finger and flipped it, holding my breath as it made an arch. It struck the ground and stood straight up like a flagpole in the dirt.

Someone clapped, and I glanced around. The girls were supposedly playing tag, but as usual, they were paying more attention to us boys. Patsy Rawlings was clapping. My face turned red. Patsy was a town girl with big brown eyes and a darker brown braid hanging past her waist. I thought she was beautiful, but I never talked to her. It made my palms sweaty just thinking about it. According to Daddy there had been bad blood between our kin back during the Civil War, but so far as I knew, we Lorings got along with the Rawlings now.

After school Sammy ran to join Laddie and started for home, but I detoured by the store and stuck my head inside long enough to make sure the guitar was still there. I gave a relieved sigh when I saw it hanging on the wall. I wanted to try it again, but chores were waiting at home and at Grandpa's. I'd be hard pressed to get them done before dark.

Miss Hilda bumped into me as she came out the door.

"Jackson, I'm sorry. I wasn't paying attention. My mind was a million miles away."

"It was my fault, ma'am. I shouldn't have been blockin' the doorway. Here," I reached for her sack of groceries. "Let me help you with those. I'm going right by your place." Actually, I had planned to cut through the woods again, but I wanted to do something nice for Miss Hilda, make it up to her for my fool mistake.

"Thank you. A sack of groceries does get heavy by the time I get home."

I didn't think Miss Hilda was feeling well. She smiled, but her face looked drawn and tired. We walked side-by-side, Miss Hilda quiet, not saying a word.

"Ma'am," I finally spoke, "is something wrong? You not feeling well?"

"What?" She stopped and blinked at me, like someone waking from a dream.

"You were just so quiet I though maybe you weren't feeling well or something," I explained.

"No. I'm fine," she said and started walking again.

Then I asked what was really worrying me. "Are you mad at me, ma'am, about calling you a spy and everything?"

She smiled. "Good heavens, no! Jackson, I hate the Nazis too. I would have done the same thing you did." She sobered and drew something from her pocket. "I keep going to the post office hoping for a letter from my family. Esther used to write faithfully, but there's not been a word in months." She looked at the picture before handing it to me. "This is all the family I have left in the world, my niece Esther, her husband and children, and my nephew Zosel and his wife Anna." She pointed and named each one.

Esther was a young, sweet-faced woman with dark hair and soft looking eyes holding a baby wrapped in a white blanket. Standing around her were three boys, stair steps, the oldest about my age and the youngest a mite smaller than Sammy. But the one who caught my eye was a pretty little girl with dark curly hair and the biggest eyes I ever saw. She was laughing and appeared to be pulling away from the oldest boy who held tight to her hand. I could just imagine her running straight into mischief.

"They're a handsome family, Miss Hilda." I looked at the big-eyed little girl again and handed back the picture. "Where do they live?"

"The Ukraine." She looked at the picture again before tucking it back into her pocket.

We were both quiet for a bit. "You were right," she broke the silence, "I do have an accent." She turned to me and smiled. "I'm Ukrainian too—and I'm Jewish." She paused and added. "Things are not good now in Europe for Jews. I don't know what has become of my family. Hitler is wicked, a very wicked man. The things he is doing...." She left the sentence hanging. Finally, she spoke again, "If only Esther and the children had come here as I begged."

I had no idea what she was talking about, but she looked at me as if I did. When we reached the gate, I opened it with caution, but Fritz's deep bark echoed from inside the shed. Lost in thought, Miss Hilda absentmindedly thanked me as I carried the groceries into the house. I took a quick look around. I wasn't often in Miss Hilda's house. I relished the chance to see all the finery. Someday I planned to have a house just like it with pretty paper on the walls and shiny, polished hardwood floors that glowed in afternoon sun coming through big clear windows. As I closed the door behind me, she opened it again.

"Where are my manners!" she called. "Here, Jackson," she rummaged in her black coin purse and pulled out a quarter. "Please take this. I do thank you so much for helping."

I stuck my hands into my pockets. "No, I was glad to do it, ma'am." I was surprised at Miss Hilda. Didn't she know neighbors didn't take money for being neighborly?

"Well, thank you again. You're a good boy, Jackson. Your mama can be proud." She dropped the coin back into the purse. "As soon as she can spare you, I have some work for you. I need some firewood split."

I was too humiliated to say I couldn't work for her anymore. And I didn't tell her that Mama wasn't proud of me at all. Lately, nothing about me seemed to please her.

She was not inside when I got home. I slammed my books onto the bench and grabbed a cold cornpone and dipped it into the bowl of molasses sitting on the table. Then I noticed the envelope. It was a letter from Daddy. I recognized his neat handwriting. I whooped and grabbed it.

"It's a letter from Daddy, Sammy!" I shouted as I pulled it from the envelope.

"Maybe you should wait for Mama," he cautioned.

"She's already read it." I pointed to the slit in the end of the envelope.

My eyes quickly went over the first page before I began reading aloud to Sammy. Daddy was fine. He was in Texas, training new recruits. When that was done, he figured they would be shipping out.

Mama came through the back door with a load of clean laundry from off the line in one arm and Timmy in the other. She took a couple of clothespins from her mouth and smiled. "I see you found the letter."

"Sounds like he's doing real good."

"Sure does." Mama nodded. "How was school?"

"Fine," I answered.

I was walking out the back door on my way to Grandpa's when I noticed a wadded paper in the kindling box. It was a brown, official-looking envelope. I whirled.

"Did the allotment check come too?" I asked, my heart pounding.

Mama nodded.

"Oh boy! Can we go to Rawlings' before he closes? I can get my overalls there, but he doesn't have Red Wing boots. I figure to get them in Clarksville on Saturday."

"Come, sit down for a minute, boys."

I turned back and went to the table. After one glimpse of Mama's solemn face, Sammy slid beside me onto the wooden bench. Mama put Timmy down where he sat on the floor with a fist crammed into his mouth, staring at her with unconcerned eyes as she faced us.

"You both know I didn't want your Daddy to join up again. But he did." She hesitated. "I wanted him to take a good job so we could save for our own farm," her eyes swept the tiny room, "and a good house." She looked back at us. "But for now we're going to make do." She waited a minute to let that sink in. "There's not going to be any spending—no new clothes," she went on, "no toys, not even candy or gum from the store."

Sammy and I exchanged puzzled glances.

My eyes slid over her shapeless brown dress; faded and thin, it looked worse than my own threadbare overalls. Daddy had said she was to buy a pretty new one, green to match her eyes, with the first allotment check, and me and Sammy new overalls.

"But the allotment checks—"

"I'm not cashing the first one of those checks."

"But Daddy said—"

"Your daddy thinks the allotment checks will make things rosy." Her voice was bitter. "If I take the easy way and spend the money like he wants, buying new clothes and frivolous toys, we'll be right back in the same shape, still living hand-to-mouth right here in this shack, when, and if, your daddy makes it home."

My stomach knotted. No new clothes....

And Mama shouldn't even hint that Daddy might not come home! It might jinx him.

Her lips thinned. "Better to do without now and eventually have better."

I frowned. Daddy wanted those allotment checks spent on lots of wonderful things.

"The only way to keep that allotment from slipping away, bit by bit, is to hoard every check. You understand?"

"Yes, ma'am," answered Sammy.

I glared, not believing how she dared defy Daddy's wishes.

"We'll all have to work hard to save for a farm. I intend to take every odd job I can get. That means you boys will have to take over lots of my work. And for a while you best get ready to see harder times than you've ever seen. But we're not going to always live like poor white trash."

She intended to make things harder than this! How much more could we do without? How could she be so mean?

Angrier than I ever remembered being, I stomped out the back door.

Grandpa was sitting on the porch, smoking, as I crawled through the fence. I ignored him and headed for the back door.

"What's yer hurry, boy?" he called. "You got a hive of yellow jackets on your tail?"

"Just running late," I mumbled, not wanting to be sociable. It did no good. He followed me inside.

"Unless I miss my guess," he studied me through hooded, bloodshot eyes, "you're mad at someone...yer mama?" he guessed.

"Could be," I snapped.

"She can be right vexing," he noted. "I been mad at her plenty of times myself."

He was smart enough not to pry, and I let my guard down. After all, he was family. "She's aiming to stash back Daddy's checks and keep us in rags, so she can keep the money," I spat out.

"She is? Then how's she figuring to feed all of you?"

"She's got a fool plan to do odd jobs and work for Uncle Roy at the sawmill."

At mention of working for Uncle Roy, Grandpa's eyes narrowed. Uncle Roy's mill was a sore spot with Grandpa. He resented Roy starting his own business instead of joining him at bootlegging. I knew making moonshine was Grandpa's business, even though Mama never talked about it.

"She ain't buying you any new school clothes?" he asked, looking shocked. "Why, them is rags." He pointed to my patched knees. "It ain't right for a boy to get laughed at cause his ankles is showing...especially if his mama has money stuck back."

I stayed quiet, but silently agreed. No one had laughed at me yet—but if my pants got any shorter, they might.

When I brought in the milk, Grandpa said, "Husky boy like you could make his own money. Buy his own clothes."

I shot him a look. "Maybe. If he had a job."

"There's always money around," he said, "if a fellow's smart enough to go after it."

Grandpa had an idea. I could see it in his eyes.

"You got any ideas how I can make some money, Grandpa?"

"Let me think on it a bit. I'll see what I can come up with."

I hoped he came up with a good plan soon. I needed a radio battery. And it was a cinch Mama wouldn't be buying one.

He pulled on his chin thoughtfully. "Yer mama is dead set agin' my business. But making shine is only illegal cause the government can't tax it. Yer kin was respected brewers back in the old country.

"Making good liquor is a knowledge that's been passed down through generations of Matthers, father to son. I learned firsthand from my Grandpa Dillon." His eyes grew hard. "Roy as good as spit in my face when he'd have no part of it." He eyed me up and down. "Could be you might be the one to take up the slack." He dropped into a chair and uncorked a jug. "I'll have to think on it."

While he took a long pull, I headed for the door. I wasn't sure about getting too involved with Grandpa. I couldn't quite trust the hard glitter in his eyes.

When Mama said, "Good morning," I didn't answer. Instead I slid onto the bench and began stirring molasses into my oatmeal. I looked up through mussed hair that fell across my forehead. "Got any butter?" I knew there was none.

She sat at the end of the table, holding Timmy on her lap. "You know Bossy barely gives a glassful every milking."

"I reckon Rawlings has butter at the store."

She gave me a steady look as she pulled Timmy's shirt over his squirming body. "And as far as I'm concerned that's where it'll stay."

I hoped after Mama had a little time to think about it, she would see how foolish her plan was and change her mind. She had not. Pushing back the bowl, I left the oatmeal and let the screen door slam behind me. Sammy soon ran to catch up.

"What you in such a blasted hurry for? We got plenty of time before the bell." He was panting. "Mama sent some cornpone for our lunch and this jar of tomatoes to go in the soup."

Every so often, we all brought canned goods from home and one of the teachers made a large pot of soup—or stew if there was meat—on the potbellied stove for all to share.

I grunted and kept walking. He kept pace with two steps to my one. My legs were longer than last year, I noticed with satisfaction. Pretty soon I would be grown, old enough to leave home. The way I felt this morning, that couldn't come soon enough.

Sammy handed me a comb. "Your hair looks awful. Mama sent this. She said be sure not to lose it."

Without stopping I jerked the comb through my thick hair.

"She sent some extra for your breakfast." He held out two golden-fried cornpones.

I poked the comb into my hip pocket and started to ignore the outstretched hand, but my stomach was hollow. I usually ate a big breakfast. When he poked them closer, I took them.

As I chewed the crispy pones, Sammy went on, "I don't like it when you're mean to Mama."

"Me mean to her!" I exploded, stopping dead in my tracks. "You got things kind of twisted, ain't you, Sammy? She's the one expecting us to starve and wear rags so she can have Daddy's money all to herself."

"No she's not." He drew his brows together, looking as if he wanted to say more, but couldn't figure out what.

I let the matter drop while I crossed the creek, out of habit using the stepping stones. The water was so low I could have crossed almost anywhere without muddying my feet. Sammy followed with Laddie right behind, the dog already panting, his tongue hanging out in the still, hot morning.

"She ain't wanting the money for herself. She wants to buy us a good house," he persisted.

I pierced him with a cold stare. "That's not what Daddy said to do with that money."

He looked troubled then, and we went on through the woods in silence.

So far Mama's odd jobs of laundry and mending had brought in only a couple of dollars. The flour and meal barrels were getting low. With grim satisfaction, I wondered what she would do when they ran out. Cash an allotment check, I was betting.

I thought about Grandpa. Mama had said I was to have nothing to do with his shenanigans. It would serve her right if I did. Mama had a plan to get what she wanted—maybe it was time I had one too.

School seemed to last forever that day. I stayed in a bad mood. It didn't help when I almost flunked a math test by not paying attention. When I got home, I slammed my books on the table. Mama looked up from the pan of peas she was shelling.

"That's no way to handle books," she began to scold, but the chickens started squawking. "Better go see what's upset them," she said. Just then Sammy sidled inside.

"What's botherin' the chickens?" I asked.

He ignored the question and stood rubbing a bare foot up and down the back of one leg. He sneezed.

"Chicken and dumplings sure would taste good, Mama," he said, looking sheepish. "Reckon we could have 'em?"

Mama turned around. Without a word, she looked at him until he slowly drew out what was hidden behind his back. It was a fat leghorn hen, her head lolled to one side where Sammy gripped her limber neck.

"Enoch spurred me high up, between the shoulder blades. Felt like he drew blood. I hauled off and rocked him. Only thing is, I missed him and got her."

"Hope you learn something from this, Sammy. A nasty temper often makes a body do something they ain't aimin' to." Mama looked at me as she dried her hands and folded the dishtowel.

My mouth watered at the rich smell of chicken stewing. I could barely wait while the hen stewed and Mama sifted flour into a bowl to make dumplings. Her lips pursed as she eyed the remaining flour. She started to put the lid back on the flour can. When she caught me staring, she flushed and then dipped another cup full and dumped it into the bowl.

After doing my chores that evening, I took my guitar, heading for the bluff to lick my wounds. I had not been there long when Charlie joined me.

"You happy now, Jackson?" I had just played a little run on the guitar when he came up and dropped down beside me on the big flat rock.

"Yeah. I'm happy." It was a lie. I was still fuming over Mama and school, but there was no need to bother Charlie. He was tenderhearted. It worried him if he thought anything was wrong with anyone.

"Joel's not happy today."

"What's wrong with Joel?"

"He got mad and yelled at me." Charlie dropped his head. "I forget, Jackson. I forget to do stuff like he tells me."

I patted his shoulder. "I forget sometimes, too. And sometimes Mama scolds when she ain't really mad. I bet Joel ain't really mad at you, just a little upset."

Charlie looked up. "Yeah. He said he was upset. That's what he said." He screwed up his face trying to remember. "Joel said it was bad today."

I nodded, not wanting to pry, but Charlie went on. "He said Sissy died today."

Joel's wife, Sissy, had been dead for several months. I supposed it was a year ago today.

"Guess that would make a fellow snappy," I sympathized. "He'll feel better tomorrow," I added, "and he probably won't yell at you any more."

I knew it was coming, but I cringed when Charlie pulled out the small watch. I sat back to endure the story again.

"Mama give me this watch." He showed me the tiny white face circled with gold. "Mama's with Jesus. She went there a long time before Sissy." He scrunched around on the rock for a better seat, and I knew I was in for more of the same. "Mama's gonna come back in the clouds with Jesus. She told me so." He looked up, his eyes searching the sky as if he thought he would see her any minute.

Charlie shoved the watch in front of my face. "What time does it say? Is it time for Jesus and Mama to come back?"

I shivered and darted a look skyward myself. I didn't like talk about dead people coming back—with or without Jesus. I'd just as soon Charlie's mama stayed put.

"It's six-thirty. But I don't know nothin' about Jesus coming." I sprang up. "I gotta go, Charlie. It's past milking time, and I have to get to Grandpa's." I scatted and left Charlie sitting on the rock holding his mama's watch and staring at the sky.

Saturday morning Uncle Roy needed us at the mill. We made enough that day to buy flour and meal. I was disappointed. I knew it was an ugly feeling, but I wanted Mama's plan to fail. I figured I hated the shack just as badly as she did, but I wanted Daddy to have the say about things. He would buy us a place when he got good and ready.

The boys stayed at Aunt Sue's while we worked. Aunt Sue had no children, and she said she enjoyed having them too much to take pay. We arrived at the mill soon after the sun popped over the ridge to find Uncle Roy already working. Cap pushed back and wrench in hand, he bent over a small gasoline engine.

"Roy, you're whistlin' that tune off key. Might help if you'd spit that twig out," chided Mama.

"Howdy, Sis. You two are here bright and early." He shot us a sunny grin but kept the sassafras twig in the corner of his mouth. "You know it's funny, I don't sing off key, but I can't carry a tune a'tall when I whistle."

"Trouble?" I pointed to the engine.

He drew a greasy rag from his back pocket and wiped his hands. "No more than usual. It's like Sue. I have to baby it to keep it purring."

Mama rolled her eyes.

"Morning," called Jake. He looked like a granddaddy-longlegs the way his long legs came reaching down the hill. He set a lunch pail in the shade and joined us.

"Howdy." Roy glanced up. "I sure got a early bird crew today. Looks like we're ready to make the sawdust fly."

I nodded my howdy, and aping Uncle Roy, plucked a twig and stuck it into my mouth.

"Howdy, Jake. How's all your folks?"

"They're fine, Miss Janie—that is all except Mama. She worries about the boys all the time."

"Having three sons in the army will do that to a mother."

"I reckon so." He scratched a head covered with curly brown hair. "She's scared to death that Hal or me will run off and join up too."

"Hal? Why, he's hardly out of diapers!"

Jake stuck out his chest. "Hal's eighteen and I'm seventeen."

"Like you said, Sis, barely out of diapers." Uncle Roy laughed and cranked the engine.

"I'm man enough to keep up with you," retorted Jake with a grin as he pulled a bandana from his pocket and tied it for a sweatband around his head. He grabbed the cant hook and rolled a log onto the saw's carriage.

"If you'd learn to wear a cap like a man, you'd save yourself some misery!" yelled Roy over the whine of the saw.

Jake scratched at peeling skin on a blistered nose and grinned. "I'll take the sunburn. I hate wearin' hats."

"Free country. But like I always say, 'there's slow-learners and then there's no-learners.'" Uncle Roy winked at me. "Reckon Jake fits in there someplace."

That day we did indeed make the sawdust fly. Uncle Roy grabbed the lever and gave a nod toward a huge slab pile.

"Sis, that pile's getting mighty high. Why don't you and Jackson start a new one over there."

Mama nodded. She drew on gloves and reached for the first long peel of bark as it dropped from a log sliding through the sharp teeth of the saw. Each time Uncle Roy pulled the lever, a long slab of bark sliced off. While Mama carried it away, Jake turned the log and it fed through again. I grabbed the next piece of bark and carried it to the pile. After the log was squared, it was ready to slice into boards. And when the boards began, we caught and stacked them into a neat pile on the bed of Uncle Roy's old gray pickup.

Jake quickly rolled another log and the process began all over again. By midmorning my shirt was sweat-soaked, my clothes and hair sawdust covered. I had blisters on my hands. Mama never complained of the work or the heat.

I loved working at the mill. I suppose sawmilling was in my blood. My great grandpa was said to be the best barrel stave maker that ever lived. We didn't mill staves now. Uncle Roy only milled lumber and crossties. The special mills for making staves were expensive, and Grandpa's had burned to the ground years ago.

I supposed making moonshine whiskey might be in my blood too. Grandpa Cole told me that his great grandpa, big Red Matthers, had passed the recipe down to his grandpa, Dillon Matthers, who passed the recipe down to Grandpa Cole. It almost made me think of all the begets in the Bible—except I don't think any of those folks were known for making fine moonshine.

Uncle Roy had departed from tradition when he went to work at my Grandpa Loring's sawmill when he was a teenager. He said he liked milling better than whiskey making, but Mama said the real reason was Aunt Sue had sworn she would never marry a moonshiner.

Daddy never said, but I always thought he regretted letting Mama talk him into selling the mill to Roy before moving off to Pine Bluff. I could tell he loved milling too, even though it didn't pay the big money that factory work did.

The day sped by. When Uncle Roy declared a break, we sought shade and sank gratefully onto the grass. Although the saw had stopped, my ears kept ringing.

Uncle Roy knocked sawdust from his clothes and sat down beside us. He pulled off the cap and let the hot breeze stir his sweaty hair as he scanned the sky. "Most folks are cussin' this drought, but I can't help dreading wet weather. Muddy ground is sure a logger's nightmare."

I knew there would more than likely soon be days too wet for the mules to skid timber. And those would be days Mama couldn't work at the mill. With winter coming on, she would have to start cashing those checks. I smiled, then sobered. Of course, I wished Uncle Roy no ill.

"Sis, you been doin' a good job this last couple of weeks," said Uncle Roy. "Makes things go a heap faster." He punched my arm. "And the apple ain't fell far from the tree. This boy is a worker like you and Keith."

We took the compliment in silence and Uncle Roy continued, "I'm thinking of trying for a government contract. They're beggin' for pine timber. Need it for making crates to ship war supplies—say they can't make 'em fast enough. Zearl Johnson says there's going be some big contracts let pretty soon." He hesitated. "I'm just a one-horse operation, and I don't know if this old junky equipment will hold up, but I've been thinkin' of hiring a crew and giving it a try. Might even be worth taking out a loan and getting a better engine."

"I think you should, Roy," urged Mama. "It may be a once-in-a-lifetime chance. When the war's over the contracts will likely disappear."

"You're right." He looked pleased. "I might lose my shirt, but I'm gonna give it a whirl!" He grinned wickedly. "Besides, Sue just loves me without my shirt."

Mama slapped his shoulder and we returned to work. I frowned. If Uncle Roy got a government contract, he would likely pay Mama higher wages. And he'd run the mill, come hell-or-high water. Mama might not have to cash a check any time soon.

The next day we borrowed Uncle Roy's pickup, and Mama drove us to pick pears at Daddy's old home place eight miles away on Minnow Creek. Years ago, when Daddy's folks died, he had moved in with an uncle, and the home place had been sold to some folks who lived in Little Rock. But they didn't mind us picking pears from the big tree that grew close to the creek.

The day was almost cool, and the black-gum leaves were turning red. I felt something in the air, something I couldn't quite put my finger on—just a feeling. I sniffed. Daddy said you could smell fall. Maybe that was what it was, the smell of cool weather coming. I shinnied up the tree and threw the golden pears down to Mama, while Sammy and Timmy picked up the ones on the ground.

"Sammy, put the bruised ones separate. In that basket yonder," ordered Mama. "I'll can them first, before they spoil, and save these good ones to eat fresh as long as possible."

I tossed a big, fat pear and Mama caught it with both hands. "Not bad for a girl," I praised. I was in a good mood, enjoying a mouthful of sugary pear.

Mama bit into one. "I declare, I forget how good these are till I taste them again. I have no idea what kind they are, but I never tasted better."

The tree was old for a fruit tree. Daddy said it was bearing when he was a boy. Being close to the creek, it always had a good crop, even in a drought.

"Don't eat too many, boys," cautioned Mama. "They'll give you the trots."

We should have listened. Sammy and I spent more time at the outhouse that night than we did in our bed. But we had been starving for something besides beans and cornbread. I rubbed my growling stomach and decided the tasty pears had been worth it. Sometime after midnight, on my way back from my last trip to the outhouse, I saw lightning flicker low in the west. I closed my window, shivered, and pulled up the sheet on my bed. It looked like the drought might soon be over. Just before dawn, I woke to the sound of rain pattering on the tin roof. I snuggled close to Sammy and went back to sleep.

Chapter 6

My fifteenth birthday, October 11th, passed with no more celebration than Mama and Sammy wishing me a happy birthday. I was not disappointed, for our family had never made a fuss over birthdays.

While a drizzling mist streaked down the schoolroom windows, I stared out, thinking of hunting and fishing—and Daddy. There had been three letters, arriving at the same time and letting us know that he was still at Camp Swift, Texas. He thought he would be there for a little longer. The new recruits, as Daddy put it, were learning to march, hit the dirt, and use a rifle. I figured Daddy probably knew more about rifles than almost anyone. His specialty was a weapon called a BAR, a Browning automatic rifle, with a bandolier for ammunition.

I wished by some miracle that the war would end before he had to go fight. That evening at supper when I mentioned it to Mama, a strange look crossed her face. After a while, I saw her reach into an apron pocket and pull out the little black book, the record of Daddy's allotment checks on deposit. Not a night passed without her opening it near the lamp. She opened it now and rubbed her hand over the total—$150 printed boldly on the first page. When she caught me staring, she flushed.

I grew sullen. "You worried if Daddy comes home those checks will stop?"

Her mouth fell open. "Surely you know I love your daddy and you children more than anything on this earth!"

My heart hardened against the hurt in her voice. I stared at my plate and pushed aside the food with my fork. It was fake sausage made from whippoorwill peas mashed full of red pepper and sage, and then rolled in flour and fried. But I was hungry for meat. We'd been without for days.

"If you're so crazy about us, how come you don't buy some meat, instead of feeding us this slop?"

She flinched as if I'd slapped her, and I felt ashamed. I wasn't about to admit that the patties on my plate did taste almost like sausage.

An extra hard gust suddenly howled between the gaping boards and fluttered the flour sack curtain hanging at the window.

"Meat would taste good,"—Mama's mouth set in grim lines—"but peas will feed a body just fine, and I aim to get us out of this drafty shack!"

She grabbed a copy of the Grit newspaper Uncle Roy had given us and began furiously folding a page over and over into a fat wad to poke between the boards.

Only a small fire burned in the cook stove. The fireplace devoured wood, so we hoarded the supply Daddy had cut against the real cold. I looked around, hating the bare, cold room. If she wanted to, Mama could make things better, buy new curtains and maybe even pictures to hang on the walls and flowered wallpaper like Miss Hilda had. I knew it would do no good to suggest it. Besides, I was feeling ashamed. Daddy would have tanned my hide for the way I had just talked to her.

Almost overnight, fall arrived. The early mornings were sharp and misty with fog. It felt good to pull up a quilt, and I winced each morning as my bare feet touched the cold floor. I sympathized with Laddie. He was frisky and wanted to go hunting. So did I. I chafed because Mama still thought I was too young to be trusted with the shotgun, but I wondered if she thought I'd miss my shots and waste shells.

The cold snap had Mama anxious to finish the cellar, which was now a fair-sized hole. But she said it would have to wait, for as soon as the weather cleared, it would be time to harvest Uncle Roy's crop of sorghum cane. It was a good thing, for our last can of sorghum had disappeared days ago, and Uncle Roy would trade sorghum for our work in the harvest. We boys loved to pour the golden-brown syrup over pancakes and biscuits, hot and slathered with butter. We had plenty of butter again. When the rains started, the grass came back, and along with it, so did Bossy's milk.

Bossy was bred to Grandpa's bull and was due to freshen in February. To grow a good calf, the cow would need turning dry soon. I didn't like the thought of being without milk and butter again. I wondered if Grandpa would have any to spare. He was mighty congenial lately. I decided to ask the next time I went over.

With evening came a lightening of western sky. Mama forecast a clear day ahead. And the next morning the sun did rise bold and yellow, sparkling on puddles in the ruts of the road and chasing away the wispy mist that clung to the low places and to the hollow.

"Jackson, you'll have to stay home from school today to keep an eye on Timmy. I need to help Roy and Sue make sorghum."

"I'd rather help with the sorghum and you could watch Timmy." I looked up hopeful. Old man Caruthers was making life unbearable lately making us diagram sentences.

Mama studied me. "It won't be long until you can do a man's work. You're muscled like my people, not slender like your daddy."

"I can watch Timmy," Sammy volunteered.

"I think we'll all go," she decided. "We'll make a picnic of it."

Sammy and I both whooped our heads off.

Mama dressed in the brown dress, an old gray cardigan, and a flowered-print scarf tied firmly under her chin. She walked briskly down the road with us coming behind. As we left the yard, Enoch made a flying dash at Sammy, but Sammy had on a jacket, so no real harm was done. Mama wasn't looking, so he hurled a rock that barely missed the rooster.

"Someday I'm gonna blow his head off with Daddy's shotgun," vowed Sammy. When I grinned, he shot out, "Just wait and see if I don't."

The sky was clear, but little warmth came from the bright sun. A gusting wind, tangy with the smell of cedars, stung our cheeks and noses, but the brisk pace kept our bodies warm.

I tried to avoid the mud, but in spite of all efforts, red clay stuck to the soles of my boots and clung there in big clumps until I finally stopped and scraped it off on a patch of grass.

"Aren't the woods pretty," observed Mama. "Since it's been so dry, I figured the leaves would just turn brown and fall off, but look at those sugar maples. They're a sight to see."

My eyes swept the woods. They were pretty. Deep-red sassafras and purple-red sumac crowded the path, and there were gold-leafed hickories everywhere. The maples, brightest of all, were every shade of orange, red, and coral.

Suddenly I smelled muscadines. I stopped and looked into the trees nearby until I spied the vines loaded with red-brown grapes. They would need picking soon before the wild things ate them. I stretched high and picked a few and stored them in my jaws like a squirrel. The husks were tough, but no grape on earth tasted better.

"Remember where these muscadines are," said Mama. "Soon as the sorghum's done, I'll make jelly." Then she frowned. "Of course that means needing extra sugar, and that means haggling with your grandpa."

There were also chinquapins growing close by. It made my mouth water to think about cracking them out some snowy night. Feeling happy, I hurried ahead, lugging Timmy on my hip.

Uncle Roy spied us and helloed from the top of the hill where the sorghum mill sat. He stood beside the mule-drawn wagon loaded high with a stack of freshly cut cane. A hot fire blazed in the firebox under the long copper pan used by four generations of Matthers for molasses making. Uncle Roy made it just the same, with only one exception. He used a small gasoline engine rather than mule power to turn the mill. I heard it sputtering as I drew near.

Rosy-cheeked, plump Aunt Sue, with soft brown eyes and brown hair peeking from under a scarf, called a cheery greeting. She was already busy poking wood into the firebox of the long, rectangle molasses cooker.

"I see you've already got a batch going. Sorry we're late," Mama apologized.

"You ain't late. We're early." Roy flashed a big grin. "The old woman cracked her whip and booted me out long before daylight. She knows this sorghum crop will bring in a little cash money, and she wants it done and in the jugs by nightfall." His eyes teased Aunt Sue. "That's what a fellow gets for marrying a working woman and turning her into a lady of leisure."

"Leisure!" Mama snorted. "Sue never sits down, and I never saw anyone as soft-spoken and sweet. As for you bein' hen-pecked," Mama scoffed, "if love weren't so blind, Sue could still be working for wages instead of slaving for you."

"Aw, you're glad you married me, aren't you darling? Just think, if you were still sitting behind that old typewriter, you wouldn't be here in the sunshine with me!"

Aunt Sue smiled softly. "There's nowhere on earth I'd rather be than out here with you."

All of a sudden, Mama looked sad. I guessed she was missing Daddy. Quickly she changed the subject. "How much sorghum do you think it'll make?"

"Won't be a great lot, but I'm lucky to have any. Sam Hughes lost his whole crop—dried up in the field. I planted late, and if mine hadn't been right by the creek, I'd have lost it too. Hope it's not bitter. Sometimes drought makes it bitter as gall."

He took a pocketknife from an overall pocket and cut off a small section of cane and handed it to her. "It doesn't taste too bad, does it?"

She chewed on the coarse stalk and, when the sugary sweetness filled her mouth, shook her head.

"It's plumb good, Roy. I think it'll be fine."

He looked relieved. "Let's head this so I can get a new batch on."

Mama selected a couple of sharp knives from some lying on the wagon tailgate and handed me one. We swiftly began lopping off the heads of grain on top of each stalk and dropping them into a bucket to be saved for chicken feed. With both of us working, the pile of stalks grew quickly. When enough were headed, Uncle Roy began feeding the stalks between the rollers of the press. Clear juice ran steadily into a stave barrel.

Aunt Sue shielded her face with one arm. Using a long handled scoop, she reached across the pan to skim a green film from the top of the steaming amber liquid and threw the bitter scum into an old lard can. When the mixture had boiled enough, Uncle Roy opened baffles located on the lower end of the long pan. Using a wooden paddle, he pushed the boiling cane juice toward the far end. Then he closed the baffles and opened a spigot on the stave barrel to turn in a flow of fresh juice. As the syrup thickened, bubbles rose and popped, and the air grew fragrant with the smell of molasses.

"I'll spell you awhile on the skimmin'," I volunteered.

"Thanks. It gets warm standing over this pan." Aunt Sue gave me the skimmer but, without resting, went immediately to help stack the mashed pieces of cane to be used for fodder into a heap on another wagon.

"Have you heard from Keith?" she called over her shoulder as she worked.

"I got three letters all at once. He's fine and still in Texas." Mama shifted the knife to the other hand and tucked a stray twig of hair blown loose by the wind back under the rayon scarf. "They're doing all kinds of training. He doesn't know when he'll be shipping out—but I dread it."

"I heard on the radio that we're whipping the Japanese on the Aleutian Islands and we're sinking lots of their ships," offered Aunt Sue. "Maybe it'll all be over soon."

"There's plenty more islands—and plenty more Japs," countered Uncle Roy, removing a sliver of chewed cane from the corner of his mouth. "I doubt Keith'll be home any time soon."

"Course," he continued slowly, cutting his eyes at Mama, "I don't rightly understand why he went in the first place."

"You nor me either," said Mama as my jaw tightened.

"He ain't gimped up like me," Uncle Roy held up the hand missing three fingers due to a saw blade accident years before, "but I doubt they'd have called him back since he has a passel of young'uns. Besides that he could have claimed a farm exemption—working part-time for Zearl Johnson like he did. Government claims to need farmers as much as soldiers."

"I know," she agreed. "I told him all that, but he wouldn't listen. You know Keith. He's always readin' and thinkin'—but sometimes without a lick of common sense. And when he gets a notion, he's stubborn as a mule."

I flashed her a bitter look and thought how the pot was calling the kettle black! Besides, Daddy had plenty of common sense. The trouble was Mama couldn't see past her own back yard. Daddy was hoping to keep the world a fit place to live.

"He read those articles Ernie Pyle wrote—the ones about the blitz over London. Keith said he painted it just like a body was right there. That's when Keith got all stirred up about the war. Then after Pearl Harbor, he wouldn't listen to me. I told him one man wasn't going to win or lose this fight."

Defiant, I jumped in. "Daddy said before it's over, it'll likely take every able-bodied man in the country."

"Maybe he's right at that," said Uncle Roy. "Did you hear about those bomb fragments that fell in Oregon the other day?" When Mama nodded, he went on, "Since they turned out to be Japanese, Uncle Sam's likely to start drafting guys with only half a hand." Uncle Roy playfully swatted Aunt Sue on the rear. "Would you miss me, darlin'?"

"Not one bit," she lied.

He laughed and changed the subject. "I hear they might start rationing gasoline. Can't get vehicle parts or tires now. It'll make it hard on the working man. I think we're in for some mighty hard times."

"I never knew there was any other kind." Mama shut her lips hard and kept cutting.

I skimmed until my arm felt ready to fall off. By the time Mama spread the blanket under the tree, I was more than ready for the picnic lunch. She had brought boiled eggs and cornbread. I ignored those and ate so much of Aunt Sue's crispy fried ham and flaky-crusted apple pie that Mama finally gave me a scolding look, which I pretended not to see.

One evening in late October, I leaned against one of the ancient oaks lining the Johnson's big yard and watched a crowd gather. Some came in cars and pickup trucks. Most arrived in wagons, on horseback, or on foot—some from miles away—to enjoy the dance, Hal's going away party. I was here only because Jake had stopped by and begged Mama to let me come.

The evening was mild, but beyond the clapboard house, the sun was setting behind a few overlapping clouds that had begun to thicken and look suspiciously like rain clouds.

"Hope them clouds ain't all show. My place is still dry. It'll take more than a rain 'er two to get over that there drought we had last summer!" Zearl Johnson, standing in the group of graybeards, spit a brown stream and wiped his long face. He caught my eye.

"How's yer pa?"

"Last we heard he was fine, but it took the letters a while to get here."

"If anyone can make it, Keith Loring will."

I nodded my appreciation of the sentiment and let my eyes drift again. I was not acquainted with the big-bellied man working the crowd passing out cards. Zearl said the fellow was running for sheriff. I didn't figure he had much chance of beating Sheriff Thompson. Daddy and Mama thought real highly of Buster Thompson, and so did everyone else as far as I knew.

My glance wandered on. In spite of chilly nights, there had been no killing frost yet, and Maggie Johnson's flowers, although wilting, still lived. Mama loved flowers neatly potted and arranged. Maggie's were placed helter-skelter around the yard sticking like quills on a porcupine from every kind of container: an old cream can, a coal-bucket, an old teakettle minus the lid. There was even a rusted foot-tub filled with red geraniums to add a bright touch to the high front porch.

The unmistakable smell of roast pork filled the air, and my stomach growled. It had been so long since I'd had fresh roast pork, I hardly remembered how it tasted. I got in line and started counting the heads in front of me, worrying that the good stuff would be snatched before I got some.

I needn't have worried. The sawhorse-and–plank tables stretching across the yard were filled with food. The rich smells made my mouth water even before I spied bowls filled with mashed potatoes floating in butter, yellow hominy, sour cabbage kraut, huge pans of baked beans spiced with molasses, and platters heaped high with steaming cornbread. There was chicken of all kinds: roasted, stewed with dumplings, and fried with golden crust.

A three-layered cake took my eye, its fluffy frosting white and mounded like snowdrifts. It was disappearing quickly as the crowd filed by. Sammy and Timmy loved cake. I wished they could be here to get a piece.

I planned to put away plenty of everything tonight. I figured the Johnsons would be tightening their belts after providing this feast. It must have nearly emptied smokehouse and cellar. But Hal was leaving for the Army on Monday, and who knew if he would ever return.

"Come help your plate, Dora," invited a frazzled looking Maggie Johnson, carving thick, pink slices of roast pork and hickory-smoked ham. "I declare," she shooed away a fly. "The way these flies are gathering, I do believe it's going to rain."

"It's bound to, fer I heared the rain crows callin', and my hens has been ruffled up all day," agreed Dora.

Dora was Delbert Slate's wife. The Slates were near neighbors, but I tried to keep my distance. They were what Mama called white trash because they worked seldom and bathed less. Dora had a little, pinched face and thin, stringy hair pulled back into a bun so tight it made her eyes squint. Years of snuff dipping had turned her broken teeth almost the same dirty yellow as her hair. I felt sorry for the kids, especially Dillard, the oldest. He was ten. At school he hardly ever raised his head, and he seemed scared of his own shadow. The other four ragged, barefoot boys clustered around Dora, clinging to her faded dress, while the baby, a girl with damp, blonde curls, sat propped on her bony hip. Using the baby's dress-tail, Dora wiped drool from its wet mouth. It looked to be Timmy's age, and I figured it was teething like Timmy was.

"Your mama here?" asked Mrs. Johnson as I stepped forward to get a slice of the juicy roast and another of the ham.

"No, ma'am. She worked at the sawmill today and she's awful tired."

"Well, you be sure and take her a plate, and take enough for the boys, too," she added. "I figure that pretty sister of yours will come out from town. Rita May loves a party."

"Speak of the devil," I muttered as Wade Lucas' Lincoln slid to a stop, flinging dust over the crowd. Wade and Rita May climbed out.

"With her pa gone, it sure didn't take Rita May long to go wild," said Dora. "Just look at that skirt—don't even cover her knees! When the sun goes down she'll turn blue as her dress—and them lips and nails! So red you can see 'em from twenty yards away."

My face blazed.

"Now, Dora." Apologetic, Mrs. Johnson glanced toward me. "Rita May ain't really wild. It's just this awful war. It's got all the young girls half crazy. Havin' to go to work and take over fer the men. Things is just changin' too fast." The gray head shook sadly.

I was pleased that Mrs. Johnson had defended my sister. I shot Dora a sullen look, but I knew if Mama had been there she would have made Rita go home and sew a few more yards of shiny blue cloth onto that dress.

"Hey, Jake!" Someone yelled toward the Johnson brothers who were hunkered under a tree, holding plates of food heaped high. "You boys can eat when you get old. Right now we wanta dance!" Hoots and whistles followed the remark.

"Let 'em eat, boys," called Zearl. "They'll need their strength to play as long as y'all will want to dance!"

The Johnsons were good musicians. Grandpa claimed it was the Matthers blood flowing in their veins from way back yonder. I reckoned I got my love of music from both sides. Daddy said he had an uncle way back then that was known all over the country for his fiddling.

Someone yelled back, "I got something will churk 'em up better than food!"

It was Grandpa. He stood with the men lounging against cars parked at the edge of the yard. With my plate loaded, I started over to join him. I gave Dora another ugly look as I walked past, but she paid me no mind. She was fussing at Delbert.

"I want to go home early before any devilment starts. And you stay away from Cole Matthers's jug, you hear?"

Delbert was rail-thin and dressed in patched overalls, faded red shirt, and decrepit brown brogans with hay twine for shoestrings. "You don't never want to have fun no more," he said bitterly.

"Yer idea of fun and mine is different!" she snapped. When she saw me looking, she shut up.

I joined the men and hunkered on the ground between Grandpa and Zearl. Grandpa looked pleased to see me.

"Howdy, boy. I never figured your mama would let you come tonight." Then he grinned wickedly. "Hey, I'll bet she don't know you're here." He slapped my back. "Good for you. Cuttin' loose from the ol' apron strings."

I kept quiet. He was right. It was high time I quit letting Mama treat me like a baby.

Before long, Hal and Jake, beanpole-thin and tall, their curly brown hair still damp and plastered down from a recent combing, went inside and came back out the screen door carrying guitar, fiddle, and banjo. They were greeted with more hoots and hollers. Zearl nodded toward them.

"My boys kin beat the birds at making music. But with three of 'em gone to war," Zearl shook his head, "it ain't the same." He pointed to a flag sporting three stars proudly on display in the Johnson's front window. "And now that Hal's going, Ma will have to sew another star on that flag in the winder. Jake there is a-rarin' to go too. Don't know if Maggie kin keep him here, but she's a-tryin'." Zearl paused to spit, making a prominent Adam's apple bob up and down.

The Johnsons could play well, but I thought Ben played even better. And where Ben's voice was deep and true, Jake sang through his nose. It was a popular style, even on the Opry, but I didn't like it.

"Turkey in the Straw" swung directly into "Under the Double Eagle." When Jake put down the banjo and picked up the fiddle,

Zearl rose to his full six-foot-two and clapped time while he called the sets of "Cotton-Eye Joe."

"I'd a been married a long time ago
If it hadn't been for Cotton-Eye Joe"

I watched the fast shuffling feet and swaying bodies—a swirl of print dresses and cotton shirts. With a touch of pride, I realized Rita May could out-dance them all. A bunch of lanterns hung from low limbs, and in their soft light her gaudy dress looked pretty. Rita May looked pretty too. Her hair suddenly glowed in the light of the big orange moon as it slipped from behind the clouds for a minute before it disappeared again as quickly as it had come. My pleasure quickly faded when Wade put his hands on her waist and twirled her around. My eyes narrowed when he smiled down into her face, but she seemed to like the attention and danced with him every dance.

Jake and Hal finally took a break from playing, and I went in search of another piece or two of Mrs. Johnson's famous peach pie. I was about to take a bite when my mouth dropped open wider. Coming toward me was Ben Tyler! Thinner and sun-baked, but unmistakably Ben, dressed in sailor uniform complete with white hat perched on the back of his head. I whooped and made for him, grabbed him around the neck and hugged him like a long lost brother. He was grinning ear to ear.

"Ben! You're back! How come you never wrote that you were coming? I thought you were in the Pacific."

"I was," he said. He held up his left hand. It was wrapped in bandages. "Until the Japs gave me a ticket home."

I sobered. "How bad is it?"

I dreaded the answer. That was Ben's catching hand, and more importantly, the one he used to fret guitar.

"Let's just say I'm lucky to be here." He gave his old, lopsided, white-toothed grin. "I should be at the bottom of the ocean, instead of talking to you and asking where that pretty sister of yours is."

When he turned to scan the crowd, I swallowed hard. I knew he wasn't going to like what he saw.

Rita May and Wade were right beside his Lincoln. The car doors were open and the radio was cranked up full blast. A boogie-woogie beat filled the air. Ben saw them too.

Wade was leaning forward, clapping to the beat, and Rita May was wiggling to the fast rhythm. Then suddenly she did a fast step and twirl, her skirt swirling high around her legs; then she slid heel and toe and cut loose dancing. My face turned red. This was sure not square dancing!

The crowd began to gather and, for a merciful minute, cut off Ben's view. He walked closer. I was sick but felt duty-bound to follow. Ben found a clear view and stopped near Delbert and Dora.

"That there's the jitterbug. I seen it done last time I was in Hot Springs." Delbert started clapping, keeping time.

Dora glared at him, then looked at Ben and dropped her voice. "You been going to dance halls, Delbert?" she hissed.

"What if I have?" he growled, flushed-face and mean-eyed.

Ben paid no attention to anyone except Wade and Rita May. Now they faced each other, and with fast moving feet, joined hands without slowing. It was plain this was not the first time they had danced together. Not missing a step, Wade dropped his hands to her waist and lifted her off the ground and then slid her first to one side and then the other. My mouth dropped open when he raised her high into the air, tossing her back between his legs and into the air again.

I had never seen such dancing. Neither had most of the crowd. Some of the older people were walking away, shaking their heads in disgust. My face burned. I peeked at Ben, wondering if he would ever speak to Rita again. I had seen him angry, but never like this. His eyes smoldered, and his jaw clenched vise tight as he watched in silence. With a knot in my stomach, I wondered what would happen when the dance was over.

When the music finally ended, Wade gave Rita May a big hug. The way Ben's face looked then, I figured Wade was in for the licking he deserved. But, with a sinking feeling, I remembered Ben's hand and realized Wade had nothing to fear for the moment.

Rita May twirled around, laughing. She stopped. Her eyes riveted on Ben and her face blanched. For a second, I thought she was going to faint. Then, with head held high, she came forward.

I wouldn't have blamed him for shaking her. I wanted to. But Ben just stared.

"Howdy, Ben," She spoke with a phony lightness. "Where'd you come from?"

"A war." His voice was low but granite hard. "Midway—South Pacific. Ever hear of it?"

Under Ben's steely gaze, Rita flushed. Laughter and talk flowed all around. Another loud, rollicking tune began to blare from the radio.

Ben looked behind her to where Wade leaned against a tree, watching them. "There's your kind of music. Your partner's waiting."

She raised her chin and gave Ben a haughty look. He turned and walked away into the night. I started to follow, but I figured he'd rather be alone.

"You idiot!" I lashed out, "letting Wade paw you. It'd serve you right if Ben never spoke to you again."

She surprised me by softly agreeing, "Yes, it would."

It had rained hard all night and was still coming down the next morning as I went to milk. The cold, gray sky suited my mood. I figured I'd lost all hope of having Ben for a brother.

I wasn't paying attention and stepped into a puddle beside the back door where the rain barrel had run over. Cold water soaked into my cracked boots, wetting my feet.

I scowled. "Maybe they'll fall apart and Mama will have to get me another pair," I griped. "Or maybe it's time I took Grandpa up on his offer," I pondered as I sloshed toward the barn. "He says I could earn enough in a few weeks to buy my own."

By noon the sky had cleared. With our morning chores finished, Sammy and I went to the store to check the mail.

"Good news, boys. Letters from your papa." Mr. Rawlings held up a stack of thin letters. I was so excited I did not ask to play the Gibson.

I let Sammy carry them home. He entered the yard yelling and waving the stack of envelopes.

"It's letters from Daddy! Letters from Daddy!"

Wearing an old sweater and scarf, Mama stood in the yard in front of a washstand. She dropped the dripping shirt back into the tub filled with hot suds and a washboard. "Let me dry first," she admonished as Sammy tried to shove the letters into her wet, shaking hands. She wiped on her apron, then carefully tore open the end of the first envelope.

Her voice trembled. "Not a word in a month and now a whole stack all at once!"

Daddy was fine. At least he had been two weeks earlier. Sammy clamored at her side, jumping up and down and demanding to know what Daddy said. She sat on the steps and read.

Daddy was now at a place for special infantry training, Camp Cibolo, Texas, learning how to do village fighting. There were mock villages built by the engineer battalion. They had funny names, Branntown, a North African type named after the division's chief of staff. And Kuhreville, the German style village.

Daddy thought the villages were just like being in a foreign country. He made everything sound like a picnic or camping out with lots of fun. We got introduced to Horseface Harry and Mugs McGilley. They were from the big city of Chicago. And there was Blackstrap Jones. No one could play a guitar like Blackstrap. The name came from the color of his guitar strap and not because he liked molasses as Sammy had first guessed. I wished I could hear Blackstrap play.

Toward the end of one letter, Daddy grew serious, and he wrote some stuff that Mama kept to herself. I saw tears in her eyes, and for a minute, I felt close to Mama. We were both missing Daddy something awful. After placing the letters into an apron pocket, she took the allotment check that had just come and looked long at it.

My heart hardened and I frowned. She fretted over that money as much as over Daddy.

Mama was never idle. Even when she sat down there was always sewing or mending in her lap. For that reason, before I left for school on Monday, I was surprised to see her sitting in the rocking chair reading a newspaper.

In the morning sun coming through the window, I noticed she had lost weight. Her cheekbones stuck out more than ever. Although her face was thin, the skin under her eyes was puffy. She had gotten little sleep lately. Timmy was teething and had been fussy.

He was asleep now, and she had made a cup of coffee. Coffee was rare these days, for we had been out of coffee beans for weeks. When Mama had last cleaned house for Miss Hilda, rather than throwing away the used grounds, Mama had put them into a can and brought them home.

Miss Hilda had also given her several newspapers, and although they were a week old, I wanted to read the articles. Mama was looking at the latest fashions on the Patterns Sewing Circle page. While I waited impatiently for her to turn the page, she studied a v-necked jumper described as one of the new conserve-fabric designs. Along with it was a picture of men's cuffless pants and the quote, "A cuff on your American trousers isn't worth a Japanese cuff on your American jaw."

Mama rubbed a hand across her threadbare dress. Conserve fabric or not, I knew there would be no new dress for her. These days, she wouldn't buy a spool of thread.

She flipped to the next page, skipping the war news. As I hung over her shoulder, the bold headlines caught my eye: Luxembourg Defies the Nazis.

"Let me read that, Mama." She waited while I hurried through the article.

"The pint-sized land of Luxembourg, one of the world's most important steel producing regions, repudiated Nazi propaganda that they were voluntarily acquiring German citizenship and entering the enemy armed forces. When the plucky Luxembourgers staged a general strike—the first in a German occupied country—German authorities declared a state of emergency and threatened striking workers with death."

I reckoned, compared with what those folks in Luxembourg were facing, the local headlines about shortages seemed less of a burden: "FDR Plans Nationwide Gas Rationing With 35-Mile Speed Limit for U.S.; Double-Time Pay Banned for Duration."

Mama showed no interest in either article and started to turn the page again, but I put out my hand to stop her.

"Mama, I want to read this too."

She handed me the paper and started clearing away the breakfast dishes while I read the Winchell column out loud.

"A nation lives by the higher values of its soul. Not by the lower prices on its store counters. Sugar is a luxury and gasoline a comfort. But liberty and freedom are still American necessities....

"It will cost most of our wealth to win this war. But all our riches to lose it. We must give most of our privileges or lose all of our rights."

With a spoon in midair, Mama stopped scraping a plate. "I thought when your daddy left, I'd get a break from war propaganda."

"Don't you care anything about the war?" I asked.

"I got enough to do minding my own business."

Mama's attitude about the war confused me. Everyone but her talked with pride about our men fighting and dying for freedom.

"Don't you think we've got to fight for freedom?" I asked.

She went back to scraping the plate. "We got no business poking our noses into Europe. That's none of our affair."

"Daddy thinks it is," I muttered.

She ignored me and started washing dishes. I was deep in thought about what Mr. Winchell had written. I figured Daddy would agree with him.

Mama jolted me back to reality. "You best get on to school or you'll be late."

"Mama, the teacher was tellin' us today that everybody's supposed to save their old grease and take it to the store. A government truck is gonna pick it up," said Sammy while helping me with the supper dishes.

"Yeah, they call it a grease salvage campaign," I put in. "And they have a slogan— 'From the fryin' pan to the firing line.'"

Mama looked up from the mending. "Why do they want old grease?"

"Teacher says they use it to make something called glycerin, and they use that to make gunpowder."

"Well, I've got my own slogan," said Mama. "From the fryin' pan to the soap kettle. I use every bit of extra grease to make the soap to wash your dirty necks."

"When we butcher can we give some lard? Wouldn't have to be much." Sammy squirmed from her look. Then he shot out, "Robby Hammond keeps bragging about how 'the Hammonds give this and the Hammonds give that' to help win the war."

Mama motioned him to her and pulled him onto her lap. "Robby Hammonds hasn't given up his daddy. You remind him of that next time he goes to braggin'."

I looked up from doing arithmetic. "Gee, Mama, you almost sound patriotic," I said hopefully. Although Daddy was in the army, I lived in dread that Mama would say something to the neighbors to brand her disloyal.

She misunderstood. Her eyes became green slits. "I've had just about enough of your smart mouth—"

Just then a timid knock sounded. It was Charlie standing on the porch holding a large parcel wrapped in brown paper.

"Howdy, Miz Janie. I catched a whopper of a catfish in Bradley's pond. Way more than enough fer us. And Joel said maybe you'd like some."

"Why, thank you, Charlie. That's mighty nice of you both." She reached for the package. "Be sure to tell Joel I said much obliged."

Charlie grew wistful. "Reckon I could stay awhile and play with Laddie?" Already his hand was on the dog's big head, but honesty made him hurriedly add, "Joel says not to be no nuisance."

"You won't be a nuisance! Come play with Laddie anytime," she offered.

"Oh boy!" His eyes lit then darkened. "But I ain't gonna tell Joel." Eyes on the ground, he mumbled, "He don't like me going places much. He thinks folks don't want me around."

Mama touched his shoulder. "You come anytime, Charlie. You're always welcome here."

His face brightened and he smiled from ear to ear. "You're always nice, Miz Janie."

I slammed my arithmetic book. He sure didn't know her like I did.

Chapter 7

It was almost noon on a mild November day. Through leafless trees I could see a clear view of a light-gray sky. There was hardly a nip in the air, but large flocks of snowbirds feeding in the fields warned of an end to this spell of good weather.

I hefted a rock on top of the pile already mounded on the sled and called "get-up" to the mule. Along with what we had gathered over the last weeks, I figured this should be enough to finish walling the cellar. For weeks, after school, I had helped do the final digging with a pick and shovel, shoring up the bottom of the walls with rocks. Now there was a fair-sized hole in the bank, as large as a small room, but it looked a bit lopsided. Uncle Roy was coming to help square the walls and to finish laying the rocks. He was also bringing white oak logs for the roof. Then all we would have to worry about was tin to cover the logs.

Most days lately were too chilly and damp for Timmy to play outside. Today was the exception, and he rode on the sled or toddled beside me. On cold days when Sammy and I were at school, Mama solved the babysitting problem by building a barricade of chairs in the corner of the kitchen and tying them together with twine. She returned often to make certain that Timmy had not scaled the walls and gotten into mischief. It made for slow progress on the digging, but her main concern was the hot stove in the other corner.

If all went well, she hoped to have beds and a stove moved into the cellar and to be able to sleep toasty warm by Christmas.

I dumped my load near where Mama knelt inside the tall walls scooped from the hillside. I went to lend a hand hoisting a flat rock into place on top of another with the clay mortar that was forming the wall. It was tiring work. I glanced toward the sun and thought about taking a break. It was almost time for dinner.

"Hello."

Startled, I whirled and then frowned. Most folks wouldn't just come up on you and scare the wits out of you. Anyone with any manners a'tall would "hello the house" and let you know they were about. But one look at this woman and I knew she wasn't country. Her high-heeled shoes were like stilts. I expected her to pitch over any minute.

While she looked Mama and me up and down, her nose crinkled like she smelled something bad. Mama stood and began brushing at the dirt clinging to the knees of Daddy's baggy gray trousers. She tucked back a lock of her hair that was sticking out of an old wool cap.

"I'm here on behalf of the State Defense Council. Have you heard about our V sticker?" The woman spoke in clipped tones. I got the impression she wanted to get shed of us as quickly as possible.

Mama's jaw stiffened. "No." Mama must have felt the same as me for she did not sound friendly.

"Well, every American wants to help win the war, and this is one way for those of us who can't go off to fight." The woman quickly rattled off the memorized speech. "I'm here to do an inspection of your home—with your permission, of course. And if it meets the criteria—uh, the rules—set up by the Council, you'll be awarded a decal to go in the window. Proof to your friends and neighbors that you're aiding the war effort."

"I've given up the daddy of my three boys," said Mama, deadpan and matter-of-fact. "If that ain't enough for the government—and the neighbors—they can go to blazes."

The woman's eyes hardened, but she was not put off. She drew a pencil from her clipboard. "Well, I'm supposed to ask anyway. There are five requirements for each home. I'll read each one, and you tell me if you comply."

"Does this home follow the instructions to conserve resources, such as keeping lights off at night?"

"I don't have lights on late. Kerosene costs money."

"Does this home conserve food, clothing, transportation, and health, in order to hasten an unceasing flow of war materials to our men at the front?"

"I don't throw away anything and I don't go anywhere."

"I'd say that qualifies on your behalf," she noted and put a check mark in the proper column.

"Does this home salvage essential materials in order that they may be converted to immediate war use?"

Mama was silent.

"Do you give to the junk drives in order for the materials to be used in the war effort?"

"I use everything I've got to feed and clothe my own."

I suppose she checked the no column.

"Do you buy war bonds or stamps regularly?"

"It's nobody's business how I spend my money."

The woman's face grew as red as Mama's beet pickles.

"Does this home refuse to spread rumors that divide our nation?"

Mama stared. "If I were you, I'd go back to the government people that sent you and tell them all their nosy questions are making folks mad."

The woman slammed shut the clipboard. "I'm afraid I can't give you a sticker. You haven't met every requirement."

We watched her stalk away.

"Dang government, always poking its nose where it doesn't belong and always wanting money. That's one thing I agree with your grandpa on—they're a bunch of leeches."

I flared up. "I hope you don't ever say that down at the store."

Lots of folks had talked anti-government before the war. I cringed recalling that Mr. Caruthers had said ignorant people were often suspicious of the government. Since Pearl Harbor everyone—except Mama and Grandpa Cole—were for Washington one hundred percent, or at least they were careful not to say otherwise.

She froze me with an icy look. "I'll say what I please."

It didn't seem right—Mama criticizing the government. She acted like Pappy Tyler, Ben's old grandpa, who was close to a hundred and had fought Yankees along Piney Creek and still considered himself a Confederate.

Daddy was patriotic. I didn't like being caught in the middle.

"You lambaste the government," my voice trembled, "but all your slaving and hoardin' and planning won't amount to a hill of beans if we lose the war! Do you think Hitler or Hirohito would let you keep your old money?"

She blinked and her eyes widened before she turned and hoisted another rock into place and dabbed it with wet clay from a nearby bucket. Maybe it was the first time she had imagined herself under the thumb of the likes of Hitler. I pressed my lips together and lifted another rock. Mama didn't say another word, but maybe I had given her something to think about.

The sun had begun to inch toward the one o'clock mark before I finally asked, "Ain't it about dinner time?"

Reluctantly she agreed to stop and eat. The way she drove herself, she acted as if someone were standing over us with a bullwhip. I figured what didn't get done today would be waiting tomorrow. No need to kill ourselves. But I didn't want my head snapped off, so I kept that thought to myself.

We washed up at the well. I lay on the floor, and while Mama made whippoorwill peas into sausage, I listened to the radio.

"Hush, Sammy!" I stopped quarreling over which program to tune in next, and cocked my head to better hear the faint voice of the radio announcer amid the crackling static.

I tried to wrap my mind around the strange place called Guadalcanal—the name sent a shiver down my spine. It might be silly, but I hoped if Daddy had to go, he would go to Europe rather than to some far-off island in the South Pacific fighting slant-eyed Japs. I had seen Germans but never Japanese—somehow the unknown was scarier.

"Mama," Sammy interrupted the commercial urging everyone to buy war bonds, "reckon Daddy will have to go to those islands?"

"I don't know. The government doesn't make a habit of telling soldiers where they're heading."

In his last letter, Daddy told us he had been transferred to Fort Benning, Georgia. He was glad. He had hated the Texas-Louisiana border. He was well, but missing us like crazy. He thought he would be shipping out in less than a week, but he did not know where.

As the sausage fried, Mama returned to hemming one of Miss Hilda's dresses with a needle threaded with pale yellow thread.

The rough skin of her fingers caught on the delicately embroidered material, so she laid the dress aside to rub glycerin and rosewater lotion into her hands.

A commercial interrupted the broadcast. I had begun to recognize the different voices of the announcers. This one sounded like the carnival huckster I had once heard when Daddy took us to a carnival in Pine Bluff.

"Ladies and gentlemen, as you know, the junk drives across the nation are a huge success! Enough scrap metal and rubber has been collected to make a big difference. Remember, one old tire provides enough rubber for twelve gas masks. One shovel will make twelve hand grenades. One plow will convert to one hundred 75 mm armor-piercing projectiles. So, although the junk rally was successful, we must not drop the ball. Keep that junk coming so we can throw it at Hitler!"

Sammy piped up, "Uncle Roy said the newspaper says to 'Jolt the Japs with Junk from Johnson County!'"

I shushed him when the news continued. "On Tuesday, Moscow released one of their most encouraging press reports since the Nazis invaded their country. Russian troops have smashed across the Don River to a point about 100 miles northwest of Stalingrad. There are reports of 50,000 German casualties. However, gloom persists in Russia with worry over the food supply for the Russian people this winter. The Germans moved trainloads of foodstuffs out of Russia."

Mama must have been thinking about us going hungry like the Russians because she began to check our supplies. There was still flour and cornmeal in the barrels. But when she raised the curtains over the cupboard, I saw rows of empty jars that were usually filled with beans, corn, peas, and kraut. I felt sort of scared when I looked at the empty shelves, until I remembered Daddy's checks. We wouldn't have to go hungry unless Mama chose to.

"I'm glad there's two shoats fattening in the hog pen," she spoke.

I had forgotten about butchering. Soon we would have plenty of meat. Daddy had asked Uncle Roy to help with the butchering when the time came, and it would soon be cold enough for that.

A few days later, when Roy came to visit, Mama asked what he thought about butchering.

"It's cold enough, but you sure you're up to it?" he asked staring at her weary face.

"I'd like to get it over with. Besides, meat will taste good for a change."

"If you're out of meat you ought to have spoken up. We got plenty of beef and pork, and I could maybe get you a venison," offered Roy. "Course deer have been mighty scarce the last few years. Folks have just about done in the game around here, tryin' to feed themselves."

"We're makin' do fine. I've still got chickens to kill." Mama refrained from telling Uncle Roy that it had been so long since we tasted beef, we could scarcely remember it. But Mama was not big on handouts, not even from family.

"If this cold snap holds—and I reckon it will—I'll be over day after tomorrow before daylight. Have Jackson lay in plenty of pine knots. You got a pot for scalding?"

Mama nodded. "I have everything we'll need, and I'll have it ready."

"Charlie Watson's been working for me, cutting firewood to sell. He ain't real bright, but he's strong as an ox. I'll bring him along to help. Sue would be glad to help, but she's down with the bursitis. I'll be goin' to town tomorrow. Want me to see if Rita May can come for the day?"

Mama chewed her lip. "If it won't put her out. I sure could use help fryin' down sausage and rendering lard."

"I'll bring her if I can." Roy waved goodbye.

I shifted positions and tried to avoid smoke. It seemed to follow no matter which side of the fire I was on. A large metal pot held water heated by a pine knot blaze underneath. The water was almost hot enough to scald. I had added a large pan of ashes at daylight to make lye. Now the water was a dirty shade of gray, but the lye would make the hog's hair come off easier.

A cold, brisk wind flapped my trouser legs, and it teased the flowered-print headscarf that held back Mama's hair. She added a few more pine knots as we waited for Uncle Roy and Charlie Watson.

A shot rang out and then silence. Shortly, a wagon pulled by the mule rounded the barn with Uncle Roy driving and Charlie walking alongside. A large black and white mound lay still on the wagon bed. Roy stopped near a block and tackle hanging from a tree above the barrel. Before he climbed down, his laugh rang out and he slapped his thigh.

"Janie, Charlie wants to know what the hoist is for. Says he don't need a block and tackle. He'll just souse the hog up and down holdin' to its back legs. I'll be dadgummed if I don't think he can!"

"I don't doubt it, Charlie. But the water's scalding hot, and you might splash yourself and get burned. I think we'd better use the rope." Mama smiled encouragingly into his gentle eyes.

"Yes 'm." Charlie ducked his head.

The door slammed as Rita May came outside. Charlie looked up. "There's Rita May. She's nice. She give me a piece of candy once. She's pretty, ain't she?"

"She sure is," agreed Uncle Roy. "Always has been pretty as a speckled pup."

"Joel says she takes after her mama," vowed Charlie.

Roy smiled at Mama's pink cheeks.

Rita stopped to give Laddie a quick pat before joining us. She wore a pair of slacks and one of Daddy's old jackets rolled up at the wrists. Even in that get-up, she managed to look stylish.

Charlie bent to pet the dog that followed with a wagging tail. "I like Laddie."

"We best get busy or there won't be any pork ready for dinner." Uncle Roy hunkered over the dead hog. He made slits in its back hocks and inserted the hook attached to the block and tackle. Then he began to pull on the rope. Without a word, Charlie walked up and took the rope.

Although Uncle Roy's broad shoulders were capable for the task, he thanked Charlie. "I sometimes forget to use your muscles too, Charlie."

The hog moved slowly upward, its tongue lolling from an open mouth. I had seen butchering done all my life, but I avoided the sight of the bloody neck where Uncle Roy had bled the animal. I had never learned to like the smell and mess of it all.

Uncle Roy raked his finger swiftly three times into the water. He said, "Water's just right. Let 'er down. Easy does it." He guided the body into the hot water and, taking hold of the hind legs, turned the hog back and forth inside the huge cast iron wash pot.

"Bring it up just a mite." He reached and gave the wet hair a tug. "Back down." He turned thumbs down to Charlie. "Ain't quite ready, but it won't be long." After a couple of minutes he checked again. "Haul her up, Charlie. She's just right."

I was thankful that Uncle Roy was excellent at knowing just when the hair would slip. If the water was not just the right temperature, the hair would not come loose, which made the scraping process—which was already bad enough—a nightmare.

Uncle Roy swung the wet carcass over a table made of planks laid across sawhorses. "Drop her down."

Charlie let the hog down, and we lost no time in beginning to scrape. It had to be done quickly or the hair seized again. In one hand I held the butcher knife handle, in the other I held the back of the blade near the end, with sharp edge straight down. In a smooth raking motion, I drew the knife toward myself as hair rolled off in front of the knife. I hated the slimy job. My appetite for fresh meat lessened considerably.

Rita May, with set jaws and a deep frown, worked across the table from Uncle Roy and me. Mama stood alongside her scraping a different portion. Charlie scraped the head. We stopped often to rake off the knives onto burlap sacks.

When the hog had cooled too much, I brought a bucket of scalding water dipped from the pot and wet it again. And after one side was scraped, we flipped over to the other. The top half finished, Uncle Roy made a hook hole in the bottom jaw so he and Charlie could souse the hog's bottom half into the water that still warmed over the smoky blaze.

"Can you all manage?" Uncle Roy asked Mama. "Good. Then we'll go kill the next one and get started on it. I'd like to have the meat in the salt by noon."

The wagon creaked away. We worked hurriedly and had finished scraping the first hog by the time Uncle Roy and Charlie were half through with the other.

"My hands are frozen." Rita May rubbed her hands together and blew on them. "I hate this stinking job!"

"Why don't you go on inside and warm up. Check on Timmy and Sammy. And make us some fresh coffee," Mama added.

"Gladly." Rita went toward the house, and I knew she would not be returning soon.

By noon the hogs were gutted, quartered, and lying in the salt to cure.

"That's a big job well done," said Uncle Roy as he stood by the wagon sharpening the butcher knife. "I'll come back in three weeks to hang the hams and shoulders and start them smoking. You get up some good green hickory chips."

"Yes sir, I will—when I get a free minute to do it. Mama don't let me get through with one chore before she's got another waiting."

Uncle Roy took the knife off the stone and shook it at me. "Your mama might push you," he said, "but she pushes herself harder—way too hard. You ought to carry all the load you can," he finished.

He was as bad as her. I figured most grownups had forgotten what having fun was all about.

He put down the stone and checked the edge on the knife by rolling up his sleeve and shaving a small place on his arm. Hair peeled off, just like a razor.

"Daddy says you're the best knife sharpener around," I noted.

"Can't abide a dull knife ner an empty gun," he said. "They're both useless." After a bit he looked at me. "Your daddy asked me to keep check on things." He glanced toward the house. "I know your mama is a proud woman, but I need to know if y'all ever need anything. I never knew you were doing without meat." He frowned. "Of course I should have asked."

"We're doin' fine." I felt prideful—just like Mama, I suppose.

Uncle Roy let it drop. "Heard your daddy's in Africa."

"Hope he likes it there," I said. "He sure hated that Louisiana border—said it was nothing but heat and bugs and misery. He vowed anywhere would be a cakewalk after that."

Uncle Roy drew his brows together. "He's liable to find out what real heat is in that African desert."

"He sure sounds lonesome. He keeps saying how much he loves gettin' our letters and to keep them coming because they're about all that keeps him going." I hesitated and added low, "I heard Mama crying in the night after that letter came. I wish he'd come home!" Uncle Roy squeezed my shoulder.

After supper I lay on the floor in front of the crackling fire while Mama and Rita stood side by side at the kitchen table chopping scraps of meat into sausage.

"I appreciate you comin'. It's been a big help."

Rita May glanced at Mama.

"I'm glad I came too."

Mama looked up startled. It was the first civil words from Rita May in a long time.

"You look bad, Mama. You been sick?"

Mama shook her head. "I just lost a lot of sleep lately." She added, "Timmy had another one of his bad earaches. He couldn't sleep."

"Poor little thing! You should have sent for me."

"I didn't want you to lose work," said Mama.

Rita May looked at the baby playing on the floor. "Some things are more important than a job," she said.

"Mama," Sammy interrupted, "you gonna put lots of sage, the way I like it, or lots of red pepper for Jackson?"

Mama sounded happy. "How about both?"

Sammy nodded. He was easily pleased today because of getting to stay home and babysit while we butchered.

Laddie began to bark, and shortly a horn blew long and insistent. Mama pulled back the curtain. "Too dark to see. Jackson, go see who it is."

"I'll go," Rita hurriedly dried her hands, but I was already out the door.

"It's Wade. He said for Rita May to get out there quick. He's in a hurry."

Rita frowned but grabbed her coat from the peg.

Mama whirled. "You're not running out there like a hound to a whistle!"

Rita's fists clenched. "We've been through this before, Mama. I'm all grown up. I make my own living, and I'll come and go as I please."

When the door slammed, Mama dropped into the rocker and stared at the fire. After a bit she gave a deep sigh and stood.

We worked late into the night. One of my jaw teeth had started paining me lately, and tonight it really bothered me. I worried it with my tongue while I sat at the table and cut meat into long, narrow strips. When there was a fair-sized pile, I fed them, three parts lean, one part fat, into the sausage grinder while Sammy turned the mill. Every so often Mama dropped a cayenne pepper in to grind with the meat. When the bowl was full of ground meat, she added salt and sage. Sammy and I both offered to taste a fried patty to check for flavor.

I winced when I chewed, but it was delicious. Mama declared it just right. She began the frying down process, using three cast iron skillets, moving the patties from one to the other as the moisture fried away. If any moisture remained, the sausage would mold, so only the grease in the last skillet was used to pour over the patties and seal them airtight in jars.

Mama scooted the skillet of frying sausage to the coolest surface of the wood stove and tiptoed to the bedroom door to check on Timmy. He was sleeping soundly, curled up into a tight ball. She pulled another quilt from her bed, and with a kiss, tucked him in tightly. Then she spoke more to herself than to us.

"It seems such a short while ago that Rita May lay in this crib, that mop of copper curls all around her face. I don't know when things took such a wrong turn between us."

I knew Mama fretted over that, for she mentioned it a lot.

She returned to the kitchen and eyed our work. "One more batch and we'll be through."

Mason jars filled with brown sausage patties, fried and layered in hot grease, covered the table. The tang of sage and frying pork filled the house, along with an occasional popping sound made by the lids as they sealed on the cooling jars.

Rendering the lard was the last big job that remained from butchering. We tackled it the next day.

Cutting the firm pieces of hard white fat into cubes wasn't bad, but as they rendered slowly over low heat the air became filled with a heavy greasy odor. Weather permitting, we used a large pot over an outdoor fire. I was glad today was fair.

The big pieces of fat had lain cooling in a washtub in the back room. I dragged them into the kitchen. Mama and Sammy joined me at the table. This time Sammy could help, for the cubes for lard were easy to cut. We listened to the radio while we worked.

"I hope Daddy's gonna shoot lots of Germans," piped up Sammy.

Mama gave a hard stare. "You'd put your mind to better use by hoping they don't shoot him."

Sammy grew quiet and so did I. I had seen many gunshot wounds in animals. It would be awful to get shot. I surely did hope it never happened to Daddy.

We finished the day quiet and tired. By nightfall there were several cans of firm, snow-white lard sitting in the kitchen corner waiting to be stored in the cellar.

Chapter 8

"Mama, could we maybe go to the Christmas program at the church?" asked Sammy. "Lizzy Pitts says it's lots of fun." He stopped shaking the gallon jar filled with cream. We were now getting milk from Grandpa in exchange for half the butter.

"You best keep shaking that jar. The butter's almost gathered," said Mama before adding, "We have no fit clothes for church going."

Sammy began sloshing the jar back and forth again.

"Lizzy don't have fancy clothes neither, but it makes her no difference. She still goes."

"Well, it makes a difference to me. We're not going and that's final."

Sammy seemed disappointed, but not surprised. He had never been to church in his life.

"Mama, what we gonna send Daddy for Christmas?" I was excited. "Today the teacher was tellin' us the size package for soldiers can't be bigger than a shoebox and can't weigh more than six pounds. I figure we can come up with some good stuff that doesn't weigh too much."

Mama tied a knot and bit off the sewing thread and smoothed and folded the kitchen curtains she was hemming for Thelma Wright. "Along with the tea towels I hemmed last night, this will bring in a quarter. No one else pays as good as Miss Hilda, but I'm fortunate to get this job. If Thelma didn't have arthritis in her hands, she would be doing her own sewing," she said, ignoring me.

"Here, let me tend to that." She took the jar from Sammy and unscrewed the lid to lift out a soft mound of yellow butter and began washing and working the milk from it with a big wooden spoon.

"What about the package, Mama?" I persisted.

"We're not sending a package. Daddy said he had all he needed with what the Red Cross gave him in their package."

"Mama!" I was stricken. "We have to send Daddy some presents. It's Christmas, for gosh sakes!"

"Presents cost money. So does postage. And if it was going to reach him in time, we would've had to mail it long ago. Besides, your daddy knows I've got my hands full trying to keep food in your bellies."

"No he doesn't!" My face was livid. "He thinks we're making out fine! He doesn't know how you're hoarding every penny of them 'llotment checks like a stingy old witch. That's what you are, a stingy old witch!" I jumped up glaring.

Her hands grew still. "I'm thinking of our future." Her hand slipped into the pocket and drew out the black book. "This money is the one chance for us to have a better life. Someday you'll understand."

As I slammed the door, I heard her tell Sammy to go to bed and not to worry because I would be back soon.

———⌇〜⌇———

I was unaware of cold as I ran through the dark night, stumbling and crying and clenching my fist. Rebellion burned hot, and I headed toward town, the place Mama would least like me going. I thought about going to see Rita May, but I would not tell her what had happened. It would be too shameful to tell even her that Mama was so stinking stingy.

Cold drops on my forehead caught my attention, and I stopped long enough to realize it was snow! Some of the anger melted, and I began to walk, for the first time noticing a chill biting through the thin shirt and flannel underwear. I stuck my hands deep into overall pockets, hunched my shoulders against the wind, and kept walking. Miss Hilda's place was just a bit farther. Besides, it wouldn't hurt Mama to worry about me for a while.

Rounding the last corner, I caught my breath. I had never seen such a pretty sight! Miss Hilda's curtains were open, and two big lamps sat on tables, one on either side of a huge Christmas tree. It stood behind the double windows, ablaze with color from floor to ceiling. Red, green, blue, and yellow balls and little glass icicles shown like dozens of stars, winking at me through the falling snow. I hunkered on my heels and drew in the beauty, amazed at my first sight of a decorated Christmas tree.

Because we owned no vehicle, not even a wagon, trips to town were scarce. I had been to town only rarely in the summer, and never at Christmas. I watched until I was half frozen, and then suddenly spoke aloud.

"Sammy's gotta see this! I hope Miss Hilda doesn't blow out the lamps before we can get back here." I stood and ran fast, forgetting the cold again.

The house was dark when I snuck back inside. When the door squeaked, I heard Mama turn over in bed. I figured she had lain awake waiting until I returned. She didn't say anything when, a few minutes later, I opened the door again, so I figured she had gone to sleep.

"What you dragging me out here for?" hissed Sammy. "I told you I want ta go to sleep. Hey! It's snowing!"

"Yeah, ain't that worth gettin' out of bed for?"

"Not really. It's so dark I can't see it. But I'm glad we're gonna have snow."

"Come on. I've got something else to show you. I hope it's still there."

"What is it?"

"I ain't tellin', but you'll be glad you came, if it's still there. Hurry!"

This time I wore a jacket, and I had warned Sammy to wear his coat and the cap with earflaps.

"This better be good. I don't like sneaking around in the dark. What if Mama catches us gone? She'll tan our hides."

I hurried along without answering. Sammy trudged behind, grumbling most of the way. Now that it was snowing harder and the wind picked up, he complained that both his nose and feet were freezing.

Finally, I rounded the bend and gave a sigh of relief. The lamps still blazed, showing the tree in all its glory.

"Jumping Jehoshaphat!" Sammy's mouth fell open. "I ain't never...." He hunkered in the wind beside me. "Oh gosh, Jackson, it's super," he said with awed reverence. "I wish Timmy could see it. Reckon we could go get him?"

"Naw. We better not. You know how he gets those earaches. Besides, if we woke him up he'd most likely cry and wake Mama."

"I sure wish he could see it, and Mama too," added Sammy wistfully.

My heart hardened. "Mama doesn't care about anything pretty. All she cares about is money."

"That ain't so, Jackson! I seen her running her hand over that fancy dress of Miss Hilda's she was hemming, and you could tell she wished that pretty thing was hers. And you was wrong to call

her a old witch tonight. You forgot all about Santa Claus! Mama
knows he'll give Daddy some presents."

I didn't have the heart to disappoint him. I knew Daddy's
Christmas would be slim, if any, but what Sammy didn't know
wouldn't hurt him. I stared through the cold darkness at the fine
house and the glittering tree and my lips narrowed. With her stingy
ways, Mama was even ruining Christmas!

————————

I looked critically at the cedar tree we had hacked on for an
hour with a dull ax. In the woods it had looked full and shapely, but
once inside the house it appeared lop-sided with bare places where
no limbs grew.

"I don't reckon Mama will let us keep this one, Jackson,"
remarked Sammy. "It takes up too much room. She won't even be
able to get to the cook stove without going way around. Besides,
the top's too tall. It's all bent over way up at the ceiling."

I glowered at him. There had been too much effort put into this
particular tree to give up easily. "I'll lop off the top."

"But it still takes up most of the room. I tell you, Mama ain't
gonna like it. We best get a smaller one before she says we can't
have one a'tall."

"I guess you're right," I gave in grudgingly. I had wanted a tree
like Miss Hilda's. Of course there would be no fancy balls and
icicles, but I had made paper chains at school from colored paper
and glue, and I planned to ask Mama for some popcorn to string.
We still had some ears that Uncle Roy had grown the year before
stored in the shed.

With more grunting and heaving, we lugged the tree back
outside and went in search of a smaller one. Most were flat on one
side or funny shaped. I had almost given up when, just before dark,
on my way to Grandpa's, I spotted the perfect tree. It was about

four feet tall, full and perfectly formed. I ran home, got the ax, and chopped it down before going on to milk.

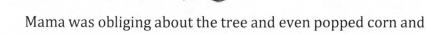

Mama was obliging about the tree and even popped corn and helped us string it before we went to bed. It helped brighten the room a bit, in spite of the bare walls and shabby furniture.

Our gifts were hidden in Mama's room. She had made a little money that week at Miss Hilda's by helping out with a major housecleaning. Miss Hilda was having guests for Christmas and wanted everything spic-and-span.

Rita May sent home three dollars along with word that there would be lots of overtime during the holidays. She was not coming home for Christmas. Mama was disappointed but said Rita May had a mind of her own and had stopped listening to her long ago.

I had wagged home a Montgomery Ward catalogue from Grandpa's—Monkey Wards he called it—and left it conspicuously opened to the pages filled with guitars. Mama frowned when she saw it. I knew it was hopeless, but I mentioned that whoever bought the one at Rawlings' wouldn't have to pay postage.

I caught Sammy looking longingly at sleds. They were said to be fire-engine red and as fast as greased lightning. How Sammy would love one!

When he showed the picture to Mama, she said I needed new shoes, Timmy needed a coat, and the flour barrel was almost empty again. But Christmas Eve, while we slept, presents appeared under the tree wrapped in some red and white checkered shelf-paper left over from Miss Hilda's last housecleaning. I was surprised Mama had bought a bag of marbles and a new flannel shirt apiece for Sammy and me. Uncle Roy had carved two wooden trucks for the boys with round wheels that really turned. There was also a large bag of hard candy. It was a mix of red, white, and green fluted ribbons and a bunch of flat, round pieces, their edges rings of red, and on each white center an image of Christmas flowers.

The other boys were excited with their gifts. I was not. I didn't want to spoil their day, so I tried to hide my disappointment. Sammy and I began a game of marbles on the floor in front of the stove while Mama made a special breakfast—hot buttered biscuits topped with honey.

The government gave Grandpa extra sugar rations for his bees. Before the government men confiscated the honey for shipping overseas to the troops, he always managed to slip some back. The night before when I had returned from milking, he shocked me by offering a quart jar filled to the brim with golden honey. Usually Grandpa was stingy as could be. But just about the time I thought I had him figured out, he would surprise me.

"Take this home so you can all have a treat." I was more amazed when he added, "Tell Janie I said Merry Christmas."

While we ate biscuits and honey, snow blew around the house, and cold drafts fluttered the curtains and occasionally puffed smoke down the fireplace and into the room. We had just finished eating when there was a knock on the door.

"Come in, Roy. Merry Christmas."

I was startled to see Mama give her brother a hug. I knew they loved each other, but they weren't much on hugging. I supposed Mama was in the Christmas spirit.

Uncle Roy grinned at us. "I passed a little fat man in a red suit a while ago. He was stuck in a snowdrift and couldn't get out. Asked if I knew where the Lorings lived."

Sammy's eyes were getting big as he stared at the package under Uncle Roy's arm. I remembered when it was fun to believe in Santa Claus.

"He asked me to drop this off for Jackson."

It was my turn to get bug-eyed. "For me?"

Roy beamed. "That's what the fat man said."

I took the box and stared at it. Mama laughed.

"You're supposed to open it," she said.

When I tore off the red and green striped paper, my mouth fell open. I grabbed Uncle Roy around the neck. "A brand spanking new radio battery!" I cried. "I've wanted one in the worst way."

He smiled and his eyes crinkled at the corners. "Let's hook it up." He seemed almost as excited as me when we turned the knob and a clear voice boomed into the room.

"Boy, oh, boy! That sounds great." I began spinning the dial and was amazed at all the new stations coming in as clear as could be.

Roy tousled my hair and turned to Mama. "Janie, I got the contract."

"That's wonderful!" said Mama.

"I know you wanted to have the cellar finished by now. Just as soon as I get this big order filled, I'll get right back to the roof."

"Thanks. I'm still looking for used tin to cover the timbers. When we pile dirt on top, I figure tin will keep it from sifting through."

"Good idea. It'll work till it rusts through. By then the dirt should be pretty hard-packed." He started to speak, then stopped. He squirmed a little, then plucked a small stem of cedar from our Christmas tree and began to pull off the twigs. Seeming to find courage, he went on, "With this cold spell, Sue and I would feel better if you and the boys came and bunked with us."

He knew how proud Mama was. Apt as not, she would bite his head off for the kindness. However, she smiled.

"Thanks, Roy, I appreciate it, but we'll make out fine."

"Well, if you change your mind, you know where my front door is. By the way," he added, "as soon as the weather breaks, I can use you and Jackson any chance you get."

"We'll be there. Thanks again, Roy." She looked at the battery and the wooden trucks. "Thanks for everything."

We spent the evening listening to the radio and President Roosevelt's Christmas greeting. With the good battery, we could pick up several more stations. Now we could always find Amos and Andy, Lum and Abner, and George Burns and Gracie Allen.

———————

"Jackson, you asleep yet?"

"Nope. Why?"

"I keep thinkin' about that pretty tree of Miss Hilda's, all lit up and sparkly." Sammy propped on one elbow. "I want Timmy to see it awful bad. I'd like to see it again myself before she takes it down. Reckon it's still there?"

"I reckon."

"We could wrap Timmy up real good in a blanket, and he could wear my cap with the earflaps." Sammy rolled onto his stomach and propped up on both elbows. "Don't ya think we could?"

"I reckon." I felt mean and selfish, because without a word to Sammy, I had detoured by Miss Hilda's almost every evening after milking.

We boys climbed out of bed and fumbled into clothes in the darkness. I drew the dubious honor of lifting a sleeping Timmy from the crib in Mama's room. I tiptoed out, freezing once when Mama stirred and rolled over. I quickly grabbed a quilt from my own bed and wrapped Timmy, who began to rouse when Sammy slapped a cold cap on his head and pulled down earflaps.

I carried Timmy while Sammy grabbed the lantern. He waited to light it until we stepped outside. The match flickered and went out in the wind. He lit another, then another. Finally, by carefully cupping his hands and turning his back to the wind, he succeeded.

"It's blowin' like crazy out here. I don't know if we ought to go," I worried aloud.

"Aw! Come on. It won't take long. If we wait till tomorrow, she might take the tree down!"

"All right, but we ain't stayin' more than a second."

In a pool of lantern light, we set off at a trot. Timmy, now wide awake and big-eyed, sucked his thumb, bouncing up and down in my arms.

"I gotta slow down. My arms is most ready to fall off." I slowed to a fast walk. "It sure takes longer carryin' a baby."

Part of the quilt dragged behind, whipping in the wind. My own ears were half frozen. I was glad Timmy had on the cap.

We arrived out of breath but excited to see the lamps lit and tree decorations shining through the darkness. Timmy took the thumb from his mouth and reached toward the tree and gurgled with pleasure.

"See! I told ya he'd love it." Sammy was delighted. "See the pretty tree, baby, see the pretty tree."

We laughed together at Timmy's delight. I ventured closer to the house. Suddenly I turned back.

"We best get out 'a here. There's Miss Hilda sittin' on the couch looking at a candle. It's a thousand wonders she didn't see us."

We hurried home, shivering in the wind, with the lantern swinging vigorously in Sammy's hand. Quietly, we crept into the house and slipped Timmy back into bed. I noticed his diaper was wet. I left it unchanged for fear of waking Mama.

The next morning Timmy was cross and about noon his nose began to run. Mama felt his forehead.

"I think he's running a fever," she worried aloud. "I sure hope you're not getting sick again, Timmy."

Before dark it became clear that Timmy was ill. His face was flushed and his throat raspy when he cried. Mama sat and held him, rocking and shushing him. He kept pulling at his left ear.

"It's one of those awful earaches!" she fretted. "No two ways about it. I have to get the cellar finished. It's a wonder we aren't all sick, sleeping in this drafty, old house. It gets cold as a tomb in here every night when the fire dies out."

Mama poured a cup of salt onto a square of flannel cloth and sewed it shut, making a small pillow. She heated the pillow and put it against Timmy's ear. The warmth made him stop crying for a while.

Sammy and I, feeling a need to be punished, sat studying at the kitchen table. We exchanged guilty looks over the open schoolbooks. Mama was too preoccupied to marvel that we were doing school assignments in the middle of Christmas vacation.

For the next three days and nights Timmy pulled at his ear and shrieked. Even the salt pillow did not quiet him for long. He ran a high fever. Mama fought to bring it down with cool sponge baths. Now he was burning up again. His face was flushed. Fear gripped my heart.

"Mama, is Timmy gonna die?"

"Good heavens no! He's got an ear infection, but he is no ways close to dying!"

"Reckon we ought to take him to the doctor?"

"I've been thinking on it." Her shoulders sagged tiredly. "It's such a long, cold ride into town, I'm almost afraid to try it. But if he's not better by morning, I'll send for your Uncle Roy to take us."

"Reckon we ought to pray?" I asked. The Bible reading at school lately had been about Jesus healing the sick.

Mama's eyes widened in surprise before they quickly hardened. "The last time I prayed for someone to get well, I was fourteen years old. Mama died. I've not prayed about anything since...except to beg God that your daddy wouldn't go off to the war. Look how far that got me."

I was in no way knowledgeable on the subject, but I had a notion if someone was bad sick, folks ought to pray. Now, because of Mama's attitude, I was terrified that Timmy would die. Wracked with guilt, I did all of the chores without a word of complaint. The weather was bitter and the fireplace devoured wood. There was still plenty left in the stack against the outside wall, but I could no longer tolerate sitting at the table listening to the creak of the rocking chair as Mama rocked Timmy. It was the only sound in the quiet house since the baby had quit screaming and fallen into a restless sleep. I grabbed a jacket and motioned for Sammy to do the same. Tiptoeing, he got a jacket and followed me outside.

"Come on, Sammy. We're gonna saw some wood." I got the crosscut saw from the shed.

He looked dubious, but followed to where oak and hickory trees that Daddy had felled and trimmed lay side by side on the hard, frozen ground.

"Them trees is gonna be froze hard as a buck's horn. They'll be mighty hard cuttin'," he observed.

My reply was a grunt.

Sammy rounded the tree and grabbed the handle attached to the long, jagged blade and pulled with all his might. It skittered across the bark without making a dent. I frowned and scolded, "Can't ya do any better than that?"

"Hey, Mr. Smarty Pants! You got one end. See how good you can do!"

I got a fresh grip and managed to set the teeth a little way into the bark. Then Sammy pulled, skipping the blade out again.

"I reckon I'll have to spend my time runnin' around this tree to do both pulls," I snapped.

"Well, I reckon you will! I can't pull this thing through unfroze wood! How you expect me to do it frozen?"

I sat down on the tree, hunched my shoulders, and looked back toward the house at the gray ribbon of chimney smoke lacing into the sky. "That's all right. I'll use the bucksaw. I just thought you might be like me and wantin' out of the house."

Sammy sat down beside me. "It is awful in there—Timmy crying all the time. He's hurting terrible. You reckon he's gonna be all right?"

I shrugged, feeling miserable.

He twisted to face me. "If he dies, we killed him."

I stayed quiet, but I looked skyward and wondered if Timmy was about to join Charlie's mama and Miss Sissy. Since Mama wouldn't pray, I wished for the first time in my life that I knew how. I didn't. But we did recite the Lord's Prayer a lot at school. I screwed up my face, shut my eyes, and silently gave it a try. It didn't say anything about sickness or healing, but it did say something about being delivered from evil...I hoped that would be good enough.

Just then Mama came to the door and called me.

"Jackson, go tell Miss Hilda that I can't come to clean tomorrow because Timmy is sick."

"Yes, 'um."

I ran most of the way and hurriedly delivered the message. Miss Hilda told me to wait. She wanted to come with me, and she soon appeared on the porch bundled in a long coat and furry hat, carrying a black satchel and a brown paper bag full of funny smelling stuff. She handed it to me.

"Mr. Krause was a good physician. But if he couldn't cure someone with his pills and needles," she turned and grinned at me, her black eyes twinkling, "I'd fix them right up with my herbs and tonics."

I knew she was teasing, but it made me feel better just knowing she had some knowledge of doctoring.

"That was a right pretty tree you put up," I said to make conversation. "I liked the colored balls a lot."

"Of course I don't celebrate Christmas, but Mr. Krause was Christian. He loved his Christmas tree. I tell myself I put it up in memory of him," she dropped her voice like it was a secret, "but the truth is, I like it too."

"You don't believe in God?" I finally asked. I had God on my mind since I had been praying for Timmy—the best I knew how.

Miss Hilda's mouth fell open. "Of course I do! I'm Jewish—a descendant of Abraham, the patriarch, the friend of God."

"Lincoln?" I asked.

When Miss Hilda's lips twitched and her face turned purple and she burst out laughing, I knew I had made a fool of myself again. My face blazed. I would have to look up patriarch in Webster's. It must not mean politician as I had supposed.

"No, Jackson," she managed to say. "Abraham of the Scriptures."

"Oh yeah," I said.

"Abraham is the father of the Jews, God's chosen people," she said.

Miss Hilda sounded more prideful of her relations than I was of mine—Grandpa Cole Matthers was no one to write home about.

A dull winter sun slanted through the west window, making patterns on the front room floor, while the fire popped and crackled in the fireplace. Mama held Timmy on her lap while Miss Hilda dropped warm olive oil mixed with mashed garlic into his ear—making Timmy smell like something to eat—and then they spooned some dark-brown herb concoction down his throat. "Keep giving him the pennyroyal and mullen. He's a strong boy. He'll be fine."

Mama beamed. "Miss Hilda, you're a godsend."

I mulled that over for a minute. Maybe God had sent Miss Hilda, her being one of his chosen people and all.

Miss Hilda reached to pat Timmy's head. "Such a pretty child. He has your eyes, Janie." She sighed. "I so wanted children." She looked at Mama. "I envy you. You are so blessed, so rich."

I batted my eyes. Mama rich! Miss Hilda must have been sipping Grandpa's shine.

"But," she went on, "I have my sister's family, my niece and nephew. They're like my own. Such a wonderful family." She beamed, then she sobered. "I don't get to see them often. They live in the Ukraine."

"Yes," said Mama, "I met your niece and her children when she visited a few years ago."

"Ah, yes, I remember. Keith got a fishhook in his neck."

Mama laughed remembering. "I was glad the doctor was home. We had tried to get it out for an hour, and Keith was getting mighty cross."

Just then I felt another sharp pain in my bad tooth. I rubbed my jaw. It had been hurting more and more lately. I wondered if Miss Hilda had a cure for the toothache. But after one look at the dark brew Mama was forcing down Timmy, I kept my ailments to myself.

By the next day, Timmy was still fussy, but he was cool and he no longer screeched and pulled at his ear. I was greatly relieved about him. Now if only my tooth would stop throbbing. Nonetheless, I kept my swollen jaw turned away from Mama.

Chapter 9

"Jackson! Wake up!"

As my shoulder was shaken, the words swirled in my sleep-fogged brain until I fought myself awake. I propped on one elbow and eyed Rita May kneeling by my bed. I could see her clearly in moonlight coming through my small window.

"What's the matter?" I mimicked her hushed tone, yet she still put a cautious hand to my lips and glanced toward Mama's bedroom.

"Grandpa Cole sent me to fetch you. He needs help."

I reached for overalls hanging on the bedpost. "Why does Grandpa need me?"

"Come outside so we can talk," she glided from the room as I shivered into overalls and followed on tiptoe. Shoes and coat in hand, I joined her in the star-filled, frigid darkness.

"Why does Grandpa need me?" I asked again. My teeth chattered and my hands shook as I put on the coat and bent to tie my boots.

"He's got the malaria again, jerkin' with chills. Can hardly stay on the bed he's shaking so." She was serious. "Grandpa insisted I fetch you, but, Jackson, I don't want you to come."

"Why not? If Grandpa is sick—"

"He ain't wanting you to take care of him. I can do that."

"The moonshine?"

She nodded. "He's got a big order to fill, going out to Little Rock. He thinks I need help to get it ready."

At my surprised stare, she flushed. "You can't tell Mama. I been helpin' with the whiskey making."

"Mama will skin you alive."

"She won't find out—unless someone tells her."

"I ain't no tattletale."

She rushed on. "I told Grandpa I could handle it and to leave you out of it, but he said to tell you and let you make up your own mind."

"My mind's done made up, and you can't talk me out of it!" I shot back. "I'm sick of doing without while Mama stashes back every penny. Just look at these wore-out overalls!"

"Grandpa swore you'd come." She took my arm. "I wish you wouldn't...."

I shook my head hard.

Rita sighed. "If you're bound and determined, then let's hurry. I'm already late."

"How long you been helping?" I asked, catching up beside her.

"Not long, just a few months."

I shivered. "Wish he didn't make shine in the wintertime."

"Makes it all year round. He has to keep steady orders filled."

She lifted a strand of barbed wire and nodded toward the pasture. "Come on, we'll cut through here. Grandpa wants to talk to you before I take you to the still."

"I knowed you'd come!" Grandpa's hoarse laugh stopped in a fit of coughing.

Rita May moved the lamp nearer the bedside, and I got a good look at Grandpa. His skin was pasty above the red beard, his blue eyes hollow in their sockets.

"You look awful, Grandpa. You need a doctor?" I asked.

He swore.

"I take it that means no," I said.

He pointed a shaking hand toward a bottle sitting on the cluttered table. Rita found a cup and rinsed it before pouring in a dose of Wintersmith's malaria tonic. The way his teeth chattered against the cup, I feared it would break.

"Ain't no wonder you're shakin'—it's cold as Christmas in here. I'll put more wood on the fire."

I stoked the remaining embers in the fireplace with a poker and threw on an armful of dried sticks, then added three logs from a stack against the wall. The blaze sprang to life and danced on the dark walls.

"That stuff really help any?" I pointed to the tonic.

"I don't know," he gasped. "But it's all I got. I run out of quinine. Been so long since I had a spell, I forgot to get more." Exhausted, he lay back against the bare pillow ticking and stared at me.

"I never involved you children in my business cause your daddy was dead set aga'n it."

I felt a shiver trace my spine.

"But," he continued, "don't seem like he cares too much what happens to you now, the way he skedaddled and left you. And since he took off, I figure all bets is off. He's got no more say in things around here." He rose off the pillow for a fresh fit of coughing. When I held out the cup, he shook his head. Finally he lay back and rasped out the words, "I was no older than you when my old man died. I made it just fine. It's high time you quit lettin' yer mama wipe your nose. Time you start making your own way."

I took exception to the part about Daddy—there were the allotment checks if Mama wasn't too stingy to cash them—but I agreed with the rest. I was almost a man now, and Mama insisted on treating me like a baby. Slowly I nodded.

"Good." He went on, "Rita May is going to take you to the still. Before she does, I'm asking your promise, boy, that you won't ever tell a livin' soul." His eyes bore hot and heavy on my face. "Don't know as you can understand just how serious hit is. I could easy go to prison if you kids don't keep mum."

My eyes narrowed. "I can keep my mouth shut, but how much is in it for me?"

He managed a weak laugh. "You got my blood flowin' in yer veins, all right!" A fit of hard chills momentarily stopped the talk, but after the spasm passed, he went on. "I'll pay you the same as I'm payin' Rita May. Probably won't need you often, but when I do, hit'll be better wages than you're makin' at the mill."

I nodded.

"Rita'll take you to where things is set up just now. I got several locations and I move regular. Don't nobody but me know 'em all—but Rita knows this one. And I've done showed her what to do."

He turned to her. "Don't forget—keep the light hid and dust out yer tracks in the clearin'. Look sharp and stop real often to listen."

"I won't forget."

As we left the room, Grandpa called Rita back and lowered his voice. I still heard the rasping words.

"Keep yer eyes peeled. Jackson's too young, I'm afeared he might not be careful enough. Keep yer wits about you. I wouldn't want anything to happen to you young'uns."

Grandpa closed his eyes, but they reopened. "I make the best corn liquor in the country. There's folks would give their eyeteeth to know how I do it." His eyes found me and hardened. "I better never find out that you two have told anything."

At times it seemed as though Grandpa was two different men. He watched as I closed the door.

Our winding path led through limbs and briars that snagged my clothes and scratched my face. I scrambled over windfalls and skirted boulders, and after dozens of crooks and turns in the darkness, I had no idea where we were. I suspected that was Grandpa's plan. Rita May had probably been instructed to take a roundabout route.

"How much further?" I hissed.

"Not too far. We'll have to get down on hands and knees and crawl here," she whispered.

After plowing through a dense thicket, I came out on top of a steep, rocky incline. Rita raised her hand to halt, and we stopped to listen. There was nothing in the frosty quiet but our own labored breathing. But the listening sent a chill over me.

Rita turned sideways and began inching her way down. Pebbles rolled beneath her feet, sounding loud in the night. Once at the bottom, she listened again and then, satisfied, motioned for me. While I scrambled down the tall ledge, she began pulling brush back from its base to reveal a small opening.

"You've got to hunker goin' in, but you can stand up once you get inside," she whispered.

Before following, I looked all around in the darkness. I saw nothing unusual, just a few patches of snow, ghostly white, clinging to the north hillside, and the outline of black trees, tall and bare, sky lighted on the far ridge. My eyes swung all around like compass needles, and then settled on the North Star hanging frozen in the cold sky. A screech owl hollered. The hair stood on the back of my neck. I stooped and entered the cave.

A sour odor revealed the whiskey mash even before Rita fumbled for a match. My lips curled. "Pew-wee! It stinks in here."

"Keep your voice down. I don't think there's anyone within a mile, but better safe than sorry," she cautioned.

When the wick caught and held flame, she returned to the entrance and made certain the heavy curtain shut in the light. My heart pounded, and although the air was frigid, my palms were sweaty.

The room was just large enough to hold the tools of Grandpa's trade—a stave barrel and two metal boilers joined with a piece of tubing, and coming from one, the copper worm of whiskey making. Their shadows loomed big and black against the cave walls.

A makeshift table of boards stretched between two white oak barrels. The wavering light glinted on an assortment of narrow-mouthed mason jars sitting on the table. Sacks of dried corn and an empty sugar barrel lined the rest of the walls.

"Let's hurry. It always makes me nervous being in here." Rita May set the lamp down and reached for a funnel. "Grandpa never waters his whiskey down. We have to mix this sour mash liquor with the sweet mash liquor, half-and-half. That's one thing that makes it so good."

I shot her a look. "You been sampling?"

"No. I hate even the smell of the stuff. Just quotin' Grandpa. Here, hold the funnel while I pour—you'd just slop. We've got to hurry. That fellow is comin' for this just before daylight, and we have to carry it all down to the road."

"What fellow?"

She shrugged. "I just leave this in a ditch beside the road." She saw my grimace. "Well, you ain't supposed to know."

"But it's Wade Lucas," I surmised, his name leaving a bad taste in my mouth.

"Yes."

"I don't know how you can stand him, Rita May! He ain't half the man Ben is."

"Well, Ben ain't exactly knocking down my door lately." She caught her lip between her teeth and poured with care.

"Even if you and Ben never make up, you ought not hang around Wade. He sweet-talks every girl in sight, even when you're with him."

She shrugged and then frowned. "If Wade's not careful, there won't be any girls to flirt with where he's goin'. He's been flashing his money, and I'm afraid folks are getting suspicious."

"Rita May, what'll happen if you get caught?" I asked, as a shiver went down my spine.

She stopped pouring for a second. "I guess I'd go to jail. That's why I don't intend to be stupid and get caught. And you'd better look sharp too."

"I never heard of them sending a fifteen-year-old to the pen," I smarted off.

"Maybe not to prison, but there's other places, places for wayward boys. Think what that would do to Mama."

"I hadn't noticed you taking much thought of her."

"Because she takes plenty of thought for herself!" Rita's eyes flashed. "I haven't seen a penny of Daddy's allotment checks, and I bet you haven't either," she bit out. "Anything's better than being stinking, dirt poor like we are, Jackson. It used to kill me seeing the girls in town preening in their fancy clothes. At least now I got a few of my own. I've already made more doing this than in three months at the cafe."

I understood. I wanted nice things too, things like Miss Hilda had, and a new guitar and britches without a dozen patches on them. If I was ever going to have anything, I'd have to get it for myself.

A slight whisper of sound froze us both. I hurriedly puffed out the light and slipped to the mouth of the cave. I listened, straining to catch the sound again. Suddenly I laughed and dropped the curtain.

"It's just an old possum out in the moonlight nosing around. Guess he's hoping for some dried up persimmons."

Rita gave a shaky laugh and then sobered. "This time it was nothing. But don't ever forget this is dangerous business, Jackson. Never let your guard down."

After the lamp was lit, we continued the job with a fresh sense of urgency. After several minutes of silence, she finally spoke:

"I shouldn't have let you come."

"Aw, Rita May, I can take care of myself."

"Grandpa's right—lots of folks end up in prison for doing this. And I don't want to see that good-looking face of yours behind bars."

Silence filled the cave.

Then I spoke. "Don't reckon Daddy would like us doing this, Rita May, neither one of us."

She bit her lip. Her hand shook, and a few drops of liquor spilled onto the table.

"I try not to think about that. Besides, Daddy might get killed any day, and then I'd have to take care of myself. May as well start now while there's cash money to be made."

That made sense. I decided for the time being to forget the right and wrong of it. The money Grandpa paid would feel mighty good in my pocket.

It took four trips, carrying two gallons apiece, to finish the job. Although the frozen ground crunched under my boots, I was covered in sweat from the strain of listening and watching as we slipped through brush and under trees that killed the moonlight. We placed the last load into a ditch near a blackened stump beside the road and covered it with leaves and brush.

I stood and cocked my head to listen. Night was hushed with the stillness that comes just before dawn. "It's almost daylight. You best get home before Mama catches you gone," urged Rita in a whisper.

"Where you going?"

"Don't worry about me," she evaded my question.

"You get caught in Wade's car with this load of shine, you'll be in deep trouble, Rita May."

"Get on home," she ordered. "Oh, I almost forgot." She reached into her pocket and pulled out two dollars. "Grandpa said to give you this when the job was finished."

I took the money and stuffed it into my pocket, then looked at her. "You take care." I wanted to say more, but I knew it wouldn't do any good. Except for usually minding Daddy, Rita May did as she pleased. Cutting through the woods, I headed for home at a trot.

I slipped into the house carrying my boots. I hoped to snatch a few minutes of sleep before Mama called me to go milk. I pulled my share of the quilt off Sammy and managed with fair success to forget Daddy's parting words, "You know right from wrong...."

Chapter 10

The next afternoon I returned from doing the chores at Grandpa's earlier than usual and met Mama on the road. "Mama, where you goin' with the shotgun?" I asked.

She flinched at the question.

"I'm taking it to your Uncle Roy."

"He has a 12 gauge. What does he need with Daddy's?"

She steeled herself. "He's taking it to town for me. The government is asking folks to bring in all their 12 gauge double barrels so they can use them for guard duty and training. That'll free up the rifles for war use."

My eyes hardened. "You ain't worried about rifles for the war. What they paying?"

"Thirty dollars." Her voice was flat.

"It ain't yours to sell! It's Daddy's!"

"Jackson, you have no idea how much money that is! Your daddy only gave ten for this gun."

I grew desperate as she stalked away, and my tone softened. "Mama, we won't have any way of killin' varmints. That old twenty-two doesn't shoot a'tall. And I could kill game with the shotgun if you'd let me." My voice trailed away as she kept walking.

My eyes narrowed and my fists knotted. "I hate you."

Her shoulders squared, the only sign that she had heard.

I stood in the shed doorway and watched the evening January sky, all pinks and purples. Quickly shadows crept up the distant ridge and swallowed the rosy glow. No matter how beautiful, twilight made me miss Daddy. It was the time he would come home from the mill, and we would gather around the supper table all together. I swallowed a lump in my throat and went back inside the shed.

"What are you two doing?" Mama questioned as Sammy and I bent over a pile of boards with a hammer in my hand.

"I'm building a rabbit gum. Uncle Roy told me how. I'll have to trap," I muttered the rest, "since you sold Daddy's shotgun."

"We can have fried rabbit!" rejoiced Sammy.

I pushed back my dark hair and glared at him. "Hold that board still. You keep wigglin' and I can't nail it right."

"Put it away for now," ordered Mama. "It's too dark to see tonight, and we can't waste kerosene. You can work on it tomorrow."

"Yes 'um."

Seeing our dejection, she added, "Fried rabbit will taste mighty good."

I doubted there would be many rabbits caught. In the last few depression years, almost everything with hide and hair had disappeared from the woods. Folks had hunted to eat. Once Mama had even resorted to cooking a possum, but it had been too greasy. Even Daddy wouldn't eat it.

Mama sat near the lamp mending Sammy's overalls. She smirked at the announcement that shoe retailers in New York's East Side had to close their doors as a protective measure when shoppers flooded the store to buy shoes before rationing went into effect the following day. Each person would now be allowed only three pairs a year.

I could not imagine what the fuss was about. I had not had a new pair in two years. It was no concern of mine that evening slippers, men's patent leathers, and two-tones would be manufactured no longer. I looked down at my toes straining against the cracked leather of my boots. I was beginning to limp. It would be so simple to cash one of the allotment checks and buy boots and some of the other things that would make life easier.

With a weary sigh, Mama laid the overalls aside and rubbed the back of her neck.

Sammy continued our argument. "I ain't gonna be no Jap again!" he railed. "Jackson, you always get to be MacArthur or Captain Rickenbacker or somebody neat—and I'm always some old Jap er German!"

"But I'm the tallest and it'd look stupid—"

"For heaven's sake! Hush boys!" Mama scolded. "War, war, war! I'm sick to death of it. Can't you think of something else to play?"

"Jackson always gets his way," pouted Sammy with his lip pooched out. "He always has to be the big shot, and he won't ever let me be the good guy."

"That's not so! Last week I let you—"

"I said hush!" snapped Mama. "Go to bed, right this second. And don't you dare wake Timmy. I don't want to hear one whisper out of you either, understand?"

We sullenly left the room, and Mama immediately called us back. "I'm sorry, boys. It's been a hard day. I'm worn to a nub after washing and ironing and mending all day, but I shouldn't take it out on you."

She motioned Sammy off to bed and told me to sit down again. Mama didn't usually confide in me. I was surprised when she began to explain.

"When I took the Baker's laundry by today, I found out they're leaving, moving in with their daughter in town. That means I'll lose a dollar a week from doing their wash." Tonight the downturned lines on Mama's face made her look old. "Mr. Baker did have some good news. He's giving us their old kerosene cook stove. It will sure make cooking simpler, especially in summer. And he's giving me the pile of tin stacked behind his barn. I had asked if he would sell it, but he insisted on giving it. Now we'll have a roof for the cellar, but I'll sorely miss the cash from the laundry."

"Don't know why you let that fluster you. We must have a gob of money from all those allotment checks."

She slowly folded the mended pants. "If I cash one of those checks, Jackson, it'll be like putting a hole in a dam. At first it'll only trickle out, but in the end it will all float away." She changed the subject. "Tomorrow's Sunday. I think we'll have pancakes for breakfast. Would you like that?"

Still smarting over the selling of the shotgun, I sullenly replied, "I don't care." As I stomped off to bed, I heard her sigh before she took the lamp into her bedroom and shut the door.

I tossed and turned. My tooth hurt, but that was not what made me restless. My conscience wouldn't let me be. I was treating Mama terrible. Not that there wasn't plenty of reason to disagree with her. She was making our lives miserable when they did not have to be. And I resented her attitude toward Daddy. She still acted as if he had deserted us to go have fun. I had said I hated her, and the way I was behaving she probably thought I did. I didn't. I wished she would be happy and smile and sing again like she used to. I had been proud when folks said how pretty she was. Now the frown on her mouth and in her eyes made her look old and hard. I wanted her to buy a new dress, fix her hair pretty, and do something besides work, work, work. I missed Daddy terribly, but in a way I was more lonesome for Mama. It seemed as if she had gone away too.

————〰———

By the next morning, my jaw was swollen double and an imp had moved into my mouth. Every time my heart beat, he used my tooth as an anvil. I arrived at Grandpa's holding my jaw.

"What's sa matter? Toothache?" The way Grandpa's words were slurred I knew he was drunk, even this early in the morning.

I nodded, not wanting to open my mouth.

"Here. Take a swig of this." He handed me a small, flat bottle filled with liquor. "Fix you right up."

I took a tiny sip. The stuff burned like fire and tasted worse than castor oil—which was saying a lot. I couldn't imagine why anyone would want to drink it.

"No, no, keep it. Take it home with you. Best stuff in the world fer toothache." He blinked, trying to focus on my face. "But don't let your Mama know." He slapped his leg and laughed as though it were a great joke.

"Thanks." I slipped the bottle into my pocket, but I had no intention of sampling any more. I might give it to Ben. I had not seen him since the night of the dance. He liked Grandpa's shine. Maybe if I gave him the bottle we could be friends again. The icy wind made my jaw throb, so I hunkered low into my coat as I hurried the two miles toward the little house where Ben lived with his Grandpa. When I knocked on the door, Ben answered. I was relieved to see his eyes brighten.

"Howdy, Jackson. Come in." He motioned me inside. I nodded to old Pappy Tyler who had just roused from napping in his chair. He had raised Ben. Ben's mother had died of tuberculosis when he was ten, and shortly after that his daddy had been killed in a coal mine accident.

"How's it going?"

Ben turned from leaning against the doorframe and stepped into the light before shutting the door. When the shirt draped across his bare shoulder slipped, my eyes widened and then stayed glued to his hand and arm. His left arm and the left side of his chest were a mess of ridged scars, but worst of all was the pale, puckered skin of his left hand.

"Not a pretty sight, huh?"

I looked up and saw him smile. "How in the world did that happen?" I asked, feeling sick to my stomach.

"I got burned when my ship was torpedoed. I got off lucky." His eyes clouded. "Lots of the fellows didn't make it." He slipped into the shirt and then slapped me on the back. "Hey, it's all right. There's hardly a scratch on my ugly mug."

With the shirt on, he looked nearly normal except for a small purple streak running from his neck to stop in front of his left ear. But the mangled hand was awful. Besides being burned it looked as if it had been crushed, the fingers misshapen and crooked. "Ben, you won't ever be able to play guitar..." I stopped as the awful thought sunk in.

"You just watch." He walked into the room just off of the front room and came back carrying his guitar. He sat down on a blue, stuffed chair and pointed me to the matching sofa. I watched, surprised as he pointed the guitar in the wrong direction.

"I put these strings on in reverse and I'm learning to play left-handed." He strummed a few chords, awkward while making the changes. "It'll take a while, but I'll get it."

"Sure you will," I agreed. But I knew Ben would never be the musician he had been. That made my heart hurt worse than my tooth.

Remembering my errand, I pulled out the bottle. "I brought you a present."

When he hesitated, I added, "I know how you like Grandpa's shine."

"That's mighty thoughtful of you." He set it on the table nearby. I was surprised that he didn't tip it up and take a swig. But it was still early. He sat silent for a moment, just looking at me.

"You got a toothache?" He pointed to my puffy jaw.

"Yeah." When I swore using one of his favorite old expressions, Ben flinched and looked at the floor.

But shortly he looked up. "You need a doc. How about me giving you a lift into town?"

"No, but thanks just the same."

"I'm going anyway," he persisted.

My face grew warm. "I got no money for doctors."

He grabbed his jacket. "I know a dentist who'll work for a song—he likes my guitar picking." Ben stopped smiling. "Well, he used to," he added soberly. "If he wants pay, it'll be my treat. My present to you."

I hesitated, but the thought of enduring another sleepless night of torture overrode pride. "I'll have to ask Mama."

"Sure," he agreed as he grabbed the car keys off a hook near the door. "Grandpa,"—he leaned over and shook the old man who had nodded off again and yelled in his ear—"I'm going to town. You need anything?"

Old man Tyler was deaf as a post. He cupped his ear with a bony hand. "No. No. I don't need nary thing, I can think of."

We stopped by the house and found Mama elbow-deep in soapsuds doing some laundry in the washtub sitting on a chair in the kitchen. She dried her hands and gave Ben a hug. "It's good to see you back safe and sound."

I bit my lip to keep from blurting out that she should see the hand tucked into his pocket. Ben might be safe but he was definitely not sound!

"Good to be home, Mrs. Loring." Ben noticed Timmy, who was playing on the floor. "That can't be Timmy! Good grief! He was a tiny baby last time I saw him."

Mama looked at Timmy fondly. "They do grow up way too fast to suit me."

"I heard Keith re-upped," said Ben.

Mama nodded. I was glad she never let on to Ben how she had been against Daddy's going.

While Ben made the offer to take me into town, Mama stared at my jaw. "Why, Jackson Loring! That jaw is swollen something awful." She was flustered. "This is the first I knew about a toothache. How come you never told me?"

"You think castor oil fixes everything," I mumbled and Ben laughed.

Mama thanked Ben for the offer, but she insisted that we pay. She went into her bedroom, returning with a wad of folded bills. I had no idea she had saved that much cash. Uncle Roy must have been paying us more than I thought.

She handed the money to Ben. "If it's any more, let me know."

Ben took the money. "I'm sure it won't be near this much. Anything else you need while we're in town?"

Mama hesitated. "If there's enough left, get Jackson a new pair of boots."

My mouth would have dropped open if my jaw had not been swollen almost shut. I was about to thank Mama, but I saw her eyes linger on the money as he put it into his jacket pocket. I figured she was just buying the boots because Ben had seen my ragged ones and now he knew that she had money.

The wind had stopped, but snow began sifting down as we drove toward town. Soon it frosted every limb, twig, and fence post and coated the tall, dead grass along edges of the road and fields, and at the rate it was coming, the ground would be covered in no time. The wipers swished against the windshield as Ben drove his old, battered Ford across Spadra Bridge and past a two-story building with green-striped awnings over the windows and doorways.

I held my jaw and dreaded the dentist as we went on down Main Street, lined with lampposts and a hodge-podge of buildings, old and new, some like Ben Franklin and Palace Drug, old enough to have false fronts. We passed The Fair Store where Mama liked to shop. I reckon she agreed with the sign on its brick wall above one big window—Clarksville's Greatest Value Store.

Ben parked across from the courthouse, a newer, impressive-looking gray stone building. Although it was more than a month after Christmas, the drug store was still decked out, bright windows full of decorations. Glistening tinsel, red velvet bows, and evergreen framed patriotic posters. In one, Uncle Sam pointed a long finger and told me to "Buy Bonds!"

I stopped to look at the poster in the next window that urged me to "Keep Him Flying." It was an American Ace sitting in the cockpit of his plane plastered with decals of the Rising Sun, each a kill to his credit. Directly above the poster hung a banner saying, "Peace on earth and good will toward men." Ben chuckled. He said he wondered if they had been placed together in jest or in real Christian cheer. Then he nodded toward a sign over some stairs.

My stomach did flip-flops, and I thought about just heading on down the street; but about that time, my tooth really went to throbbing, and I figured a dentist couldn't hurt much worse. If I had seen the needle that was coming at me in a few minutes, I would have skedaddled. The doc was a tall, skinny fellow with wire-rimmed glasses perched on the end of his nose. I guessed him to be about Daddy's age, but he and Ben were buddies. After pounding each other on the back and catching up on the past two years, they got around to me.

Before long I was sitting in a funny chair, sort of how I imagined the electric chair down at Tucker Prison must look. I don't think I would have sweated more if it actually had been. He pried open my mouth, none too gentle, and began poking around. I let him know with a loud holler when he got on the sore tooth.

"Needs to come out," the doc said, and then he began filling a needle from a little bottle. That needle was about as long as my arm and big around as my finger. I would have bolted if Ben hadn't laid a hand on my arm. Squeezing shut my eyes, I decided not to look. The shot burned like fire, but in a bit my jaw was easy for the first time in days. The doc pulled and pried a few times before the tooth popped out, but I didn't feel a thing.

When Ben started to pay, the doc pushed the bills away. Then we went out on the street, and I was feeling pretty good, in spite of the wad of stuff packed inside my mouth. Ben pointed to my feet.

"We better get your new boots now."

I followed him into Young's Shoe Store where there were enough shoes to outfit every person in Johnson County with two or three pairs. I had never seen so many shoes: men's, women's and children's—fancy and plain—brogans, slippers, and fancy high-heels like the government lady had worn. I saw the price on them and my eyes popped. The government must be paying good wages to nosey ladies who pried into other folks' business.

The salesman took one look at my feet and led us to a rack where boots stood in neat rows like soldiers on parade. There were cowboy boots on a rack nearby, one pair about my size, black and gray and shiny as a new penny. The summer before, Rita May had taken me to the movies to see John Wayne in *Stagecoach.* He had worn a pair of boots just like these. Ben saw me eyeing them.

"Don't think that's what your mama had in mind."

I knew he was right, but my eyes stayed glued while I imagined swaggering into class like John Wayne with those boots on my feet. I wondered if Patsy Rawlings liked cowboys.

My feet were soon laced up in a brand-spanking-new pair of Red Wing work boots. I would have been mighty proud to have them—if only I hadn't seen the black and gray cowboy boots, which, along with my holey brogans, I had left behind in the store.

I hoped I would be working more for Grandpa. He had needed me twice lately. If that kept up, soon I would be able to buy the things I wanted.

On the way back to the car, I saw Ben stare across the street toward the cafe where Rita worked. I wanted to tell her howdy, but I didn't want to ask Ben. He solved the problem for me.

"I need to go to the hardware store—it'll take about fifteen minutes. I figure you'll want to see your sister."

Rita was surprised to see me. She quickly asked, "Is anything wrong?"

"Naw. Except I had to get a tooth yanked. Ben brought me in to the dentist." Her eyes grew large as she looked behind me toward the door and I added, "He's over at the hardware."

She relaxed. "After getting a tooth pulled, I don't guess you could handle a piece of pie?" She nodded toward a glass case holding several kinds: apple, cherry, and some yellow pie with puffy white stuff piled about a mile high on top. Lemon meringue, she called it. I would have dearly loved to try some, but I had spit out the gauze and my jaw was hurting again.

"I reckon not," I shook my head sadly. Time was short so I changed the subject. "Rita, you're gonna make up with Ben, aren't you?"

Her eyes flashed. "Mind your own business, Jackson." She turned and began walking away. But she turned back, biting her lip. "I shouldn't snap at you. Truth is, Jackson, we did talk, and I'm just not Ben's type any more."

"What's that mean?"

"After he got hurt, Ben got religion. Now he's too good for the likes of us."

My mouth opened and closed like a catfish out of water, my mind unable to imagine Ben had become a Bible thumper. Finally I spoke. "You gotta be wrong...he's been mighty nice to me. Took me to the dentist and offered to pay. Never said a preachy thing all day."

"He sure preached at me—told me the way I dressed and acted at Hal's party was downright sinful."

I cocked a disbelieving eyebrow.

"Well, what he actually said was that I acted scandalous," she admitted. "At first I thought he was kidding—but he's dead serious about this religion stuff."

"He ain't said a word about it to me." I knew I was treading on dangerous ground here. "But he's right about Hal's party. You were awful. Everyone was whispering. And Dora Slate outright said you had gone wild."

Rita's green eyes blazed. "Jealous old cat. She's a fine one to talk. Everyone knows Delbert isn't the father of that oldest boy."

Everyone but me. Now I understood why Dillard didn't resemble Delbert and why I had always liked him.

Rita tilted her chin defiantly. "Let 'em talk. And Ben Tyler can go to blazes. I'm not about to start wearing high-necks and long skirts to please him! I intend to have fun and not get old and sour like the pickle-pusses down at the Baptist Church!"

The few times I had been around when the Baptists spilled out the church door, it seemed as if almost everyone was smiling and happy, but I wasn't going to argue the point now.

"When you see Ben, you can tell him I said so!" she finished hotly.

I turned to go. She quickly came after me and touched my arm.

"Hey, I'm not mad at you. It was good to see you. How are the boys? Have you heard from Daddy lately?"

I noticed she hadn't asked after Mama. "Daddy was fine last we heard. Timmy's putting on weight again, but he's spoiled rotten. Wants Mama to sit and hold him all the time now."

"I miss the little squirt." Her eyes grew soft. "Give him a hug for me."

"Why don't you come home sometime and hug him yourself."

The bell over the door jingled and Ben walked inside. Rita whirled and disappeared into the kitchen.

Ben looked after her as he spoke to me. "You ready?"

"Yeah."

I followed him to the car, and we drove awhile with hardly a word passing between us.

I wasn't convinced Rita was right. I hadn't seen any halo floating over Ben's head. He wasn't as rowdy maybe, but that could be because he had been sick. Then I remembered how he had set the shine aside without tasting it. The old Ben would have tipped the bottle no matter what time of day it was. My curiosity got the best of me.

I looked out the window at the white-coated fields flying by. "Rita May says you got religion."

He didn't answer right away, and I looked at him. He watched the road, acting as if he hadn't heard me. "Well, did you?"

Before answering, he took a stick of gum from his pocket, unwrapped it, stuck it into his mouth, and chewed a bit. "You ever see anybody die?"

I shook my head.

"It's not a pretty sight. There's an old saying about no atheist in a foxhole," he said, "and it's pretty much true. When my ship got torpedoed, all around me were flames, men running, screaming, crying out to God—arms and legs blown off—my own clothes on fire." His eyes narrowed with the telling.

"You know what went through my mind?" he asked.

I shook my head.

"I'm headed for hell."

I swallowed and squirmed around, wishing I hadn't asked him that stupid question.

"That's the last thought I remember," he said, "until I woke up. I was mighty relieved to not be in hell. I was aboard the ship that came to our rescue. Later, in the hospital when a chaplain came around quoting scripture, I listened." He grinned that big white-toothed grin that made a dimple at the left of his mouth. "Ever hear John 3:16?"

I nodded. It was one of Mr. Caruthers's favorites.

Ben went on, "I never was much for listening to preachers before. I'm no Holy-Joe now, but it's good being ready to meet God."

I didn't have much to say after that. When I got out of the car, Ben stayed inside and handed me the change. There was more than five dollars. As I stuck it into my pocket, he grinned.

"Make sure you give all that to your mama."

I knew he was joking. I might have lots of faults, but I would never steal from Mama.

I had a hard time going to sleep that night. Rita was right. I didn't figure Ben would enjoy my company now, and frankly, I wasn't wild about his either. I didn't like thinking about God and hell and such. I punched my pillow into a new shape and pushed Sammy. "Hey, scoot over, bed hog."

He grunted and moved only an inch or two. I determined to ask Mama again if I could move into Rita's room. Last time she had said no, but maybe she would change her mind if I pointed out that Timmy was outgrowing his little bed and could move in with Sammy.

I was almost asleep when a loud thump hit the outside wall and echoed through the quiet house. I jerked awake and cocked my head to listen. Laddie growled deep and then began furiously barking. He was tied to the end of the porch because Zearl Johnson had set steel traps along the creek this trapping season.

There was another thud, this time near the door. Someone was out there!

"Revenuers!" I thought with my heart in my throat. Coming to arrest me! I looked around for a place to hide. On bare, cold feet, I crept to the bedroom door. It opened with a loud creak. Mama stood in the kitchen, her long white gown outlined in darkness.

"Mama," I hissed, "don't light the lamp! The curtains are open. A body can see in the windows. It's better to keep it dark." My voice shook.

"Shhh," she shushed me. "Stay put."

She was halfway across the floor when another blow landed against the wall and she froze. Then total mayhem broke loose. There was a screeching squall and a thumping against the wall and then a terrible clanging overhead. It began at one side of the house and traveled across the tin roof and back again.

That was no revenuer! But it was something. Timmy began to wail.

"What is it?" cried Sammy. Shivering from fear and cold, wearing long-sleeved red underwear, he stood huddled in our bedroom doorway, his frightened face white in a pool of moonlight.

"I don't know," Mama whispered, "but you two stay in there and try to quiet Timmy. He's scared."

So was I. My heart was pounding fit to bust. I racked my brain for a possible weapon. There was none since Daddy's 12 gauge was gone, except for a long butcher knife in the kitchen.

"I told you not to sell the shotgun!" I hissed.

Mama stopped fumbling for a match and faced me.

"This is one time you're right. Roy hasn't gone to town yet. I'll go get it back tomorrow."

"Sounds like a haint draggin' a chain across the roof," whimpered Sammy, still shivering in the doorway.

"I told you there's no such things as ghosts," Mama muttered through chattering teeth, but right at the moment I had to agree with Sammy.

The baby's howls added to the frightening noise.

"I may as well light the lantern," said Mama. "Whatever's making that racket isn't human." Her hands shook as she struck the match and held it close to the wick. The flame caught and burned a crooked, smoking blaze. The wick needed trimming. There wasn't time now, so she replaced the globe. The noise overhead had not lessened.

"I wish your daddy was here, but there's no help for it. I'll have to go out and see what it is or sit huddled inside like a scared chicken."

"No, Mama, I'll go." At her refusal, I shook my head. "Daddy would expect me to."

I took the lantern, gripped the butcher knife, and headed for the door. The mist-covered sliver of moon gave the night an eerie glow.

I figured it would be a good idea to turn Laddie loose. He sounded more than willing to attack. I set the lantern down on the porch and crept to the far edge and narrowed my eyes trying to see into the blackness. I could hear nothing but Laddie. His ruff straight up, he lunged, pulling the chain too tight to unfasten. I stepped cautiously down onto the ground and pulled him back to me. He ignored my whisper to settle down. I fought to hold him as he fought to pull free. I was afraid to put down the butcher knife, so I held it and Laddie with one hand and wrestled with the clasp on the chain with the other. Suddenly a hissing came from the darkness. It came straight for me. I jumped away.

Laddie went berserk and knocked me back onto my backside. Now I was tangled with dog, chain, and butcher knife. Frantic, I grabbed the porch post. A loud screech filled the night. I went stiff with fear. Something landed right at my feet. I yelled and scooted back on my rear. Then, in wavering lantern light, I saw it.

"Jackson, are you all right?" cried Mama from the doorway.

I grabbed Laddie by the scruff and held him. "I'm fine. Come see the booger."

She stepped onto the porch. "Well, my lands," she said.

"What is it?" called Sammy fearfully.

"It's just old Tiger with his head stuck in a fish can." It was Grandpa's fat, yellow tomcat with his head stuck deep into a salmon can. I hoped no one noticed my voice shaking. "Mama, bring me those leather gloves and come help."

Grandpa opened tin cans by spearing them with a knife, cutting an x, curling back the metal, and leaving the jagged lid on the can. He pitched the emptied cans out the back door and only took them to the junk hole when he took a notion. Tiger had slipped his head into the can to enjoy a feast of salmon scraps and gotten stuck.

"Poor thing! His neck is bleeding," said Mama as the cat ran along banging his head on the ground. "He's scared to death."

I felt like laughing and crying. The crazy cat would be hard to catch. "Circle around and see if you can head him my way, Mama, but don't try to catch him. He'll scratch like thunder," I warned.

I hurried past the porch and stooped to head him. But Tiger went flying past with pitiful yowls, his tail straight up in the air.

"There he goes around the house. He's headed for the cellar. Maybe we can corner him in there. Grab the lantern," I yelled.

We headed for the cellar just as Tiger ran smack into the rock wall. With lightning speed, he started to climb, but I managed to grab his tail just before he reached the top.

"Ouch!" I screeched as sharp claws sank in. I landed in a mad whirl of cat-claws, fur, tail, and a dynamite spurt of diarrhea that flew everywhere.

"Grab hold of the can," I yelled. "I can't hold him much..."

Mama grabbed the can. It popped off and Tiger sprang from my hands. He sat blinking in the lantern light and began to gingerly lick his fur as though nothing unusual had happened.

Mama sank to the ground. She eyed me and then she laughed. "You ought to see yourself! Pew-ee and how you stink!"

Soon my small grin grew into a smile, and before long I sat on the ground beside her and howled. We laughed until Sammy called loudly from the porch.

"Mama, is Old Tiger all right?"

"He's fine," she called back and then laughed again.

"Timmy won't quit crying and it's awful dark and cold in here."

"I'll be right in."

"You strip off and leave your clothes outside."

"But it's freezing out here," I protested.

"I don't want that smell in the house. I'll have Sammy bring you out a blanket."

When Sammy arrived with the blanket, and in spite of the cold, I shucked my long johns and tossed them over the cellar wall. With chattering teeth, I headed for the house wearing nothing but a blanket. I stood shivering by the stove while water heated for a bath.

"Since we're all awake, I reckon I'll make us a hot drink," said Mama. It wasn't cocoa, but the hot milk with vanilla and sugar was tasty. While we sipped it and laughed about our scare, Mama's eyes looked soft again in the lamplight. I realized this was the first time we had all really laughed since Daddy left. It felt good.

"When you get the shotgun back, can I start hunting?" I asked.

In spite of the fact that I had faced danger tonight like a man, she merely said, "We'll see." I figured that meant no.

Chapter 11

On Monday after school I dropped by Rawlings' for a peek at the Gibson. I was hoping Mr. Rawlings would let me play it again, but he was busy. The new ration books for sugar and meat had just been issued, and the store was a beehive. I swallowed a lump of disappointment and headed out the door just in time to see Grandpa riding up on Old Dan.

"Howdy, boy," he called as he kicked free of the stirrups and stepped down. "Leaving empty-handed?"

"Yep. I didn't need anything." I looked down and kicked dirt, reluctant to tell him about the guitar. He might laugh.

"How about a sody-pop on me?"

I grinned, grabbed a Grapette from the cooler, and followed him inside, wondering why he was clean-shaven, slicked up, and in such a good mood. While he jawed with Rawlings and a couple of other fellows, I drank the pop and eyed the guitar. It was all I could do to keep from touching it, but I wouldn't dare without Rawlings' permission, so I swallowed my pop and dreamed.

After I had drained the last drop, I put the bottle in the wooden crate that held the empties. Grandpa finally got through visiting and bought a can of Prince Albert and an extra book of cigarette papers. As I followed him out the door, I glanced back at the Gibson. I decided to stop by the next day. Maybe Mr. Rawlings wouldn't be so busy.

A cold, dust-filled gust hit my face as I stepped outside. Gray clouds flew across the wintery sun almost as fast as airplanes. Delbert Slate came shuffling down the road, wearing holey pants and a greasy jacket that was much too thin for the weather. I turned up my jacket collar against the biting wind and waited while Grandpa held on to Dan's reins and had a confab with Delbert. I could not imagine anyone choosing to stand close to Delbert. Grandpa was practically whispering in his ear. I couldn't hear what he said, but I could see the stupid grin on Delbert's face. He kept nodding while he scratched under one arm. I imagined cooties and backtracked to put more distance between us. Before long, Delbert headed into the store. I wrinkled my nose against the smell of sour sweat as he passed.

"Hey, wait up," I called as Grandpa swung up on Dan. He pulled up and stared down at me. I looked around and dropped my voice. "How long you reckon it will take me to earn thirty dollars working for you?"

"Price of that guitar hanging on Rawlings' wall," he said.

"You don't miss much do you, Grandpa?"

He laughed. "Have to have sharp eyes in my line of work. About the money," he looked back at the store, "if this deal works out that I'm dickering on, you'll make thirty dollars long before anyone around here can afford that there guitar. I'll for sure need you lots next month." He kicked Dan's flanks, and the mule trotted down the road, each hoof stirring up puffs of cold dust.

"Thanks for the soda pop," I called. He waved without turning. In the fading light, I walked home pondering what kind of deal Grandpa was hatching and how much money I would make out of it.

When I got home, I was surprised to find Miss Hilda in our front room in the rocking chair drawn near the fireplace. She rocked back and forth, moaning more pitifully than the wind that howled around the house. When the door shut behind me, she looked up. In the flickering light of the fireplace, I saw her face was blotched red and swollen from crying. There was a picture in her hand. It was the picture of her family.

"What's—?"

Mama shook her head and shushed me. She knelt beside Miss Hilda, cradling her with an arm around her back. Timmy, big eyed and whimpering, stood clinging to Mama, but she paid him no mind as she tried to comfort Miss Hilda. I scooped him up and headed for the bedroom where Sammy was motioning to me from the doorway. I shut the door and whispered, "What's going on?"

"Miss Hilda's just found out," his voice quivered, "that her kin over there in Europe was killed! They was rounded up in the town where they lived and lined up against a wall and shot with machine guns by a bunch of Nazi soldiers. Her niece, Esther, her three boys, her little girl, and her brand new baby!"

"They killed the kids?" I asked, horrified.

"Yep," he said, bug-eyed. "Everyone—men, women, kids, and old folks. And then they dumped all the bodies in a big ol' hole and covered it over."

I felt sick. That pretty little girl murdered! I hugged Timmy tight and shuddered while Sammy went on. "One of Miss Hilda's friends who lived there...well, he was hid out in the attic of a building and he saw it all. It happened a good while back. For months he's been hiding and sneaking, trying to get away. He finally made it to a safe place and just now wrote to Miss Hilda.

"Mama was coming home from the mill, and she come across Miss Hilda coming home from the post office. She was taking on so that Mama brought her here."

I stared at the closed door where muffled voices filtered through, Miss Hilda's filled with tears and Mama's soft and gentle. I shook my head. "How could anyone be so stinkin' mean as them Nazis?" Blood pounded in my ears as I felt white-hot anger.

Mama opened the door and put her head in. "Boys," she spoke low, "do up the chores and tend to the milk. Sammy, you watch Timmy. I'm going home with Miss Hilda and stay with her for a bit until she settles down. I'll take the lantern. It'll be after dark when I get home." She turned and then turned back. "Be careful with the stove. Keep the damper closed. And don't put too many logs in the fireplace. Windy night like this, a spark can burn the house down in no time."

My mind was not on milking. I was taking aim at dozens of German soldiers and plugging them one after another. Bossy took advantage of my wandering mind and kicked over the milk bucket, spilling the milk. I drew back and socked her, but it hurt my hand worse than it hurt her bony hip. I wished once again that Daddy had not forbidden forking her. A good jab with a pitchfork would make a bull behave, let alone a milk cow.

The new calf needed plenty of the milk, so I turned it in with her and left the barn with an empty bucket. In deep twilight, I could barely see the smoke roiling from chimney and stovepipe before it whipped away on the wind. Before going inside, I looked carefully and saw no sparks. Compared to the biting cold outside, at first the room felt toasty. But on such a night, both fires would be needed to keep the drafty shack anything close to warm. I would be glad when the cellar was ready.

We ate leftover cornbread and beans. I stoked the fire and then tuned in the war news on the radio. At nine o'clock I sent Sammy to bed and tucked Timmy in beside him. It was too cold for the baby to sleep alone.

I turned the radio low to hear the news. "Reports from secret sources inside Germany reveal there is a rising anti-Hitler movement. Students in Munich have passed out hundreds of flyers condemning the Nazi Regime."

My ears perked up when I heard the announcer mentioning Jews.

"And it has been reported that hundreds of German women—with more arriving daily—are gathering in Berlin outside a government building to demand the release of their husbands. More than a thousand Jewish men are being held there for deportation. Thus far, the German high command has taken no action, but clearly these brave wives and mothers are risking their lives."

I wondered if the Nazis would machine gun these women too. Apparently they had no qualms about killing women.

Mama came home just as I had pulled off my shoes and headed for bed. I stopped with my boots in my hand. "Miss Hilda all right?"

"Yes." Mama hung her coat and hat on the peg behind the door and warmed her hands at the fireplace. With shoulders sagging, she dropped into the rocking chair and propped her feet on the hearth. "She'll have to grieve for a while, but she's a strong woman. She'll get over it."

I sat down on the hearth with my back to the fireplace. I had banked the fire for the night with ashes heaped over the coals, but there was still some warmth coming from the banked logs. But Mama's face was pinched and blue, so I raked back the ashes and poked up a blaze. She kept her eyes glued to the fire. She was quiet for a while and then she spoke. "I met them once—Miss Hilda's kin."

"I heard you say so," I said.

"It was a few years back when your daddy got that fishhook caught in his neck." I nodded, remembering, and she went on, "I couldn't get it out so we went to Doc Krause's, and he got it out slick as could be. Esther and her husband were visiting—she was a shy, sweet person. I think she had three kids then. I remember the oldest boy was about your age."

We were both quiet for a spell. Finally I said, "Wish I was old enough to join up." When Mama said nothing, I went on, "Maybe Daddy will get the fellows that killed Miss Hilda's family."

Mama sighed and surprised me by saying, "I hope so. They do need killing."

Mama was glum all week. I figured she was worried about Miss Hilda or Daddy or both. Her long face was getting on my nerves. On Friday night I slipped out again. Grandpa didn't need me, so I dropped by Jake's and asked if he would like to go coon hunting. He always let me use his gun. But Jake said he had a hankering for pool. I shrugged and tagged along.

I wasn't sure they would let me inside. The roadhouse was no place for kids, but Jake said I was big for my age. Most folks thought I was sixteen or seventeen—or so Jake said—and he vowed no one would pay me any mind if I kept my mouth shut.

No one raised an eyebrow when I stepped into the crowded, smoke-filled room. Jake bought us a coke and then we headed for the pool table. Before long two sailors finished playing, and it was our turn. I imitated Jake and rubbed some chalk on the end of my stick—a cue, Jake called it. He went first, and I watched how he played while he explained the rules. When it was my shot, I bent over and sighted, lining the white ball up with another that was striped. Holding the stick sort of loose, like Jake had said, I tapped the white ball. It bumped the striped ball and sent it across the table and into a pocket on the other side. Jake slapped my back as the ball disappeared down into the pocket.

"I think you'll make a fair-to-middlin' pool player one of these days."

I got excited and missed the next shot, but after that when it was my turn, I forced myself to calm down and take my time. One after another, I put three balls right down the pockets. Pool was a great game, I decided. No wonder Jake liked it. Studying the table, I picked my next shot and leaned over the table just as a commotion began across the room. Wade Lucas had come through the door. He drew two jugs from under his slicker, and waved them before the crowded room. Whistles shrilled above the blaring jukebox.

My eyes widened when I saw Rita May. I hoped she wouldn't notice me through all the cigarette smoke. When she saw what Wade was doing, she grabbed his arm and said something in his ear, but he shook her off. I knew she was warning him to hide the jugs. I knew they were full of Grandpa's moonshine liquor, and as illegal as all get-out. Wade lurched to the bar near the pool table, so I slouched and looked down to hide my face.

"Wade," Rita May had followed, speaking low and desperate, "You don't know who's here. Look. There's soldiers, sailors, flyboys...all kinds of strangers in here."

I didn't figure revenuers would be wearing service uniforms, but I peeked up through my lashes and quickly searched the room with cautious eyes. There were a couple of fellows sitting together who might be revenuers. They were older and nicer dressed than the young loggers and miners who made up the rest of the crowd. Wade seemed to have their complete attention.

"You think I can't handle things!" he railed, thick-tongued.

Rita looked nervous. "It's just that—well, maybe you're not thinkin' straight tonight. You've had a lot to drink."

He glared. Rita May turned away and, not bothering to take off her coat, sat down at a table.

Wade slapped the jugs onto the bar. "Here it is, Shorty! Best in the country." He leered at the large, bearded man frowning behind the bar.

"Lucas, you're a fool." Shorty quickly swept the jugs under the counter out of sight.

Wade looked around bleary-eyed until he spied Rita May. Dragging back a chair, he joined her at the table and stuck his long legs out, halfway blocking the aisle. A flashy redhead left a crowded table to join them.

I was not surprised. It was always that way with Wade. Women flocked to him like ants to sugar. I never liked him. He was a loud-mouthed braggart, but I had to admit most females would find him good-looking with coal-black hair, white teeth, wide shoulders, and solid muscles. He was certainly popular with the ladies.

I got so busy watching that I got caught when Rita glanced back around. Her eyes widened and she choked on her cola. She marched straight to me.

"What in tarnation are you doing here?"

I leaned back against the pool table, acting far cockier than I felt. "Shooting pool."

She wheeled on Jake and her green eyes shot fire. "Jake Johnson, you ought to be horsewhipped for bringing a kid to a place like this!"

Jake's face turned redder than a turkey wattle, and I felt my own ears grow hot. Folks were staring.

"Rita," I lowered my voice, "see them two fellers over there." I nodded my head just a tad. "They seem overly interested in Wade and those jugs."

She paled and cut her eyes hurriedly, but she kept right on scolding. "Jackson, get out of here! Jake, take him home right this minute!"

He didn't argue, but I did. "You ain't my boss, Rita May," I snarled. "I'll go anywhere I take a notion."

She set her mouth hard. "If you don't leave right now, I'll go get Uncle Roy."

"You want him to know you were here?" I asked, figuring that would shut her up.

"He knows I'm old enough to make my own choices—you're not."

I figured Uncle Roy would drag me out by my ear. I grabbed my jacket and followed Jake outside feeling like a whipped pup.

———————

February was a bitter, cold month. Johnson's pond had ice thick enough for skating. Although Mama had strictly forbid it, Sammy and I sneaked over a few times to slide around. After he fell and almost broke his wrist, we left off skating and went straight home after school.

We listened to the radio each evening, eager for news of the Allied advance in North Africa. We thought that was where Daddy's division was.

"Perhaps at no time during the last three and a half years, not since the German march into Poland, has there been such a feeling of tension as marks the present day. This feeling, then, is the main news for today's report.

"Amid the Allied push into North Africa comes the cry for invasion of Europe. British newspapers are urging that the Allied forces capitalize on the Russian advances on the continent." I strained to hear the rest of the report, but the station faded.

I tried turning the dial. There was only music on the other stations.

"It's time for bed anyway," said Mama. "I'm exhausted. Five o'clock comes early, and tomorrow's another long day."

"Guess Daddy's right in the thick of that push into North Africa," I said.

"More than likely," agreed Mama with a puckered brow.

"Hope they'll get Africa over with and get on to Germany and kick Hitler's tail. I bet those Jews hope so too."

"I'm sure they do," said Mama as she lifted Timmy, already half-asleep, from the table and carried him into the bedroom. "Jackson, bank the fire and go to bed," she called.

I knelt in front of the fire and hugged the heat, dreading the icy bedroom. I was thinking how, according to the news, people were freezing to death in Russia. I was thankful for the roof over my head and the flames dancing in the fireplace.

In March we had a warm spell. The sun shone and birds chirped and flitted from tree to tree. Along the front yard's edge, green tips of daffodils poked through the thawed ground.

Mama worked for Uncle Roy almost every day. I joined her at the mill on the weekends. Every spare minute we worked on the cellar. It was almost finished. Mama said the cold might be over, but there were still the spring storms to endure. We hurried to finish it before gardening took all our time. I still managed to work for Grandpa, mostly late on Friday and Saturday nights. That earned me a dose of sulfur and molasses; Mama was worried because I was always tired. I swallowed the awful stuff without a word.

Grandpa was teaching me the art of moonshine making. And I knew I had really earned his trust when he showed me all the different locations where the still could be hidden. At first I felt proud and happy over the stash of bills and coins that were collecting in my Prince Albert can, but lately I began to doubt my decision to work for Grandpa. He was about as unstable as nitroglycerin and about as nerve-racking to work around. Even more worrisome than that, I felt guilty for breaking Daddy's trust. If he found out, I knew he would be mighty disappointed in me. All the worry made me nervous and jumpy, and I kept looking over my shoulder and imagining a revenuer behind every bush.

Late one night, halfway to Grandpa's, I heard something slipping through the brush behind me. I stopped and tried to listen through blood pounding in my ears. When I stopped, it kept coming, making too much noise to be a revenuer. It might be a panther. They were rare, but there were still a few in these woods. Charlie had killed one two years before. If it was a panther, how I needed the shotgun! My mouth was dry as dust as I quickly searched for a weapon. I settled on a big rock. It wasn't the thing to fight a cat with, but it was the best I could do. No need to try climbing a tree. I raised the rock over my head and waited.

"Hey, silly. It's only me."

If I could have reached Sammy, I'd have clobbered him with the rock. Not taking any chances, he hung back laughing.

"Why you followin' me?" I lashed out.

"What are you doing sneaking around out here?"

"None of your business. Get back home before I tan your hide."

"You're moonshining with Grandpa, ain't you? Don't lie. I heard you and Rita May talking one night." He set his jaw a stubborn jut. "I want to work too. I'm big enough."

"You ain't no such thing. Besides, Grandpa wouldn't hold still for it. Now scat before I use this rock on you."

He sulked, but turned and started toward home.

"Sammy, if you say one word to Mama, I'll get you good."

"I ain't gonna tattletale," he shot back.

I frowned. Me working for Grandpa was one thing, but I intended to keep Sammy far away from this business.

Grandpa had a bad back—or so he said, so I lugged sacks of cornmeal, barrels of sugar, and buckets of water to the still, and every so often when he took a notion, I toted the still and all to a new location which was always down in a brushy hollow in a hidden limestone cave.

Each time we ran off a batch, Wade brought Rita May out from town. He always dropped her off and drove away. Grandpa would not let Wade know any of the hiding places. I suppose Rita rode back to town with him when he picked up the shine. I never stuck around to see. After we carried it to the road, I took off for home.

Grandpa was mighty edgy. He spent most of his time dusting out tracks and keeping an eye peeled. But he alone tended the mash, not letting me touch it. I studied how much sugar and cold spring water he mixed with the cornmeal.

"That's right, boy," he said, "watch and learn. My grandpa taught me how to make the best corn liquor there is. Learn to do it right, and you can make a living easy, without having to slave all yer life like yer ma and Uncle Roy." He set down the water bucket and wiped his hands down his pant leg. "It's the recipe I'm passing on to you. Roy don't want it," he said with bitterness. "He don't want nothing from me."

"How come?" I asked.

"His mama." Grandpa grew hard-eyed. "She poisoned him agin' me. I wasn't never good enough fer that woman. That religion of hers!" He puckered his mouth. "Baah! Made me gag." He turned and began stirring the mash again. "A woman marries a man and sets right in trying to change him. When that don't work, she'll turn his young'uns agin' him."

I reckoned he was right. Mama had always tried to change Daddy—but she could never turn me against him!

We finished the cellar the last day of March. It was actually a dugout, the kind the pioneers had lived in on the prairie, with stout rock walls and a wood stove with the pipe sticking out the roof. Uncle Roy had even built bunks against one wall. When Rita May came home for a visit, I showed her around. I thought she would be impressed. She wasn't.

She wrinkled her nose. "It ain't decent, having to scurry for a hole in the ground like a rat when the weather turns cold."

Mama had stepped through the cellar door in time to hear Rita's remark. For a second her eyes showed hurt and then they snapped.

"Some of us ain't as lucky as you are with a good job and a nice, warm place to live." With that Mama spun on her heels and headed back toward the house, and Rita May headed toward Grandpa's.

I made my way slowly back to the house, wishing things didn't always explode every time Rita May and Mama got within shouting distance. I could remember when they had good times together.

Mama was at the clothesline pulling down the wash and stuffing it into a basket. I could barely make out what she said for the clothespins in her mouth. "The wind's about to blow my washing off the line." She reached for a sheet that whipped in the wind. As the sun dipped low, lightning danced in the west and dark clouds began to overspread the sky. Mama dropped the clothespins into a pocket in her apron and raised her voice to be heard above the roar. "After supper we'll gather our bedding and sleep in the cellar tonight."

It seemed like there should be some kind of celebration for using the cellar the first time, but Rita May's remarks had sort of taken the pleasure out of it for me and I figured for Mama too.

"What's for supper? I'm starving." I reached to help carry the laundry basket.

"Salt pork and dried peas."

A gust of wind blew me sideways. The house shook as if struck a mighty blow.

"I'm sure glad we finished the cellar," I yelled.

"We'll eat in there. Get your brothers and I'll get the food," Mama ordered as she began to run.

I grabbed Timmy and an armful of quilts, and headed through the storm for the cellar. Sammy and Mama came right behind. Wind jerked the door from my hand and battered it fiercely. I stooped to set Timmy onto the floor and struggled to close it.

The storm howled and shook the tin, but we were snug. In spite of what Rita had said, I thought the critters that burrowed into the earth probably had right cozy homes.

Friday night Grandpa wanted my help again. He wanted to move the operation to a different cave and needed my strong back to tote stuff over the hill and into the next hollow. I had slipped outside and started climbing through the fence.

"Where do you think you're going?" Mama spoke almost at my elbow. I had thought she was asleep, but she was headed for the outhouse.

"I'm meeting Jake," I told the first lie that came to mind, "to play pool." I knew she would be mad, but it was better than her guessing the truth.

I couldn't see her face, but I heard the displeasure in her voice. "Only pool hall open this time of night is that sleazy roadhouse." She jerked my arm and pushed me back toward the house. "No son of mine is going to hang out in that place! And you can bet I'm going to have a talk with Jake Johnson for taking you there. You stay away from him, you hear me?"

"Guess that means I can't work at the mill any more," I smarted off. "And you won't get my pay to stash in your bedroom."

She gave my arm a shake. "Young man, you keep a civil tongue in your head. Working with Jake and chasing around with him are two entirely different things." She lengthened her steps and dragged me along through the back door. "What was your daddy thinking—going off and leaving me? How I'll ever live over both you and Rita May is beyond me."

I managed to sneak out later that night. Grandpa was anxious to move the still. He needed to get a batch ready to bottle. We stayed late in the cave getting set up. I was rubbing my eyes fighting sleep when a soft whistle came from outside. We both jumped, and in a flash Grandpa held the shotgun pointed at the cave's mouth. When Rita May scooted inside, he lowered the gun, sat it down, and wiped his forehead.

"You scared the liver out of me, girl! You ain't supposed to come for days yet."

"I know." She blinked her eyes getting used to the lamplight. "I needed to warn you about something."

When he heard that, Grandpa reached for the gun. He held it in both hands and waited.

"You don't need that." Rita pointed to the gun. "I just came to tell you about a fellow who's been coming into the cafe. He laughed and joked around, real friendly like. Then he started asking questions—where I live, who are my folks. He came back every day, always interested in me. I never thought anything about it. Fellows are always trying to make a date." Out of breath, she stopped and drew a deep breath, pushed back her windblown hair, then hurried on. "But he kept asking nosey questions, and I got to wondering if he might be a Fed. It might be nothing—" she stammered.

Then Grandpa snapped, "Or it might be plenty!" His eyes set hard. "You sure you weren't followed?"

"I'm sure. I slipped over to Wade's place, and we drove all around before he dropped me off down at the road. I got out of sight in a flash. I waited for a long time. There was no one following."

Grandpa rubbed his hand along the gunstock. "We got to be careful." Then he cussed a blue streak. "Just when I got new contacts in Hot Springs wantin' all I can make."

I felt the hair standing on the back of my neck. "We better knock off for a while, Grandpa. That fellow might be a Fed."

Grandpa cussed some more, but he agreed.

From then on I dreamed about federal agents, and I saw one behind every tree and fence post.

Chapter 12

"How come they call them redbud trees, Jackson?" asked Sammy pointing at a flowering tree. We were fishing after school one afternoon. "They're purple as can be."

I lazily dangled my line over the clear pool and shrugged. "They're sort of red when they first bud."

He looked skeptical. "And dogwood. Reckon where they got a name like that for such pretty white flowers."

I raised an eyebrow. Sammy was always surprising me with his questions, asking things I had never thought about.

He shivered. "Since the sun got low, it's turning plumb cold."

I drew in my line. "Yeah. Likely this is dogwood winter. It'll be cold for a few days before it warms up and stays that way. We best get home. The fish aren't biting, and Mama doesn't see any need in wasting time if we come home empty handed."

"She does always have a heap of chores waiting for us," agreed Sammy.

May apples bloomed, and an early spring gave way to long, warm days. When school ended I felt like a prisoner set free with visions of long days filled with fishing. But Mama kept me busy almost every minute plowing, planting and tending the garden, and working for Uncle Roy.

The garden was doing fine with rows of leaf lettuce, curly mustard, red radishes, and green onions. For the first time in ages, my belly felt satisfied, for there was more than pork and cornbread to eat. Every night we had killed greens. Some folks called it wilted lettuce salad, but we called it killed greens. Mama chopped up the greens, radishes, and onions and stirred them into a skillet with a dab of hot bacon drippings. If there was bacon left from breakfast, she crumbled it in too. Served with a piece of hot, buttered cornbread, nothing tasted better.

Daddy never planted corn until the whippoorwills began to call. They had called early this year, so risking a frost we had planted early. The birds were right. Now leaves on the young corn unfolded as it shot up straight and green—and along with it, the weeds. I spent most mornings hoeing, beginning while the air was fresh and cool and keeping on until the freshness faded into heat.

Now the sun was midway up a clear sky, and I was soaked with sweat. Taking a break, I leaned on the hoe and swatted at buffalo gnats attacking my eyes and ears, while thinking soon there would be beans to pick and kraut to make.

At the end of the field, a flock of crows made skittish takeoffs and landings, their flapping feathers purple-black in the sun. I couldn't see what had disturbed them until Laddie, fresh from a dip in the creek, came loping across the cornfield as frisky as a pup. He stopped nearby and shook, sending a spray of water all over me.

"Dang dog! Do your shaking somewhere else!" I scolded.

"Jackson! Hey, Jackson!" Sammy came bounding across the yard as Mama waved to me from the doorway.

He arrived breathless. "Mama said you could take a break and go with me to the store. She needs three boxes of them new kind of canning disks, the kind with the sealing stuff right on the lid." Sammy held high a shiny nickel. "And I'm gonna buy us a strawberry Nehi with my birthday nickel Uncle Roy gave me."

Already I could feel the cool sweetness slipping down my dry throat. I hurried toward the well, calling over my shoulder, "I gotta wash up a little. I'll be right there!"

I propped the hoe and then drew water, pouring what was left inside the leaking bucket into a basin sitting on the rock wall.

"Mama ought to get a new one," I muttered, too happy over the unexpected mid-morning break to be as disgusted as usual over the leaking bucket.

I took the small lard pail full of eggs from Sammy. "Better let me carry these. You'll forget and start running."

With Laddie at his heels, Sammy pelted down the road. "Come on, Jackson!"

"You know I can't run with this bucket. Mr. Rawlings won't trade for cracked eggs."

In no hurry to return to the cornfield, I ambled along behind. The shady road felt cool to my hot, bare feet. I hoped Rawlings would let me play the Gibson today.

But there was a letter from Daddy, so after drinking the strawberry soda, we quickly headed home. I gave the guitar a parting look and followed Sammy outside. I almost ran over Jake.

"Whoa! Where's the fire?"

"Sorry, Jake. We got a letter from Daddy."

"Hey," he called after me. "I was thinking about going frog gigging."

"Kinda early in the season ain't it? They won't be much size yet," I yelled back.

"I know, but it'll still be fun." He walked back to me and talked low. "If you want to go, you can meet me somewhere. I ain't coming anywhere near your mama. She about took my hide off with that tongue lashing."

I hesitated. I didn't think Grandpa would need me, but I would have to ask. "If I can make it, I'll meet you on the bluff above the narrows at the creek tonight, right before dark."

When we got home, the house was full of sweet strawberry smell. Mama slapped at my hand as I reached for the long-handled spoon lying on the stove.

"I'm not through using that yet." She took it and stirred down a pot about to boil over with frothy red jam.

"I'll trade you this letter from Daddy for a lick."

She left the spoon in the pot and quickly wiped her hands on her apron. In spite of me holding the letter high, she grabbed it.

Daddy's news was really not much news at all. He was well. He loved us and missed us. Mama said the censors would not allow him to tell about the actual battles or where he was exactly. After she read the letter, Mama wore such a long face I wanted to get out of the house. I asked if I could go frog gigging, but I left out the part about Jake going too.

I loved fried frog legs better than fried chicken. Mama hated to cook them. She claimed it gave her the willies the way they shivered and jumped in the pan, but knowing how much Sammy and I loved them, she would fix them anyway along with hot cornpone. Mama made delicious cornpone by mixing cornmeal and a little salt with boiling water, making it into patties, and then frying them in hot lard. I could eat a platter full.

"There's still plenty of chores to do if you're bored," said Mama. "I could use some help around here after near killing myself canning jam. Tomorrow I have to do all this laundry for the Bradleys and finish putting up that basket of berries."

"All you ever think about is work," I grumbled. But I hurried to fill the washtubs with water, and I hauled out the ashes and filled the woodbox with short stove wood. "Everything's ready for the washing," I said. "If I get up early and cap those strawberries, can I go now?"

Mama looked up from pouring hot jam into clean jars. "I suppose so. If you were tired as I am, you'd be glad for a chance to sit down."

Sammy begged to come along. I told him no.

Trying blackmail, he whispered, "I could tell Mama about you slippin' out lately."

"You do and I'll gig you instead of a frog," I growled low.

Just after dusk I set off to meet Jake. He was hunkered on the top of the rocky bluff above the narrows, holding a pocketknife and plug of tobacco, staring at the creek far below. When he offered me a sliver, I declined. Since my introduction to snuff, I had no hankering for tobacco and doubted if I ever would.

Jake had a jim-dandy torch made of pitch pine split into widths about the size of my fingers and lashed together into a long bundle. It would burn for hours. I hunkered and swatted at gnats as he fumbled for a match. Laddie came trotting down the path and began licking my face.

"Aw, heck! I forgot to tie up the dog." I pushed him away. "He'll have every frog within a mile jumping into the water before we even get close."

I told Jake I'd be right back and hurried home holding to the scruff of Laddie's neck. When I tied him to the porch, he let out a mournful howl that brought Sammy and Mama to the door.

"He followed me. Don't turn him loose, Sammy, or he'll be right back after me."

Sammy came to sit beside the dog, and from the sad look on his face, I almost expected him to howl too. I decided right then to take him frogging soon.

It was not quite dark by the time I returned, but Jake had the torch burning brightly. The smell of turpentine rose in a cloud of black smoke drifting into the twilight. There was a distant rumble in the west. Somewhere down in the hollow a wild turkey gobbled.

"Daddy says wild turkeys almost always gobble at thunder."

"Really?" said Jake. "I never knew that."

I scanned the sky and was relieved to see no clouds. I didn't want rain interfering with our hunt.

While we stood on the bluff, I looked into the shadowy hollow, dark and heavily timbered, and hooted like an owl, just the way Daddy had taught me, "Wha-wha-wahho." Way off, from the head of the hollow, a turkey gobbled.

"Hey, that was pretty good," said Jake. He hooted, but he didn't get the right ring to it. Disgusted, he shook his head. "I can't seem to get it right. Never have had a gobbler answer." He squatted and looked down into the black hollow. "Wonder why they gobble at an owl?"

"Daddy says it's because they're natural enemies. Owls kill the turkey's young."

I figured Zearl must not be a turkey hunter. At least he hadn't taught Jake all the things Daddy had taught me.

"Call again and see if he answers," urged Jake.

I hooted. The last note had barely faded before, far away but distinct, another gobble echoed. Then, nearby, an owl hooted. Daddy had taught me so well that I had fooled an owl. He was coming to find one of his own.

It thundered far off again and the turkey gobbled. In the gathering darkness the shrill song of tree frogs joined the loud hum of katydids and crickets, and in the direction of the creek, I heard the deep-throated notes of tonight's prey—bullfrogs. The air was warm and moist, and as we neared the creek, I smelled the watery scent of the creek bottoms.

We had no actual gig, so we used stout hickory sticks to club the frogs. I picked up my hickory stick and followed Jake along the stream. We had decided to start out along the creek bank and then finish up at the Johnson's big pond.

Under thick, black, bending trees, the path into the creek bottoms grew dim, but I followed with sure-footed familiarity. My bare feet hardly slowed, except once when a dark shape lay across the path, and I stopped to make sure that it was a limb and not a snake. Tall bluffs now rose on both sides of the creek as the path grew narrow.

"I hear a granddaddy of a bullfrog just ahead," Jake declared.

We had not gone far before, on the bank just ahead, sat a dark lump blinking bugged eyes. It stayed perfectly still while Jake held the torch high. I drew back my stick and, with the blood-thirst of a young savage, pounced on my victim. I grabbed the limp body and stuffed it into the flour sack that hung tied at my waist with twine. It was not a huge frog, but the legs were plenty big for frying.

Sometimes the critters would hear or feel a fellow coming and plop into the water, but as often as not, they'd just sit and wait in the torchlight until it was too late. It seemed strange to me that a frog stayed put like he never saw trouble coming. As I followed along behind Jake, I got to thinking. Maybe I was being like that frog. If I stayed put moonshining much longer, I might get trounced.

Jake held the torch and we went on. It took a lot of frog legs to make a good mess. I hoped Mama would fry potatoes and cornpone to go with them.

"You hear that?"

"Naw, I didn't hear anything. What was it?"

He shook his head. "Listen."

As he was doing, I faced west, and this time I heard a low rumble.

"More thunder," I guessed. "Hope it don't rain us out. I'm lookin' forward to a mess of frog legs."

But in the next quarter mile we killed only two more frogs. "Maybe we should head on back to the pond," I suggested just as a streak of lightning split the sky right above us. The thunder was loud and constant—more like a low roar.

Jake froze. "That's a flash flood!" he cried. "Let's get out of here!"

"Why, it ain't even raining!" I disagreed as I bolted after him. Proving me wrong, a big drop splattered on my arm, and several more shortly peppered my face. The tall, rocky bluffs hid the approaching storm, but the sound was growing louder every second. Wasting no more time arguing, I made for the bend up ahead, right on Jake's heels. We were in the worst possible place for climbing out. There were bluffs on both sides, and the one on our left was almost straight up. As the roar grew louder, I almost trampled Jake's heels, and he was moving fast himself. Rain suddenly poured down in sheets, and lightning split the sky, filling the narrow passage with an eerie glow. Within seconds, a crash boomed against the bluff, shaking the ground. As the roll of thunder faded, the roar of floodwater grew ominous.

"We aren't gonna make it," I yelled as a flash lit the sky. "This bluff goes on for a quarter mile, and that water's right on our heels."

"There's a place to climb out over yonder," screamed Jake above the deafening thunder. He plunged into the creek, splashing water over me as I followed right behind.

The water tugged at my overalls and washed swiftly almost to my hips as I fought to keep my footing on the slick rock bottom.

Jake pulled ahead until through the driving rain I saw him slip. Everything went pitch black as torch went under. I screamed his name and frantically felt my way in the darkness.

"Over here!" he yelled. In a lightning flash, I saw him threshing toward the shore just a few feet ahead. I floundered after him.

I ran, stubbing my toe on a tree root, too scared to feel pain. I made out Jake's outline. In the almost constant light from the storm, I saw him grab a limb of scrub brush sticking from a crevice in the rock wall as he began to climb. I came right behind, slipping but clawing my way up the wet cliff. From down below came a sound like an explosion. Not slowing, I looked around to see a wall of water round the bend and sweep past. The lazy creek had turned into a churning monster, its teeth snapping right at my feet. If I slipped, I was a goner.

Above me I heard Jake. "You all right?"

"Don't you fall or we're both dead!"

"There's a little ledge up here," he hollered. "Let me get wedged in and I'll help you up."

"Hurry. I ain't got a good hold!"

Jake soon reached to grab my arm and dragged me up onto the ledge. There was room to sit but no protection from the storm. Like wet rats, we hunkered against the rocks, faces bowed, while rain beat onto our backs and heads.

"Do you think it'll keep rising?" I yelled, fear strong in my voice.

"I hope not. We've got nowhere else to go." Jake's whole body shook.

I looked up. There was no way to climb farther. Looming above us, the cliff face was one giant rock. It was slick as a bald head.

After a moment I asked, "You ever pray, Jake?"

"You bet. I'm praying hard right now."

Maybe, since I was alongside of Jake, God would spare me too. I felt somewhat comforted, until I recalled that Jake frequented the pool hall instead of the church. I didn't reckon he was on such great terms with the Almighty either.

A watery grave and then burning hell...I wished I had listened closer when Ben talked about God. I figured it was too late now, me being such a sinner. As I watched the water, I squeezed my eyes shut and fought back a sob.

I thought of Daddy. I had been so afraid that he might die. I had never thought that it could be me instead. And Mama. I wanted to tell her I loved her. She would never know if I drowned.

The water's roar was deafening. I put my hands over my ears, hoping to shut it out. In the darkness, I shivered and squirmed to find a more comfortable perch, drawing my knees up under my chin.

"Better keep still," warned Jake, speaking loud above the water's noise. "That water won't give no second chances."

In spite of the cold rain, hot sweat poured down my armpits as the water crept over the lip of the ledge and wet my toes.

"We're both good swimmers...."

"That current would suck us under like quicksand," warned Jake as he braced the slick wall with white-knuckled hands and stood. I tried to stand but floundered and quickly sank back to the ledge. Strength had fled from my legs. Wild-eyed I stared at the water, hypnotized as it buried my feet and crept up my haunches. Jake jerked me up.

"We got to do something!" he cried.

Churning water, tugging at my overalls, was dragging my feet from the slick rock.

"Look!" I yelled as my hand found a crevice. "There's a little foothold here. Maybe we can reach that tree limb yonder and find a way to climb up over there."

"I don't know—"

"It's worth a try!" I yelled hugging the flat wall and reaching for the crack with my curled bare toes. My foot found the niche, and I stepped over and then flung myself toward the limb.

As I plunged into blackness, I heard Jake yell. When I hit the water, my breath exploded in a hiss. End over end, like a piece of driftwood, I tossed on the current, first on top and then dragged under, cold and threatening darkness closing over my head. Bobbing like a cork, I gasped for air, drawing in a mouthful of water—then with giant hands the creek pulled me under again. Everything went black.

———⁓———

The bell rang. I was late for school. No. My ears were ringing. I was tired. My head ached. I wanted to rest, but something kept prodding me. Rain. It was pounding my face. Water washed over my legs. I put out a hand and felt sandy gravel while I drew my legs out of the creek and started coughing and vomiting water. When I managed to pry my gritty, stinging eyes open, the sky was black as midnight. With a groan, I rolled over and struggled to sit. I was on the creek bank, but I had no idea where.

Slowly memory returned. Jake! I tried yelling but only managed a hoarse croak. I heard nothing but thunder and roaring water. Staggering to my feet, I stumbled from the water's edge and then crumpled to the ground and cried like a baby.

I must have finally dozed, in spite of rain still pouring on my face. When I awakened, I heard someone shout.

"Over here!" I squeaked and tried to yell louder.

Before long Ben was bending over me.

"We thought you had drowned." He pulled me up, hugging me fiercely. "You rest here while I go to the car and tell Zearl and Roy. They're searching not far away." Ben eased me down onto a rock and then rushed off. In a few seconds I heard three shots, the signal that I had been found.

In no time he was back, and soon Uncle Roy and Zearl were stumbling over the rough ground, rushing toward me. Uncle Roy's face fairly glowed.

Uncle Roy hugged me, squeezing out what little breath I had left. "Your mama is almost out of her mind."

Zearl's eyes darted all around and his face fell. "Where's Jake?"

"You ain't found him?" I asked.

"We was hopin' he was with you."

I dropped my head and shook it slowly. "He was, but I fell in the creek. I don't know what happened to him."

"Where did you last see him?"

"We were stuck on a ledge a couple of miles below home. Where am I?"

Uncle Roy was astonished. I had washed downstream more than a mile. "A body doesn't live over a ride like that in this kind of water!"

Zearl bolted back through the woods toward the road, and with Ben and Uncle Roy half-carrying me, we hurried after. My legs were wobbly as a new calf. I collapsed into the cab of Roy's pickup, and we tore down the muddy road with me giving directions. Ben followed in his old Ford. I made several false calls. It was hard to pick the exact spot. Each time we stopped and yelled there was no answer. My heart climbed high into my throat. I stopped looking at Zearl. He was trying not to cry, but his Adam's-apple worked up and down like a pump handle.

Through the rain, I finally recognized the bluff. It was high and straight, and the creek took a bend just beyond.

"That's it!" I screamed. We all tumbled from the truck, but Zearl beat us to the brow.

"Son! Son! Are ya down there?" His echo came back. He looked at me. His voice cracked. "Ya sure this is the right place?" When I nodded, he dropped to his knees and craned his head over the edge. "Son!"

"Pop!" Jake's voice rang.

"Sit tight. We'll pull you up," yelled Uncle Roy. Zearl, with head bowed, was too overcome to speak. Uncle Roy ran to the truck and got a long rope, and he and Ben quickly tied it making a bosun's chair. They pulled on it testing the knots before letting it over the cliff.

Roy, Ben, and Zearl all hung on while Jake climbed into the makeshift chair, and then they hoisted him up the cliff. I tried to help, but I was as weak as a baby.

Soon Jake was on solid ground and being helped out of the rope. Zearl, unashamed of his tears, pounded him on the back before gathering him into a bear hug.

For the first time Jake saw me. "Jackson!" Joy blazed in his eyes. "I just knew you was dead!"

"I just about was," I said with a grin. "I'm sure glad you made it. When we yelled and you didn't answer, I got to sweatin'."

"I must have drifted off—I reckon y'all woke me."

Jake took a step and crumpled with a groan, grabbing at the calves of his legs. "My muscles are knotting something fierce!"

Zearl stooped and began rubbing Jake's legs. "Ain't no wonder after hunkering on that ledge all night."

Uncle Roy coiled up the rope and returned to the truck taking out a rifle. He fired three shots into the sky. "Half the country is out looking for you two."

"Jackson, how'd you get out?" asked Jake still grimacing from pain.

I shrugged. "I don't remember. I just woke up on the bank, spewing like a whale."

"I almost started to jump in myself so I wouldn't have to face your mama." He grinned.

I don't recall the trip home, but later Uncle Roy said I snored all the way. Ben took Zearl and Jake home in his car.

Mama met us at the door. "Thank God!"

Roy held my arm. "Let's get him into dry clothes. He's half-drowned. Him and Jake are both lucky to be alive."

Mama stared. "You were with Jake?"

She frowned when I nodded, but she said no more and got my dry clothes. There were tears in her eyes while she poured hot soup down me and tucked me into bed. The last thing I saw before drifting off again was Sammy peering at me, his freckles standing out on a pale, worried face. Sammy was a good kid. I needed to take him frogging. No, maybe that wasn't such a good idea. I'd had enough frogging for a while.

I caught a whopper of a cold. My nose poured and my throat was too painful to swallow. Every time I coughed it was agony. I stayed in bed, miserable from head to toe. Now my toenail was making its absence known—it had been torn off when I stubbed it running from the flood. Mama forced cough syrup down me that was concocted from mullen and herbs brought by Miss Hilda. As a matter of fact, most of the neighbors dropped by. It was attention I would have enjoyed if I had felt better.

Much of the county had flooded, closing many of the businesses in town and flooding Rita May's boarding house. She came home to wait for the mess to get cleaned up and the cafe to reopen. She sat on the foot of my bed and read aloud from the Herald-Democrat, the weekly newspaper. The highway to Ft. Smith was closed and badly damaged. She turned the paper to show me a picture of Main Street. Cars parked across from the courthouse had water over their tires.

"You and Jake are lucky to be alive."

I nodded agreement.

"Want me to read some more, or are you sleepy?"

"Keep reading," I croaked.

She read the details of Prime Minister Churchill's visit to this country, the attack by United States troops on the Japanese-held island of Attu in the Aleutians, the wrecking by the British Royal Air Force of the Mohne and Eder dams, and the damage by flood to much of Germany's industrial territory. The waters flooded more than fifty towns and cities and left fifty thousand homeless in the Ruhr valley.

As Rita went on to read about the invasion jitters now affecting much of Europe, my mind stayed on the story about the bombed dams. I was thinking about all those folk in the path of the flood, and somehow I couldn't keep from feeling sorry for them. I guess my brush with death was just too recent. After all, just as Miss Hilda had pointed out, Doc was a German. All Germans weren't evil. Granted, they had an evil leader and they shouldn't be following him, but Miss Hilda said lots of the common people hated him, and they were fighting in the underground to stop him.

Ben poked his head into the room. "How's it going?"

"Fine," I croaked.

"You don't look so fine, red nose, watery eyes. I'd just about bet that you're feeling rotten."

I grinned.

Rita May stood. "I promised Timmy I'd take him outside to play." On the way out, she stopped in front of Ben and looked into his face. "Uncle Roy said you stayed out all night looking for Jackson, and you were the one that found him. Thanks."

Ben's eyes followed her.

He borrowed a chair from the kitchen and sat down. "Guess you'll never forget this frog hunt."

"I reckon not! I thought sure we were goners when that water got to lappin' at our feet." I plucked at the covers on my bed for a minute before going on. "Remember what you told me about no atheist in fox holes?"

Ben nodded.

"There's none on flooded bluffs either," I said with a little grin. "I was praying hard—the best I knew how."

Ben laughed. "Being scared will start a fellow praying as quick as anything I know." Then he grew serious. "I'm glad you're alive—but a fellow never knows when his number's up. Like that chaplain said, you need to get ready."

Such talk made me nervous. Besides, now that I was safe and snug in my bed, I didn't want to think about the promises I had made to God on the ledge that night—how I would quit moonshining, quit going to the roadhouse, quit doing anything wrong ever again—so I changed the subject.

Ben hung around all afternoon, giving Mama a hand with my chores. Rita May avoided him as if he had lice, and although Mama asked him to stay, he left just before supper.

That night as we listened to the radio, I leaned forward, tensed and straining. The sound was not good and the static made my nerves raw. It was news about the big victory in Africa. The German command had surrendered its force of 40,000 on May 9th. That had been days ago, and it might be weeks before we knew if Daddy had come through the fighting unharmed.

"Reckon where they'll send Daddy next?" asked Sammy as he rolled over off his stomach and sat up. He brightened. "Maybe he'll get to come home now."

"I hope not," said Mama. She threaded a needle in the dim lamplight and rubbed her eyes before noticing my look of horror. "Silly goose," she added, "That would mean he'd been wounded. I want him home all in one piece."

Maybe the war would end and Daddy could come home soon. I wondered if he would bawl Mama out for making us do without. Then again, I hoped when he got home, they wouldn't argue all the time. I wanted us to be a happy family like we used to be. I slipped outside onto the porch and began playing my old guitar, slow and gentle. I was thinking about how God had let me live. Although I wasn't sure if the Bible said anything particular against making shine, I figured it would be best to quit. After a bit I noticed Mama in the doorway and figured she was about to send me to bed. I started to stand.

"No, keep playing. It's pretty." She came out and sat on the steps beside me and gathered her knees into her arms, resting her forehead on them.

The soft night breeze carried the tangy scent of cinnamon vine that climbed the porch post, and it teased Mama's hair where it had straggled loose from the pens. In the distance, a mourning dove cooed, the sad notes lingering in the dark. I found the same key and softly strummed a tune called "Red Wing." The mournful song about dying lovers seemed to fit the night. When the song ended

Mama turned her eyes to the stars. "I wonder what your daddy is doing right this minute."

Chapter 13

A few days later, one bright June morning, Sammy rolled me out of bed at the crack of dawn.

"Get up, Jackson!" He shook my shoulder. "There's worms on the catalpa tree!"

Without rising I grunted and rolled over. He grabbed my shoulder and shook harder. "Come on, let's go fishing. You know how fish love catalpa worms. Looky here, I already got a whole can full."

My eyes opened. I was nose to nose with a short, fat, pinstriped, green worm crawling from inside a tin can full of half-eaten leaves.

"Get that out of my face," I growled. "Mama said I could sleep in because I didn't feel good last night. And you just had to go and wake me up!" I trounced him on the side of the head with my pillow. It was a bad move. The can and the worms went flying all across the bed.

By the time they were rounded up and herded back into the can I was wide-awake, and fishing sounded better than sleeping. I followed Sammy out to study the yearly happening that took place on our tall catalpa tree. Overnight an army of hungry worms had appeared. Soon there would be no leaf left. The tree would be stripped bare and the worms gone as quickly as they had come. Daddy claimed they hatched from some kind of larva, but we had never seen the bug. The worms never appeared on any other sort of tree, and stranger still, never on the other catalpa that grew just beyond the garden.

Daddy loved to fish, and the appearance of the first catalpa worms had always been cause for a fishing holiday. Thinking about it, I ached for Daddy. Maybe next year he would be here to go with us.

Fish favored catalpa worms over just about any other bait. We caught a mess and feasted on golden fried bream for breakfast. Along with them, Mama made cornmeal gravy and hot biscuits.

On my way to the mill, I took Grandpa some fish for breakfast. I intended telling him I was through moonshining, but he was hung over and still asleep. Leaving the fish on the table, I headed on to work relieved, for I dreaded the telling.

Things were not as cheerful now at the mill. Mama still gave Jake a cold shoulder, and he was nervous when she was around.

Uncle Roy was tinkering with the engine. It was purring like a kitten. I hung at his elbow and watched.

He talked loud over the racket. "I bet your daddy will be marchin' across Europe pretty soon. News is full of talk about an invasion."

"If there is an invasion, will the war end quick?" I asked.

"No way to tell for certain. An invasion may still be a long ways off, but if the reports I'm hearing are true, when it does happen, it'll be the end of that German bunch and their Axis."

Just then Jake came up and handed him a piece of paper. His face grew black as a thundercloud.

"What's the matter, Roy?" Mama called.

"Dang it!" He jerked off his cap and mopped his forehead with a red bandana dragged from his back pocket. "The War Production Board is yellin' for production, jabbing us with less and less contract time. And now the *Office of Defense Transportation*," he snarled the name, "is hell-bent to penalize us for overloaded trucks!" He threw his cap onto the dirt. "I'm breaking my fool neck to do two jobs, saw out lumber and cut pulpwood too. Then Jake gets a ticket yesterday afternoon and another one this morning! They claim both of those loads of pulpwood he was delivering to the train were overloaded! Now I got two blasted fines to pay!"

"Like Pappy Tyler says," mused Mama, "there's plenty of carpetbaggers and scalawags still around."

Just that morning I had seen a picture in the newspaper of soldiers unloading food shipped in big wooden crates, and I had wondered if the boards might have been sawed right here at Uncle Roy's mill. The paper said Uncle Sam wanted more trees cut. Wood was desperately needed for lots of things including containers for ammunition, rations, and blood plasma. Plywood was even used to make the big cargo gliders that carried war supplies to the front.

I put in, "The government swears it needs this wood mighty bad."

Uncle Roy scowled at me. "Then why don't they let me get the job done!" He spit out a twig, muttered something under his breath, and grabbed the lever. Jake grinned at me and then rolled a log onto the carriage. After that the whine of the saw drowned everything.

During the noon break, while Mama and Roy talked, Jake managed a few private words with me. "You aught to come over on Friday nights. I got a card game going in the barn with some fellows I been playing pool with."

Just then Mama cut her eyes at me and frowned. "I'll see," I mumbled as I walked away. I wished Mama didn't have it in for Jake. He was a great guy.

There was not much time for fishing when the garden began to bear. Mama and I came home exhausted from the mill each day to face all the chores plus a big garden that needed tending. Although I was dog-tired most nights after supper, I still managed to slip away for a few minutes to my spot high on the bluff to play my guitar.

That evening when I returned in the late dusk, the swinging beat of a big band drifted through the open window. Mama usually tuned into Chicago. I preferred WSM Nashville and its country music on the Opry.

She turned off the radio.

"Please, Mama. Just a few more minutes." Sammy and I both begged. We couldn't wait to hear *The Lone Ranger*. The last episode was to be continued, and I was in a swivet to know what happened next.

"Well, turn it off just as soon as it's over," she relented. "Tomorrow is a long day. Kraut making."

I groaned. Kraut making was not my favorite chore.

When the Lone Ranger rode off with a thrilling, "High-ho Silver, away," I reckon my eyes were big, for Mama looked up from her mending and smiled.

"Glad to see you're still my little boy."

"I'm no little boy, Mama. I'm almost sixteen. Pappy Tyler was fighting Yankees when he was my age."

Smarting over her remark, I went to bed. I had no cause to be mad at Mama. Mostly I was mad at myself. That morning I had found the beginnings of a beard on my chin and had felt all grown-up and manly. But now, for gosh sakes, I had been pretending to be The Lone Ranger! Embarrassed, I sat on the bed, dropped my head into my hands, and groaned. All the foolish stuff I had said and done lately rose to haunt me. Worst of all was my capture of that dangerous spy, Miss Hilda, and her deadly clothesline. No wonder Mama didn't trust me with the shotgun!

I crawled into bed, but I couldn't relax in the stuffy room. After tossing and turning, I finally got up and slipped outside, carrying my overalls with me. It sounded as if every bug on earth was hollering. The moon looked as if someone had sliced it squarely in two and stood it on end. In its faint light, the house was small and dark. My manhood was smarting. Card playing and hanging out with Jake seemed like a good idea tonight...then I felt a prick of conscience. But I didn't recall the Bible saying anything against card playing. At least Mr. Caruthers had never mentioned it, I convinced myself. With a quick look back at Mama's window, I headed for Jake's and the card game he said would be taking place in his barn.

Most of the fellows were strangers from the Navy training program in town. But there were two guys I did know. They had gone to school with Rita May. I hung around watching them win and lose until long after midnight. Although I never thought I would, I followed Jake's lead and had a big slug of moonshine. Hot fire and a nasty taste burned my throat and settled smoldering in my belly. I shook my head. Why did Grandpa like the stuff? And why would people pay good money for it! When the jug made the rounds again, I took another slug. I didn't want to shame Jake in front of all the fellows.

I headed home, already dreading hearing Enoch crow.

The next morning, bright clear day streamed in my window. My head pounded.

I shielded my eyes and groaned when Mama called. As I tried sitting up, the greasy smell of frying bacon brought on a retch. I'd have to take care or Mama would dose me with castor oil, and there was only so much a body could endure. A moonshine hangover was worse than a tobacco misery. I knew now why Daddy left them both alone.

I got a little scared realizing the deal was off that I had made with God. I knew there were words in the Good Book against getting drunk. Mr. Caruthers had read them.

When I returned from milking, Miss Hilda showed up carrying a dishpan and a butcher knife. She was thinner and had aged considerably since the last time I had seen her.

"You came!" Mama beamed from the doorway. "Good. Come in. Have some oatmeal."

"No, thank you. I just don't have an appetite these days."

"Well, a glass of milk then? Bossy is giving so much now." Mama filled a snuff glass brim full and set it on the table. "I do appreciate you coming to help."

I stopped pushing oatmeal around in my bowl and looked up surprised. Mama never asked the neighbors for help.

Miss Hilda dropped into the chair and shook her finger at Mama. "Don't think you can fool an old woman. You don't need help. You're just trying to get me out of the house."

"Maybe so," said Mama, "but I can use the help. Kraut making is a big job."

That was a fact. I was glad Miss Hilda was going to help chop cabbage. Mama always made lots of kraut, and it was hard work.

"Why, Janie, it won't be fit to eat!" exclaimed Miss Hilda when we went outside and Mama explained her method for making it right in the jar.

"Wait until you try it," said Mama. "It's good—not as sour as the crock-made kind, but it's crisp and tangy."

"It is good, ma'am," I agreed as I came from the garden with two big heads of cabbage and dropped them onto the plank table that was set up under the catalpa tree. The pointed heads cradled in large dark leaves were beginning to split open.

Miss Hilda, looking doubtful, began trimming the outer leaves with her knife.

"I'll go inside and sterilize jars while you two chop," said Mama.

I had made my own chopping tool by cutting the rim from a tin can, sharpening the edge, and poking a few holes in the remaining end to prevent suction. Now, trying to ignore my busting head, I made one for Miss Hilda.

"What a novel tool," she said, examining her can. Then she noticed my face. "You don't look so good." She reached to feel my forehead, but I shied away.

"No, I feel great," I hurried to say. Not wanting any more of her nasty herbal concoctions, I rushed off to gather more cabbage.

I stood in the shade and removed the bug-riddled outer leaves and threw them to the chickens. Enoch grabbed one and, holding it in his beak like pirated gold, fled around the house. After cutting chunks from the heads, I put them into a metal dishpan. I loved to eat the crisp core, so I trimmed one, but realized I didn't want anything in my stomach just yet, so I gave it to Sammy.

"The can works very well," said Miss Hilda after several chops.

It did work great, but each chop jarred my head almost beyond enduring. To make matters worse, gnats had found me and started buzzing around my ears. I brushed them away from my sweaty face.

"Hey, Sammy," I called. "Bring me that turkey feather and something to tie it around my head."

He left off playing marbles on the other side of the catalpa tree and went running. Soon he returned with the feather and a ball of string. I wrapped the string around my forehead and tied the long bronze feather to the back of my head. In no time the gnats had left my face and were hovering at the top of the tall feather. I had learned that trick from Daddy.

"Upon my word. It works like a charm!" declared Miss Hilda.

"Would you like—?" Before I had finished offering to make a headdress for Miss Hilda, Sammy hollered.

"Copperhead!" he yelled.

Still clutching the chopping can, I bolted around the tree to see Sammy dragging Timmy back from a snake, bronze-patterned and blunt-nosed. It inched across the bare ground where the boys had sat playing only moments before. It was big around for a copperhead and about a foot long. Miss Hilda scooped up Timmy.

I had bolted for the house and grabbed the shotgun. "Copperhead!" I called to Mama.

"Leave that gun be!" she ordered. "A hoe will do just as well."

My lip poked out as I put the gun back on the hooks.

"Look careful now, they almost always travel in pairs," she cautioned, following me outside.

The snake coiled and began flicking its tongue as its beady copper eyes followed us. Laddie ran up barking ferociously. I raised the hoe.

"No, Jackson, let Laddie. I want him to know we count on him tending to snakes," said Mama.

In a flash, Laddie darted. He jumped away as the snake struck. Three more times Laddie lunged. But the fourth time, he grabbed the snake right behind the head and threw it high into the air. As the copperhead fell, the dog leaped up and caught it. He popped the snake as a man would pop a whip. The snake landed dead at my feet. Laddie was just a cur, but he was the best snake-killer around.

"Good dog! Good dog!" bragged Mama while I ruffled his fur and patted his head. After the snake was dead, Laddie kept snapping at it and worrying it around on the ground.

"I hate snakes." Miss Hilda shuddered. "Any kind. That's one reason I keep Fritz. He won't tolerate a snake."

"In this snaky country, a body needs a good snake dog," said Mama. "We've had dozens of close calls with copperheads and rattlers. And with us living this close to the creek, even moccasins are a problem."

We searched all around but found no mate to the snake. I rigged Miss Hilda a feather, and we returned to work. I began chopping cabbage into pea-sized pieces with my sharpened can. Each chop jarred my aching head. I looked at the sun, wishing it were farther up the sky. Tonight I would gladly go to bed early—and I wouldn't be sneaking out anywhere.

I didn't feel like talking. And I was trying hard not to bring up Miss Hilda's family. But she wanted to talk.

"All those people, Jackson, it's hard for me to believe they're dead. I grew up in the village where Esther lived. I knew them all."

I swallowed, trying to imagine everyone in Hagarville murdered by Nazis.

Miss Hilda was a good storyteller. As she talked, Esther's children—John, Mica, Amos, and Marta—came alive for me.

"John loved sports. He could outrun anyone at his school. He always won the medal in competitions. And he was a musician like you."

She noticed my wide eyes. "Yes, I've heard you play at the store. But John played the violin. His Uncle Zosel, my nephew, is a concert violinist. He started teaching John when John could barely hold the bow. He said John would take his place in the orchestra someday." Miss Hilda paused. "I guess Zosel is dead too. He married a German girl. They moved to Berlin before the war to work in her father's factory." She stopped to swallow tears. "A family is a wonderful thing, Jackson. Never take it for granted."

As she talked, our pans had grown full. Soon Mama brought steaming jars and packed them full of the chopped cabbage. After adding a teaspoon of salt and a pinch of sugar to each one, she filled it with boiling water. I capped each jar with a new lid, screwed it loosely, and then set it on the ground against the tree to ferment for a couple of weeks before it would be ready to seal tight and put into the cellar.

Enoch went flapping past, soon with Sammy in hot pursuit.

"Ouch! You ding-blasted piece of—"

"Sammy, watch your mouth," ordered Mama, "or you'll be tasting some lye soap."

"I'm gonna kill 'im!" Sammy returned with angry tears in his eyes, rubbing his bare back. He wore only overalls, their frayed bottoms dragging in the dirt.

Mama sighed. "I've always been partial to Enoch. He's so spunky. But the way he torments Sammy, I guess we ought to wring his neck."

"Reckon why he only picks on Sammy?" I asked.

"I have no idea..." Mama's eyes squinted. "Come to think of it, when Enoch was just a chick, Sammy dunked him down in the water pan trying to make him drink. He dunked him so many times that Enoch almost drowned."

Miss Hilda laughed. "The bird is still getting even," she said. "Aw, Janie. It's good to laugh. Thank you for inviting me." Then Miss Hilda wiped sudden tears onto her apron, and I looked away, feeling a lump in my own throat.

Soon the garden was bursting with vines loaded with fat pods of limas, long green fingers of string beans, and tomato plants bowed over—in spite of being tied up to stakes—from the weight of ripe fruit, red and juicy.

There were already dozens of jars filled with jellies and jams, strawberry, blackberry, wild cherry; cucumber pickles, sweet and dill, and bread and butter. And there were beets yet to pickle, corn to can, and relish to make.

This year the corn had outdone itself, standing taller than my head with at least three full ears to every stalk. It was almost as if nature were apologizing for last year's drought. I explained to Grandpa that I couldn't be spared just now. I dreaded having to tell him I was quitting, so I put it off with the excuse that Mama needed me. We worked from morning till night, picking, stringing, snapping, peeling, and shucking.

I especially hated picking up potatoes. I didn't mind hitching the middle buster to Old Dan and turning out the potatoes—I liked the good, musty smell of fresh-plowed dirt—but I hated crawling down the rows and gathering them. Most of all I dreaded digging down the sides, getting grit under my fingernails while rolling out the hidden potatoes. I tried pawning that job off on Sammy, but Mama said he left too many hidden in the banks of dirt.

"Mama, ain't we ever going to take a break from this blasted garden? I'm sick to death of it."

"The ant works now and eats later," she said.

"We've got enough put up now to last two years," I complained.

She turned cold eyes on me. "I guess you've forgotten the drought and not having enough to eat. Well, I haven't."

"We would have had plenty to eat if you had cashed some checks," I muttered. Another check had just arrived that day, and it galled me to see it sticking from her apron pocket.

She whirled on me, lips narrowed and eyes shooting sparks. "I'm sick and tired of your attitude. Do you think I enjoy working like a dog and doing without? Well, I don't!" she snapped as I backed up a step. "It's got so I hate waking up every morning, knowing there's nothing ahead but work! But when your daddy comes home, I intend to have something to show for it—not just the good times we had with his money!"

I bent back down, grabbed another potato, and tossed it into the basket. Maybe she did hate all the extra work and the doing without. I thought about that a bit. But I still figured we could spend some of those checks without hurting anything.

While I crawled down the long, dusty rows, I dreamed about when I could buy the guitar. Any way I figured it, the money I had earned from Grandpa was still a long way from thirty dollars, and if I quit there was no telling when I would ever have enough. That evening I decided to count again, hoping I had miscounted and hoping there was more than twelve dollars. There wasn't. Actually there was a little less than twelve dollars.

At first Grandpa had paid me good. Lately it had been change instead of bills and less each time. He said his profits were down because one of his local contacts had quit buying. I had been stashing my Prince Albert can of money between some planks of the bunk in the cellar.

I sighed and wondered if moonshining was really bad. And maybe it wasn't really all that dangerous. Grandpa had been doing it for years without any bad luck.

I knelt beside the bunk to put back the money when Mama, her arms full of canned goods, came through the door and bumped into me. The can flew out of my hand and landed on the cellar floor. Dollars and a pile of silver spilled out.

"Jackson, where did you get all this money?" Mama's nails dug into my flesh where she gripped my shoulder. She shook me hard. Her voice was brittle. "Where'd you get it?"

I shook off the hand and my eyes blazed. "It's mine, and you've got no call to go snooping in my business."

"I've got no call! I've got every right in the world! If your daddy was here—"

"But he ain't!" I spit out.

"No, but your Uncle Roy is, and he can tan your hide just as good." Mama's eyes were fear-filled. "Now answer my question."

"I worked for it."

"Doing what?"

I fidgeted. I supposed Uncle Roy might whip me, but that would be nothing compared to facing Grandpa if I told! My lips grew tighter.

Sammy stood behind her, his arm full of jars too. Mama whirled. "Do you know anything about this?"

Big-eyed, he shook his head.

"Sammy, tell me the truth."

Tears filled his eyes. He wilted under her piercing look and stared at the floor.

"You know something. Now out with it."

"I just know sometimes he sneaks out at night after you go to sleep." He avoided looking at me. "And once, a while back, Rita May slipped home in the dark and got him. They were gone most all night long."

I glared at Sammy while Mama set down the jars. She knelt and picked up some of the bills and coins. Slowly she let them fall back onto the floor and then she looked at me. There was pain in her eyes.

"You've been helpin' Pa, haven't you? You and Rita May both."
Despair filled her voice.

I kept my lips shut. It did not seem fair. Why did Mama have to
find out now, after I had made up my mind to quit? God must be
punishing me for getting drunk. I lowered my eyes in misery.

I passed an almost sleepless night, tossing and turning on one
of the bunks in the cellar. The next morning, heavy-eyed, I trudged
back to the house. Without speaking to anyone I grabbed the milk
bucket and headed for the back door. Uncle Roy stuck his head in
the front door.

"Can you two work today? I've got a big order—" He spied
Mama's blotched face. "Janie! Is Keith—?"

"No." Mama motioned him inside. "Come in, Roy."

I barely nodded. Uncle Roy was the last person on earth I
wanted to see just now—except maybe Daddy.

Uncle Roy took the coffee she offered and held the cup until
she also took a seat. He sipped the coffee and waited.

With a pained look, Mama broke the silence.

"It's the kids, Roy—Rita May and Jackson." She chewed her lip
and looked into her cup before setting it back down again. "They've
been moonshining with Pa."

Roy swore under his breath.

Mama looked hopeless. "What if the law gets involved, Roy?
Rita is no child—she'll go to jail." She quickly searched his face.
"Maybe she'd listen to you. Maybe Jackson would too."

My face grew hot. I took the milk bucket and stomped outside
to do the chores. I hoped he would leave, but when I returned from
the barn, he was waiting in the yard.

"You're worrying your mama to death."

My jaw jutted. "Don't see as that's any of your business."

His green eyes cut right through me. "Your mama has asked me to talk to you. Your daddy would expect it."

I shrugged and looked away.

Uncle Roy had plucked a twig of forsythia growing nearby and stuck it into his mouth. Now he took it out and pointed it at me. "You got no idea what a peck of trouble you're buying. Do you think we don't know what we're doing, steering clear of Pa's shady business?"

I spat out, "I think you're all dirt poor, that's what I think. Grandpa ain't. He's got plenty."

"You've got a lot to learn, boy," he said as he bowed his head and shook it. "Pa is poor, poor as they come, in what really counts. Moonshine is nothing but trouble for those that drink it and those that sell it."

"Didn't know you'd took up preaching," I smarted off.

I wanted away from here, away from Mama's bossiness and Uncle Roy's meddling. I slammed the screen door and left him standing in the yard.

———————

The house was as quiet as a funeral. Mama had forbid me leaving the yard. I sat on the porch steps playing a tune from the radio. When the song ended, I plucked a few more notes and listened to the benefits of Tanglefoot flypaper. *"Babies sick? Feel low? Maybe flies brought disease! Use Tanglefoot!"*

Mama was frying ham. The hickory smell lingered at the open window. The way the flies were gathering, I thought we could use some Tanglefoot. The curtains billowed out and then suddenly sucked back inside. I glanced at the sky. It was gray and threatening rain. In the early dusk the chickens had roosted. I decided to get them fastened in the coop before Mama called me to supper. As I stepped inside to put up the guitar, I heard squawking outside. I looked out Mama's bedroom window at a red fox bolting from the chicken coop with Enoch barely one jump ahead.

I grabbed the shotgun where it hung on pegs above the bedroom door, thankful that it was always loaded. In a flash I was back at the window. For a split second I had the bounding fox square in the sights. Before I could shoot, he lunged at Enoch's colorful tail and came away with a mouth full of black and purple feathers. In terror the rooster flapped wildly. Neck stuck out, Enoch dashed first one way, then the other.

Taking another bead, I squeezed the trigger. The house shook with the blast. Elated, I saw the fox drop in its tracks, Enoch's feathers still stuck to its mouth.

"Jackson!" Mama burst into the room, her face drained of color. Knees gone weak, she suddenly sat on the bed and put her head down into her hands. "I thought you were outside...I was afraid Sammy was playing with the gun and had shot himself!" Then she looked up, her eyes angry.

"What do you think you're doing, shooting that gun without permission?"

"It was a fox, Mama." I pointed out the window. "He was after Enoch and almost got him."

"I told you to never touch that gun!"

"Good gosh, Mama, Charlie is a halfwit and he goes hunting all the time with a shotgun."

"You leave that gun alone."

"If Daddy was here he'd let—"

"Well he's not! And I don't want to hear any more about it."

"But the fox—"

Mama's lips were thin. "Jackson, I knew a girl who was killed when her daddy shot at dogs chasing his cows." She pointed to

Sammy, big eyed, standing in the doorway. "Did you know where your brother was? Did you check to see?"

I looked at the floor. "No." Then my bottom lip poked out. "But I knew where that fox was—after our chickens! And he won't be any more. I'm glad I killed it, whether you like it or not."

Mama's mouth dropped open. "You know I won't tolerate that kind of disrespect. You need a switching and a taste of lye soap!"

"I ain't taking a licking. And you ain't washing my mouth out with soap," I vowed, gritting my teeth.

"What's gotten into you?" she asked. "I hardly know you any more."

I didn't tell her that I was hurt. Hurt because I had done a noble thing, and all the thanks I got was the sharp side of her tongue. I was almost sixteen and taller than she was, but she insisted on treating me like a baby. Well, I would prove I was no baby. From now on I would do as I pleased! I spun on my heels and stalked outside.

I waited until Mama was asleep before slipping back inside and then leaving with a bundle under my arm and my guitar slung over my back. It bounced against my back as I hurried across the dark pasture. Since God was through with me, I figured I might as well join up with Grandpa. Besides, Mama and Uncle Roy seemed determined to think the worst of me. I decided to let them! I headed for Grandpa's. I wondered if he would be glad to have me.

Chapter 14

I stood in the dark swatting at bloodthirsty mosquitoes. Grandpa, holding a smoking lamp, finally answered my knock. He gave me a sour look and scratched at his side through a faded red union suit. "Don't know why ya couldn't wait till morning to run off. Feller my age has a hard enough time sleeping as it is." He stepped back and jerked a thumb at the far back bedroom, before he stumbled back to bed. "You can bunk in there. Used to be your mama's room. Mose has taken to sleepin' in there—you'll have to fight him for the bed."

I took the lamp and, stepping across piles of clutter, examined a room about the size of a postage stamp. There was barely room to squeeze between the beat-up bureau and the rusted iron bedstead. Sure enough, Grandpa's redbone coonhound was sprawled out on the striped mattress ticking. There were no blankets or sheets, but Mose didn't seem to mind. I did. Wrinkling my nose against the strong dog odor, I looked around for something to cover the mattress and spied an old quilt wadded up in one corner. When I pushed the dog off the bed, he gave over without a fuss. He slinked into the front room and flopped down in front of the fireplace alongside Old Tiger.

I held the lamp close to the mattress. Even though there was no sign of vermin, I could already imagine stuff crawling on me. I liked things clean. Living at Grandpa's was going to be a sore trial.

Using my jacket for a pillow, I rolled up in the quilt and tried to sleep, but I kept rehashing the scene with Mama. All she cared about was working her fingers to the bone for a better life someday. The more I thought about it, the more foolish that seemed. There was money to be had now, practically for the taking. Grandpa made more in a week than Uncle Roy made in a month. Of course he had to be careful—but heck, he'd been making shine for years and never gotten caught. And the more I thought about it, the more I figured the revenuers had never heard of Clarksville, let alone Little Piney Creek.

About daylight I drifted off, trying to decide if I would even go back to school. As far as I could tell, making good moonshine didn't require an education.

That afternoon I tried to straighten things up, and did a good bit, until Grandpa yelled at me for interfering with his things.

"Bring that back here!" he cried as I started out the back door, my arms loaded with junk.

"Grandpa, I can't even sweep the floor with all this stuff piled around."

His voice was raspy. Blue veins stood out on his red nose and forehead. "If I wanted my life and house tore apart, I'd a married me a widder woman," he growled. "Leave things be! Put it all back where you got it—that's where I want it!"

There was so much junk piled around, even he had no idea where anything was. Having me around was making him nervous. That was the real reason he was yelling. I dumped the stuff. A black book slid out of the pile and landed on Grandpa's foot.

He drew back and kicked it across the floor. It crumpled into a heap against the far wall.

"That's one thing you can burn," he snarled before stomping outside.

I picked up the book. It was a Bible. The flyleaf said Jemimah Matthers, 1902. There was something scribbled beside the name. I held the page toward the light of the grimy window.

I softly read Deuteronomy 12:28 aloud, "Observe and hear all these words which I command thee, that it may go well with thee, and with thy children after thee for ever."

I looked up half expecting to see God frowning down on me. I wasn't about to burn a Bible, so I quickly stuffed it back into the pile of junk, grabbed my guitar, and headed for the creek.

It was a mild evening. The days were long, and the hollow was alive with frogs and peepers. My special rock was warm from June sun. I dropped down on it and stared off the bluff at the creek, swelled by recent rains, rushing past below. Idly I dropped a twig into the white foam. It bobbed and spun and rode the water to disappear around the bend, going someplace far away. I wished I could follow. It was hard to admit, but I had jumped out of the frying pan into the fire. I hated living with Grandpa. At times Mama had been gripey, but Grandpa was downright surly. And he was lazy. Today I brought in the wood, hauled out the ashes, milked, fed the chickens, washed the dishes, and cooked the meals. I didn't like my own cooking, and I was already sick of his pigsty—and to be honest, I was getting homesick.

I tossed another stick into the rolling creek. A silver flash and a splash down below made me wish I had brought a fishing pole instead of the guitar. I sighed and strummed a few chords.

"Howdy, stranger." Ben was carrying a rod and reel and a bag of tackle hung from his shoulder.

"Howdy, Ben."

He leaned the rod against a tree and then squatted near the edge of the bluff and looked down at the swift water. "Piney's rolling today."

"Yeah. All that rain we've been havin'."

"I've tramped up and down the creek all afternoon. Too muddy to catch fish, but I've got cabin fever and wanted to be outside." He pushed back his cap. "Heard you playing. Hope you don't mind me joining you."

"Course not," I assured him.

"Any word from your daddy?" He asked.

"Yeah. Last letter, reading between the lines, we could tell he's seeing lots of action. All that fighting—guess he's lucky to still be alive." I kicked at a clump of dead grass where shoots were greening beneath.

"That's a fact," agreed Ben as he settled on a rock nearby, "but your daddy is a smart and careful man. He won't be foolishly risking his neck."

We fell silent, both lost in thought.

"Seen your sister lately?" he finally asked while I was looking across the creek at a redbird perched in a sweetgum tree. It was whistling a cheery call.

I shook my head. "Nope."

Ben turned to me. "Why not?"

"I reckon she's just busy." I shrugged. "How's your guitar picking coming?"

He came over, took my beat-up guitar, and turned it to fret with his right hand. Of course it sounded awful with the strings being upside down. In spite of it, he made a lively run.

I laughed. "You play better than I do—even upside down." But it hurt me to see the warped left hand.

"I've been working at it." He handed it back with a grin. "Of course I won't have much time for that anymore. Had you heard that I'm going to work for your Uncle Roy?"

"Really?" I was surprised and a little hurt that Ben was so quickly taking my place.

"Since Jake signed up, Roy's short-handed with that government contract." He eyed his maimed hand. "I can still roll logs. Sitting around the house is making me crazy, and I'm driving Grandpa crazy too."

"Jake signed up?" I was disappointed.

Ben nodded. "Marines." Then he shook his head. "I sort of hated to hear it...nine times out of ten, the leathernecks get the worst of it."

"He leavin' right away?" I wanted to tell him goodbye.

"Next week. I think his folks are planning another big send off on Saturday night—a double shindig. Charlotte and Frank Cummins are getting married. Frank joined up the same time as Jake, and they're leaving on the same train."

Charlotte was Jake's older sister. She and Rita May were friends.

"You goin' to the party?"

Ben's face clouded. "I sort of doubt it."

Recalling the last party at the Johnson's, I was not surprised. Rita May would likely come with Wade again. I said no more about the party.

"I'm glad you'll be working for Uncle Roy."

I wished I was still working for Uncle Roy. That thought made me even more miserable. I began strumming an old Irish ballad, "The Parting Glass." It was a mournful tune Grandpa was fond of singing—or bellowing—if he was drunk.

"A fellow's mood shows in his music. I'd say you're sort of blue," said Ben.

"Could be."

"Want to talk about it?" he asked.

"Naw, I reckon not."

Ben's eyebrows drew together, and then he nodded slowly. "Ok. Well, I'm a good listener if you change your mind."

After a bit, he tried again. "I ran into Sammy at the store this morning. He said you were staying with Cole."

Before I knew it, just like the old days, I was blurting out my troubles to Ben. Oh, I didn't tell him about the bootlegging, although I figured he had guessed that already. But I did tell him about my trouble with Mama and about her hoarding the checks against Daddy's wishes.

He propped the fishing pole against the big oak at his back and then leaned against the tree himself. "Instant gratification versus long-term security."

"Huh?" I wrinkled my brow.

"Instant gratification versus long-term security." Ben smiled. "Had a buddy in the Navy, Robbie Styles. He used to say that when I wanted to jump ship for a wild night on the town."

"What does it mean?" I asked.

"Usually, that I didn't listen and had a wild time on Saturday night and woke up in the brig on Sunday morning in big trouble."

My brow furrowed deeper, wondering what that had to do with my troubles. Ben reached up into the oak tree and plucked a small green acorn. He held it up. "One of two things is apt to happen to this nut—a squirrel will eat it, or it'll grow into a tree and make lots more acorns."

"I don't see what that has to do—"

"Your mama wants to grow an oak instead of eating the acorn. And truth be told, I'll bet your daddy would agree with her."

"He wouldn't agree with her treating me like a shirttail kid who needs his nose wiped—"

I stopped short, facing the real reason I had run off. It wasn't about moonshine or money or allotment checks. It was because no matter what I did, how hard I tried, Mama intended to keep me a child. I had run off to show her.

I stood, backing off while I spoke. "I better get on back to Grandpa's. He'll be wanting supper."

"Jackson, we're friends, right?" he asked.

I nodded, growing suspicious. Usually a body was getting ready to lecture when they said that.

"I'm going to tell you straight out—you've got no business being at Cole's. He'll bring you nothing but trouble." When my chin came up, he hurried on. "You are growing up, Jackson, getting old enough to know your own mind. But you don't have a lot of experience yet."

He went on. "You're lucky enough to have a good home and a good mama and daddy. You ought to respect them—listen to them. It would save you a heap of trouble."

I hurried off, leaving him sitting there frowning. Things seemed to be getting more and more messed up. Of course since I had gone back on my deal with God, I didn't reckon things would ever be good again.

"Supper." I sat the pan of soggy fried potatoes in the middle of the table and hacked off two pieces of cold cornbread. I put one on each of the blue willow plates sitting on the table.

Grandpa reached for a glass and filled it to the brim with shine and plopped a jug down beside his plate. Frowning, he eyed the table. "Why you usin' your grannie's good dishes?" he asked sourly.

"Everything else is dirty." I pointed to the mountain of dishes piled beside the sink. A big green fly buzzed around the pump handle and then lit on an unwashed plate.

"How come you ain't washed 'em?" He had already been drinking and his tongue was thick.

"I been a little busy lately, in case you hadn't noticed."

He took a bite of potatoes and made a face. "It's fer certain you ain't been busy learning to cook. This ain't fit fer hogs!"

I had a comeback on the tip of my tongue, but I held it in check. When Grandpa drank, he was mean. I forked food into my mouth and began to chew. He was right. It didn't taste like Mama's. I looked around the dim, dirty room and wondered what they were doing at home. Probably listening to the radio and sitting down to supper. I missed the radio. I could have taken it. It was mine. But somehow I could not take it away from Sammy and Mama. Each evening Mama would listen for news of the First Division. Although troop movement was guarded, sometimes she could find out where Daddy had been.

Daddy had sent two v-mails lately—soldier's letters that were microfilmed in Europe to save hauling bulky mail sacks on the transports. When they arrived in the U.S., they were printed on small cards. There was not much room for news on them, but at least we knew he was alive and well and somewhere in Italy.

When the dishes were finished, I could not endure another minute in the house. I left and headed for home, circling around behind the shed to make sure I was not seen. Laddie met me and barked, jumping on me and wagging his tail. I hushed him by patting his head and then slipped over to an open window and sat on the ground. There was a clatter overhead of Mama washing dishes, and there was music from the radio. Timmy and Sammy were playing inside. Mama shushed them when the news came on.

I wiped a tear that slid down my face. Hiding like this was more lonesome than staying at Grandpa's.

Sun was full on my face from the east window the next morning when I woke to the sound of arguing. Mama! I heard her angry voice and sat up.

"You just couldn't wait to get him in on your dirty business, could you, Pa! You don't even need the help—ya just did it to spite me and Keith."

I slipped to the door and peeked out. Mama held a basket of folded laundry on her hip, and Grandpa sat on a chair pulled away from the table tugging on his boots. He was ignoring her and the pile of money she had just slapped onto the table.

"Here's your money back—Jackson ain't working for you anymore. And he's coming home with me."

She slammed down the basket. Her voice shook. "I ain't doin' another lick of work for you—I figure I already done enough to pay for the loan of the mule."

He shot her a mean look, and with hard eyes still on her, reached for the jug on the table and took a long pull. He wiped his mouth.

"He's old enough to decide fer hisself whither he goes or stays."

"No he ain't; he's still just a baby!"

My ears burned.

He looked toward my door. "Boy! Come out here."

I stepped out.

"Yer mama wants you to come back home. You goin' or stayin'?"

I had been dying to go, but now my temper flared. I was no baby! Defiant, I looked Mama right in the eye. "Stayin'."

"No you're not. I figured to give you a day or two to come to your senses, but it appears you got none. You're coming with me." She grabbed my arm.

Grandpa stood. "Boy can make up his own mind, Janie." His steely voice sent shivers over me. Mama jerked me toward the door. Grandpa took a step forward, and she gripped my arm tighter.

"It's all right, Grandpa. I changed my mind," I said quickly. "I reckon I'll go." I knew Mama and I knew Grandpa. Neither would give in. I didn't want anything bad to happen. I grabbed my bundle and my guitar.

When Grandpa glared at her, her own eyes hardened even more. "Keep away from him, Pa." She turned on her heel. The screen door banged behind us.

I was relieved to be home, even though Mama hardly said a word all day and I said even less. Wide eyed, Sammy, looking like a frightened rabbit, tiptoed around us both.

The next day Uncle Roy wanted us at the mill, but Aunt Sue was sick. I had to stay home with the boys and do the housework and the laundry. Babysitting and housework was not my idea of a good time. I looked around at the tiny rooms with a sigh. At least things were easier to clean here than at Grandpa's. This time I did not even try to cook supper.

As soon as Mama got home, I took off for the bluff. I played guitar awhile, then sat still, enjoying the freedom of being away from housework and the boys. I picked up a tiny acorn and bounced it in my hand. Ben's words tumbled in my head as I craned my neck toward the top of the tall oak. There was a mighty big difference between it and this one little acorn.

Just then, Sammy ran up out of breath. "We just heard on the radio that Daddy's division is in a real big battle. They're in Sicily, facing lots of resistance. Mama is worried sick." He wiped sweat from his forehead and sat down.

I stared down at the creek and thought about Daddy. He was in danger, and it might be weeks before we knew if he was alive.

"You think he'll be all right, Jackson?"

"How would I know!" I snapped.

Sammy's eyes filled with tears. "I wish you'd go back to Grandpa's!" He swiped at his tears. "No, I don't, not really—but I wish you and Mama would make up. I hate it when you fight. Mama mopes all the time, and you're a big grouch." He took a deep breath. "Couldn't you just tell her you was wrong or you're sorry or something?"

I flipped another stick into the creek and watched it bob away. I didn't answer. With slumped shoulders, he sighed and headed for the house.

My overalls were more than ankle high, so I bought a pair of jeans with my wages Grandpa had returned to me. The jeans were dark blue and stiff, with creases sharp as a razor down both legs. I wanted them to wear to Jake's party.

My blue Christmas shirt still looked new. Being flannel, it would be hot, but it was the best I had. I washed it and hung it to dry in the sun while I heated water and had a bath in the washtub. When the shirt was dry, I lifted the iron off the stove, licked my finger and quickly touched the iron the way Mama did to test the temperature. It sizzled, so I figured it was fine.

A strange smell drifted up. I managed to tuck most of the scorch down into my jeans that evening. Mama's eyes went over me when she came in from the mill.

"Where did you get those?"

"The store."

Her lips thinned, but she never said a thing as I left without asking. A good ways down the road, I looked back at the house and smiled. Maybe she had decided to let me grow up a little.

There was a big crowd at the Johnson's. I had invited Grandpa, but he had stayed home—said he hated weddings, hated to see a man lose his freedom.

I hunted up Jake and told him off for joining up without telling me. "Gosh Jake, I wish you weren't going. It'll be awful around here without you. I won't have anyone to go gigging with."

Jake swallowed hard. "I'll miss that too, but I reckon there's more important things to gig just now than frogs."

I thought about Miss Hilda's family and felt ashamed. "I reckon you're right. But be careful Jake. Frogs don't gig back. Nazis do."

"That's a fact," he agreed.

More folks came up wanting to speak to him, so I went looking for Rita May.

"Hey, Rita."

She turned around. "Howdy, Jackson. I looked for you before and didn't see you."

"I was late." I grimaced and pointed to the brown spot on my shirt.

She laughed. "Not finding women's work easy, huh?"

"Nothing easy about it. I hate housework." I looked around. "Where's Wade?"

People were standing near, so she dropped her voice. "Where do you think?"

"I thought Grandpa was knocking off for a while!" I hissed. Rita had seen the same man in town again lately, asking nosey questions at the roadhouse. She had warned Grandpa. Now we were all pretty sure the fellow was government.

"He's going to after he fills this big order. You know Grandpa. He's more greedy than scared. He can't pass up that much money. I'm as nervous as can be. Even Wade is spooked. He's being extra careful for a change."

I was worried. "Grandpa should quit right now."

She agreed then suddenly changed the subject. "You been helping Mama enough, Jackson?"

I shot her an amazed look. "Since when did you start worrying about Mama?"

She looked away. "Lately I have been. I passed her on the road last week, and she looked so old and tired—it sort of scared me."

I fidgeted. "If you're so worried, you come back home and help."

Rita rounded on me. "I don't like being under Mama's thumb any better than you do, but the truth is, Jackson, she worries about us because she loves us."

My eyes grew big. "You get struck by lightning?"

"Sort of," she gave a grim laugh. "In the form of Ben Tyler."

I raised my eyebrows.

"He came to see me the other day and tried to—as he put it—talk some sense into my empty head."

"You listen?"

"I acted like I didn't. But I did." Rita smiled and waved back at someone in the crowd before looking back at me. "My head's not nearly as empty as Mama and Ben think."

"Mama says you're smart—too smart for your own good sometimes," I put in. "Did you and Ben make up?"

"Not hardly." She looked behind me and her eyes widened. "Speak of the devil," she said before hurrying away. I looked around to see Ben headed my way.

He slapped me on the shoulder. I liked Ben a lot—even if he didn't always mind his own business.

"Glad you made it, Ben. You look sharp," I added.

"Decided it was time to get the civvies out of mothballs." He smoothed the white shirt and tie. "Guess your sister wasn't too impressed. She saw me and took off like a scalded hound."

I looked after Rita May. "I don't think she's near as mad at you as she lets on," I encouraged.

Ben cocked a disbelieving eyebrow. "Then she's got me fooled," he said.

Zearl called for folks to gather for the ceremony. I stood beside Ben as the crowd pushed in close. My face turned red when the groom kissed the bride, not because of the kiss, but because Patsy Rawlings caught me staring. She had on a yellow dress, and I thought she looked prettier than a daisy.

After the ceremony Jake came up to Ben and punched him in the shoulder. "Think you can keep the mill going without me?"

"Probably not, but I'll try," joked Ben before growing serious. "Take care, Jake."

The light faded from his eyes. "I will." He looked over at Maggie. "Mama's having a rough time of it. Even though Charlotte will still be here, the house will seem mighty empty with all of us boys gone. Would you two stop by once in awhile to visit? It'll do her good to have you."

"Sure thing," we both agreed. I wondered how many of the Johnson boys would ever make it back.

"There comes Daddy with my guitar. Guess I better go tune up. See you later, fellows."

I did not enjoy the party, not even the music. I don't think anyone did. Folks were talking, laughing, acting happy, but just below the surface I could feel the sadness. Charlotte didn't even pretend. She hung on to Frank and cried. There had been too many telegrams lately with bad news for folks in Johnson County. I personally knew three fellows who were never coming home. All evening there was a lump in my throat. Daddy or Jake might be number four.

Rita May danced with some of the fellows, but she did not make a spectacle of herself. For a while I stood around watching, too self-conscious to dance in public, although I sometimes danced with Rita May at home. I managed to spend a few minutes with Patsy. Neither of us had much to say. Mostly I kicked dirt, and she twirled her hair around her finger. It was still early when Ben offered me a lift back home.

As I turned away, Patsy called, "Jackson, you look real nice in those new jeans."

Like a ninny, I answered, "So do you." Of course I meant her dress was pretty, but my ears were burning too much for me to turn back and correct things. Instead, I hurried after Ben. We found Rita May helping Maggie Johnson clean up the tables.

"Are you about through?" asked Ben. "I'll give you a lift home, if you'd like. I know your mama would be glad to see you."

She spun around holding a stack of unwashed plates.

"No, I'm not going home. And I'm not ready to go at all. I'm not a holy-roller like you, Ben Tyler, running away from a good time."

Ben's ears turned red. He looked over at the fellows getting ready to play another song. Delbert Slate stood watching them with anticipation on his face like a hound awaiting scraps.

"Delbert loves your sort of good time—and since Wade isn't here, I'm sure he'll dance with you," shot out Ben before stalking away.

He threw his coat into the back seat, and as soon as we pulled away, jerked off his tie and threw it on top of the coat. His squared jaw kept me mum. I didn't say a word until he slowed at the store and asked, "Looks like Rawlings is still open. Want a pop?"

"Sure." Besides wanting a cold pop, I wanted to show Ben the Gibson.

The bell above the door jingled, and Rudy Hayes lifted a curtain and came from the back room. I was heading for the guitar and happened to be standing near as he entered. Just beyond the curtain, I caught a glimpse of someone's back. The fellow was wearing a fancy hat, a fedora, the kind city men wore. I was certain no one around here had one.

Rudy started talking, jovial and loud, not at all his usual unfriendly self, although I noticed he still had the same mean eyes behind his wire-rimmed glasses. Ben never noticed Rudy's odd behavior. He was too wrapped up in his own misery.

The fedora bothered me. I remembered Delbert telling Grandpa about a mountain dance awhile back. Delbert's cousin from Hot Springs had shown up wearing one of those fedoras, and no one would dance with him. They figured he was a revenuer. Delbert had slapped his leg and had a big laugh.

I glanced at the curtain. If this man was Delbert's cousin, why was he in Rawlings' back room?

I thanked Ben for the pop, hardly enjoying it. My worry made it as tasteless as branch water. I climbed back into the car, even the guitar forgotten for the moment. I didn't want Grandpa getting into trouble. But what if I was just imagining things—like Miss Hilda

being a spy. I didn't want to make a fool of myself again. I decided
to keep my mouth shut and my eyes open.

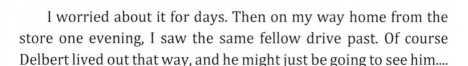

I worried about it for days. Then on my way home from the
store one evening, I saw the same fellow drive past. Of course
Delbert lived out that way, and he might just be going to see him....

I got an uneasy feeling in my gut and finally decided to tell
Grandpa. The next morning, after Mama left for the mill, I ordered
Sammy to stay in the house with Timmy, and I hurried over to
Grandpa's.

"That's all I saw, Grandpa, just a glimpse. But I'm wondering if
he's the same fellow Rita saw at the diner." I dragged a sack of
sugar out of the wagon and followed Delbert into the barn and
dropped it alongside one he had just toted inside. I tried to stay
upwind of Delbert. He hadn't had his spring bath yet.

I turned to Delbert. "Remember how you said your cousin
wears a fedora—said folks mistook him for a revenuer at the dance
a while back. He been visiting lately?"

Delbert spit a stream of tobacco juice between two fingers.
"Nope. But he's Dora's kin, not mine."

"You seen any strangers lately?" asked Grandpa, keen-eyed.

Delbert had pale eyes, watery-blue the color of skim milk, and
now they darted around nervously. He scratched a dirty chin.
"Can't recollect any of recent. There was a heap of folks at the
wedding, but I knowed all of 'em."

"I never liked that Rudy. He's a sneaky sort. Shifty eyes. He
ain't to be trusted," vowed Grandpa.

I almost laughed out loud but caught myself just in time.
Grandpa was serious. Cole Matthers, the biggest moonshiner
around, passing judgment on someone else's honesty! That seemed
funny to me, but he wouldn't appreciate the humor.

Delbert went outside, and I had a moment alone with Grandpa. "Grandpa, Delbert ain't to be trusted either. I wish you'd get rid of him."

"I know Delbert's a snake," he agreed. "I don't trust him a'tall. But just now I need him. That cousin of Dora's is my new buyer. He's a right influential feller, owns part interest in some dance halls and gambling dives in Hot Springs."

I didn't like Grandpa dealing with Delbert or any of his kin—or with Dora's either.

"Keep your eyes peeled," Grandpa interrupted my thoughts, "especially for any strangers hanging around. I'll keep an eye on Rudy."

I nodded and hurried back home.

Chapter 15

We finally got a letter from Daddy. He had made it through so far, but at the big battle at Sicily, he had gotten a piece of shrapnel in his shoulder. He vowed it was not serious, and after it was removed, he went back to duty and was doing fine. I couldn't help but wonder if he was making light of it, trying not to worry us.

I had returned to the mill, thankful to be back, for I had missed the feel, the sight, the sounds—everything about the sawmill. Ben was fun to work with, but I sorely missed Jake. Mama and I didn't talk much. At least we had no fusses. From time to time I caught her looking at me with a pucker on her brow, but she never said what was worrying her. I had quit going to Grandpa's. He had said to lay low for a while. Since he had cut back on orders, he didn't need me.

By mid-summer the peach crop was coming on. Johnson County was covered with orchards, and there was always work for anyone who was willing to brave peach fuzz. There was a choice between picking or working in the sheds sorting and packing. Mama and I stayed too busy at the sawmill to do any picking for hire, but we borrowed Uncle Roy's pickup and spent one Saturday in late July at Elmer Bradley's big orchard picking for ourselves. Peach pickles and canned peaches were a real treat in the wintertime.

By the time the sun had crept halfway up the cloudless sky, I had eaten my fill of sticky ripe Elbertas. In spite of the itching from the fuzz, I picked gladly. I was imagining peach jam and peach cobbler.

On the way home, we stopped off at the store to get sugar. Now that Mama and Grandpa were on the outs, she had to buy it. Inside the dark, cool store, the Gibson hung temptingly on the wall, but I was too covered with sweat and fuzz to touch it. After giving the guitar a wistful look, I went back outside to wait on Mama. Rudy was clerking, and I wanted nothing to do with him. Besides, I hoped Mama would hurry. I couldn't wait to get home to the tub of water we had left warming in the sun.

Mama was just pulling away from the store when a car passed. It turned in and circled behind the store. I sat up straight and stared when I noticed the driver was a stranger—wearing a fedora. I must make a trip to Grandpa's.

Grandpa was not at the house. I finally found him at the cave. I was surprised to find him running off a new batch.

"Something strange is going on, Grandpa. I think you ought to stop making any shine." At his sour look, I hastily added, "At least for a while."

"Look out, there!" he yelled. I had tripped over the copper worm running from the still and collided with the barrel half filled with mash. I grabbed at the barrel as it tipped over and spilled mash all over the floor of the cave.

Grandpa's face turned purple. He came at me with a jug in his hand. If I hadn't slipped under the plank table, he would have bashed my brains out. The jug crashed and splintered just inches from my head. I managed to scoot under the planks and out the other side and bolt outside into the sunlight.

"Get yore sorry hide outta here and don't never come back!" he railed.

I reached the trees and slowed to look back, and then stopped to draw a deep, shaky breath. Grandpa had not followed. I scurried over the hill. My legs were trembling. Sinking down, I leaned against a big hickory and panted. I had seen Grandpa's temper before, but this was my first sight of his rage. Now I knew what Mama and Uncle Roy had meant. They said at times Grandpa was plain old crazy. I figured he was more than a little upset over my news about strangers hanging around the store. I knew he would cool off and want me back. I was cheap labor.

Gnats were already swarming the cold sweat on my forehead. Swatting did no good. As usual they hurried right back. I needed to think, so I buried my head in my knees to hide from the pests.

Lately I was mighty nervous myself. My conscience bothered me. I had done so much wrong lately, I felt guilty all the time. I didn't like the feeling. It was no use praying. God was finished with me. Something bad was bound to happen. I just knew it. I bit my lower lip and worried, finally deciding there was nothing to do but let the chips fall where they may.

I took a deep breath and stood up, deciding to head on into town. I had told Mama I was going with Rita May to see a movie. A good movie would help me forget my troubles—at least for a while.

Circling through the woods to avoid home, I came out on the main road about a half-mile from the store where I hoped to hitch a ride. Up ahead, I spied Miss Hilda sitting on a rock. As I got closer, I saw she was reading a letter. A huge smile lit her face. In spite of tears streaming down her cheeks, I knew this had to be good news.

"Oh, Jackson," she noticed me and jumped up, waving the letter. "This is from Zosel! He's alive!" She beamed. She held the letter to her chest and looked up. "Thank you, God." She looked back at me. "He fled Berlin. He's still in Germany. He didn't say exactly where, but he is safe and well." Miss Hilda had to stop and get her breath. "His friend smuggled this letter to England and mailed it to me."

"That's wonderful, ma'am," I said, meaning it. I had felt sorry for her being so alone.

"His escape is such a story, Jackson—a miracle! A real-life miracle!" she said.

I was all ears. Mr. Caruthers had read about the Bible miracle of the parting of the Red Sea and such, but I had never heard about a miracle of recent.

"He had gone to work at the factory, just like every day. But that day the SS—Hitler's police—stormed the building. They gathered all the Jews, asked them a bunch of questions, and then separated them. They put a white card around Zosel's neck. He said it was because he was married to a German. They shoved him into a truck with other Jews who also had white cards and took them all to a big building." She paused. "He doesn't know what happened to the others—the ones without the white cards." Miss Hilda grew grave. "I think Hitler intends to wipe the world free of Jews just like one wipes a plate."

I could not imagine why Hitler hated Jews. Miss Hilda was a Jew, and she was a real nice lady.

"Many Jews married to Germans were arrested that day. His Anna gathered with other wives outside the building where the men were being held. So many came, soon there were hundreds of wives yelling, screaming at the SS to set their husbands free," said Miss Hilda.

"Why! I heard something about that on the radio, months ago," I burst out, amazed.

"Yes, yes, I did too." Miss Hilda nodded, her short gray hair bobbing. "Little did I know that Anna and Zosel were part of it!" she exclaimed.

"Did they turn the men loose?" I asked.

"Yes! After a week of this, they finally turned them loose!" She shook her head in disbelief and added, "They risked their lives, those women. Zosel said the first day the SS pointed machine guns at them! But they did not dare shoot them like dogs in the street—good German women, some from influential families." She added, "Anna's father is a wealthy man.

"When the war is over," her broad face fairly glowed, "Zosel says they will come here to live."

She put her arms around me and sobbed. I did not know what to do. Embarrassed, I patted her back. Soon she let me go and looked at the letter.

"I must get home. My heart is beating so hard, I think I might collapse," she said with a laugh. "Be sure and tell your mama my wonderful news."

I nodded. "I sure will, Miss Hilda. She'll be mighty glad to hear it."

I had gone about a mile when a horn tooted behind me. Ben leaned out the window, grinning. "Hey fellow, need a lift?"

I hurried through the dust and climbed in. "Gosh I'm glad you came along. I'm about roasted."

He nodded. "Supposed to top a hundred degrees today."

I wiped my forehead. "I think it already has! You heading for town?"

"Yep. You?"

"Yeah. I'm going to see Rita May."

He glanced over. "Anything wrong?"

"No. Just paying a visit."

He unwrapped a stick of gum and offered one to me.

"Been catching any fish?" I finally asked.

"Not many. How about you?"

"I caught a few perch for supper yesterday."

"What bait?" he asked

"Grasshoppers."

"They're as good a bait as there is," he said. "One of these evenings, I'd like to go with you."

"Sure thing," I agreed.

Ben sobered as we approached the cafe. I noticed that he wiped his palms on his jeans. I wondered if he was nervous. Surely a fellow who had faced Midway wasn't afraid of facing Rita May.

The bell jingled when we entered. Rita May glanced up. She saw us, but she kept taking an order from a coalminer with black face and hands seated at the counter. There was a cap with a carbide light on the seat beside him. We had sat down at a booth before she turned.

"Well if it isn't Big Ben!"

Ben reddened, not from what she said, but how she said it—sarcastically.

She called an order of chili and crackers to the cook and then came to our booth, pencil on pad.

"What you havin'?"

Not even a howdy. I guess she was still fuming over the night of the wedding.

"Coffee." Ben wasn't exactly smiling himself.

"Want pie?" Looking bored, she rattled off. "Peach, apple, cherry, lemon meringue."

"Guess I'll have apple. What'll you have, Jackson?"

The thought of peach made my mouth water until I glanced at the glassed case holding slices of clear yellow pie topped with fluffy white peaks. Ever since my toothache I had wanted to try that lemon meringue, so I chose it.

"When you get a break, I'd like to talk," Ben said quietly.

Rita May shrugged. "No telling when that'll be."

"I'll wait."

She brought Ben's pie, flaky crusted and warm from the oven, and as she passed the glass case, she opened it, took out a saucer, and then sat the lemon meringue in front of me.

I tackled my pie. I wasn't a big fan of coffee, but it went down smooth along with the tangy sweetness of the lemon.

Rita ignored us and chatted with the miner. When he finally left, she slipped into the seat beside me and pulled a pack of cigarettes from her apron pocket. She leaned forward waiting for a light, her green eyes only inches from Ben's.

"I don't have a match," he said.

"Oh yeah, I forgot, preachers don't smoke." She made the word preacher sound slimy like reptile or toad.

"Ben ain't no preacher, Rita May." I kicked her under the table and got glared at in return as she slipped the cigarette back into the pack and put it back into her pocket.

"Oh well," she said, "I just started, and I'm not sure I like it much anyway."

Her long hair was drawn back on her neck and tied with a green silk scarf just the color of her eyes. With elbows propped on the table, she twirled a strand of golden-brown hair around a finger and studied Ben's solemn face.

She asked acidly, "What did you want to talk about?"

"Look, I'm sorry I made you mad. I'd like to see you alone sometime so we can talk."

"Why? So you can tell me again what a hussy I am?"

Ben looked as if a knife twisted in his middle.

"There's another customer." Rita stood, still looking frosty. "Is that all you wanted?"

He watched her for a long moment. "No, but I guess it'll have to do."

She flushed and turned away. In a split second she turned back. "I might get off early on Saturday, but I'm not promising."

Ben nodded.

"Iced tea, please, dear." The new customer was a woman built like a battleship, big and gray, gray haired that is. She knew Ben and swooped down on him with all guns blazing.

"Ben Tyler! I've been hoping to run into you. So good to have you back, but I heard you had a harrowing experience. Your grandpa told me about your citation from Admiral Nimitz. I tried to get the details from him, but he said I'd have to wait and ask you. I want to hear all about it. Now, no scrimping on details!"

I grew owl-eyed. That was the first I had heard of Ben being a war hero.

"There's not much to tell, Mrs. Geer."

"Oh, come on! All you boys are mum as clams. That won't work with me. The motto for my column is 'Your hometown wants to know.'" She took a notepad from a canvas bag slung over her shoulder and sat down at the nearest table, looking confident that facts would follow.

I sat up straight and more owl-eyed. This woman must be a real live newspaper reporter!

"Now what happened?"

Ben squirmed. "It was nothing special. Lots of us guys volunteered to stay with the ship after it was hit—try to get it back to port."

"The Yorktown, your grandpa said."

Ben nodded.

"But you knew she was barely seaworthy and a sitting duck for an enemy sub," she said.

"Well, that is what finally sunk her," he admitted.

"Now about the injury. How did it happen?"

"Well, Mrs. Geer. I reckon I was in the wrong place at the wrong time."

"Ben Tyler! That won't get it. Of course you always were the least talkative boy, couldn't string more than three words together at a time!"

Before the war, Ben had worked at a peach shed for a man named Geer. I guessed this was his wife.

"Now Ben," went on Mrs. Geer, "I'm no Ernie Pyle, but I do write a fair-to-middling column, and a newspaper columnist has to have facts."

He shrugged. "I was on the ship when it got those last torpedoes."

"Lucky you weren't killed."

"I would have been except for the intervention of the good Lord."

Mrs. Geer's eyes widened. I didn't reckon Ben had used the Lord's name—except maybe to take it in vain—back when she knew him.

For the first time her bifocals focused on me. "And who are you?"

A bite of pie lodged in my windpipe, and by the time I had coughed it loose, Ben had answered for me.

"This is Keith Loring's boy, Jackson. His daddy joined up in August. Now there's a real story for your paper, Mrs. Geer. Keith has four kids and yet he volunteered."

She jotted on the pad and then took aim at me.

"Where is your father and what branch of the armed forces?"

"Army infantry. First Division. Last we heard he was in Italy."

Ben jumped in, trying, I think, to keep focus off his own military exploits. "Mr. Loring is quite a marksman."

"He sure is," I agreed. "He wins every turkey shoot he enters," I flushed as honesty made me add, "unless Charlie Watson shoots against him. Nobody ever beats Charlie."

Ben stood. "I'm sorry, but I really have to be going, Mrs. Geer." He turned to me. "I'll see you later, Jackson."

"Sure." I gulped down the last of my pie and drained the cup of coffee.

"I'm not through with you, Ben." Mrs. Geer's triple-chins waddled as she shook her head and poured a mountain of sugar through the flap of the chrome lid into her tall glass of iced tea. "You may as well tell me soon, or I'll corner you every time you come to town."

Just before he went out the door, Ben stopped in front of Rita. "See you Saturday."

Rita May shrugged.

When Mrs. Geer left, Rita joined me at the booth. "What are you doing in town, Jackson?"

"I thought we could maybe go to the show. Then if I can't get a ride, I could stay over till tomorrow."

"I don't know...Miss Sharon doesn't allow guests, especially males." When my face fell, she added, "Guess I can slip you in. You'll have to be real quiet. If she catches us, I'm out on my ear."

"Thanks! I'll be still as can be." I gave her a quick hug.

That night it was cool inside the Strand Theater, in spite of the fact that the dark room was packed with folks coming to watch pretty Greer Garson play Mrs. Miniver. Soon I was caught up in the story and held my popcorn uneaten. When brave Englishmen climbed into little boats to cross the Straits of Dover and save their troops at Dunkirk, I gripped the arms on my seat with white knuckles and held my breath. In amazement, I watched as a great fog rolled in, hiding them from the Germans.

A man sitting in front of me spoke right out, "That really happened. A bonafide miracle. The Good Lord's on our side!"

Several folks clapped and I got chills. At the end of the show, when the lights came on, Rita May was crying. I sat perfectly still, so proud Daddy was helping to win this war.

On the way back to the boarding house, we threw off the serious mood and strolled along Main Street, gazing into store windows. A car loaded with Navy men came by, honking and whistling at Rita May. Town was full of them for they were getting radar training at the College of the Ozarks at the edge of town. When one of them stuck his head out the window and begged her to elope, she grinned and shook her head. Good naturedly, they drove away, with the fellow still hanging out the window, begging. We walked on past store windows, choosing all the things we wanted to buy. At the dress shop, Rita chose a ridiculous bright red dress covered with stars and stripes like a flag. At the secondhand store, I stopped and pointed.

"Hey! That's for me!" I stuck out my chest, swaggering. It was a gray pin-stripped suit with a tie almost as broad as it was long.

"You'll look great going to milk. But Bossy is sure to kick the living daylights out of you." Rita laughed and took my arm. "I'm glad you came, Jackson. This has been fun."

"Yeah, for me too."

We managed to slip past Miss Sharon and hurry up the stairs while she yelled into a phone hanging on the front room wall.

"She's deaf and she thinks everyone else is too," explained Rita. "But you'll still have to be quiet. Miss Sharon's sister, Miss Wanda, has ears like a wolf."

I looked around Rita's room. It was certainly nicer than her little back porch room at home. There was a bed, a table, a chest of drawers, and a stuffed chair with blue-flowered upholstery. The floors were hardwood with braided rugs scattered around.

"This is nice. I see why you don't want to come home."

Her nose flared with an unladylike snort. "My room isn't why I don't come home." Then her mouth turned down. "Ben has been dropping by the cafe a lot lately, talking to me about Mama—about lots of things—and even though I hate to admit it, he's making a lot of sense."

"Does he know you're helping Grandpa?"

"I never told him, but I'm sure he's put two and two together. He knows I go out there with Wade—and he's bound to know Wade runs shine. I think everyone in the county knows that." Her shoulders drooped like a wilting flower. "Oh! I'm all mixed up, Jackson. Sometimes I don't even know my own self. I act like I hate Ben when really I'm crazy about him."

"For Pete's sake, I wish you'd tell him. You've got him acting like a poisoned pup."

"I'd like to," she twisted a fake pearl ring on her finger, "but I'm scared."

"Scared?" I asked, "Of what?"

"Scared I'm not good enough for him, scared he'll expect me to change and be something I can't be." Her eyes met mine. "Not that I don't want to change. I'm miserable. Being tangled up in this business with Wade and Grandpa makes me feel downright dirty.

"I want to get married, have a family," she went on. "I don't want my kids finding out someday that I was a bootlegger."

She drew a deep breath and let it out slow, like the telling was hard. "Mama may have a lot of faults, but she's never done anything to shame us. It's us that have shamed her."

I dropped my eyes. "Yeah, I know what you mean." I squirmed, doubting Patsy Rawlings wanted a moonshiner for a boyfriend.

True to my word, I stayed quiet as a corpse, seldom moving about the room, and then only on tiptoe. Rita left for a while then came back and slipped me hamburgers and pop from the cafe for a late supper. It was the best tasting thing I'd eaten in a long while. I decided then and there that when I had money, I'd buy plenty of juicy hamburgers and pop.

It amazed me how the single bulb dangling from a cord in the middle of the room gave as much light as three lamps. I could see to read as if it were the middle of the day.

"Golly," I said, "I wish we had electric at home."

"Brady Wilson comes into the cafe all the time. He works for the power company, and he says they're planning to put the lines out to Hagarville soon."

I shrugged. "Won't do us any good. Mama would never want the bill."

"That reminds me, Miss Sharon's last bill was over three dollars, and she had a conniption, so you best stuff a towel against that crack under the door. She has a hissy if there's any lights on after eight o'clock." When Rita went to bed, she put a pillow over her head and grumbled about the light, but she let me read. I wasn't a bit tired, so I stayed up late reading a copy of *Tom Sawyer* I found on the bookshelf. I slept on the floor and woke up with a sore back to find Rita already gone to work.

I had all the tiptoeing I could stand. I thought about Zosel and pitied him if he were still in hiding. I put the book on the shelf along with a note telling Rita I had headed home, and sneaked down the stairs and out the door without seeing either of the old maids.

It was good to be outside in the open—even if it was already ninety degrees at seven o'clock.

Town was always crowded on Saturday. Today it was fairly bulging at the seams. I figured folks were coming for the big war rally at the courthouse. There were posters stuck up all over town—"Come buy a pie and slap the enemy in the face." I decided to stay and see the sights. I didn't figure Mama would be too worried. Since I had come home from Grandpa's, she had given me lots more slack, and I had been taking full advantage.

The rally was for selling war bonds and pies to buy a fighter plane. Arkansas had a quota of forty to reach. I watched the pie raffle awhile from the edge of the crowd, but I did not have money to bid. One pie went for ten whole dollars!

At noon I stopped by the cafe for another hamburger and pop. I spent the rest of the afternoon wandering through stores and jawing with the men waiting around while their wives shopped. I was in no hurry to get back home. Sammy could milk Bossy pretty well now. It was getting on toward dusk when I finally decided to leave town. Rounding the corner of the bank, I saw Rita May. She was talking to Ben. They were standing on the sidewalk beside his old Ford. From her soft mouth and shining eyes, I knew they weren't arguing.

I was about to detour and leave them alone when Wade drove up. He pulled up behind Ben's car. "Hey, let's go!" he called out the window and tooted the horn twice.

Rita turned and her smile died. She walked over to Wade and had a few words before returning to Ben. She put a hand on his arm and said something before walking back and climbing into Wade's car. Ben slammed his door and drove off before I had a chance to ask for a lift. I shook my head. Rita May was an idiot!

I caught a ride with Zearl and Maggie. They had news from Jake. He was fine and loved the Marines. He hadn't shipped out yet but was chomping at the bit to get into action. It was getting dark when they dropped me at Rawlings'.

Chapter 16

The Saturday evening checker crowd had gathered, so the store was open. I was tired, hot, and dusty. Since there were no Grapettes in the chest, I grabbed an ice-cold Strawberry Nehi. When I went inside, no one was at the counter.

When I called, Rudy came from the backroom. "Jackson!" He quickly glanced over his shoulder toward the storeroom. Sweat beaded on his pimply face, and he kept swallowing, like he was nervous.

"Hey Jackson," called fat old Mr. Jones. "How about a few licks on that guitar? Liven things up around here."

I grinned before turning back to Rudy. "Mr. Rawlings here?" I asked.

"Naw. He's gone home for the day."

I didn't want to hang around where Rudy was anyway. I paid for my stuff and went out on the porch to have my Nehi, cheese, and crackers. I ate sitting on the steps. After dusting crumbs off my jeans, I put the bottle in the case of empties and headed toward home, cutting through the woods behind Rawlings'. I was surprised to see vehicles parked behind the store. No one ever parked back there. There was a shiny, new car plus a couple of older cars and a pickup. I puzzled on it, surmising Rudy might have started a card game in the back room. Mr. Rawlings would pitch a fit if he found out. I started on. Then I got an odd—step on my trail—feeling.

Whatever was going on in that back room had something to do with me.

I couldn't reach the window. There was an old wooden crate nearby. I dragged it over and climbed up. Remembering Miss Hilda's shed and all my foolishness, I was very careful not to poke my head too near the open window. I wanted to see who was inside. Very cautious, I peeped inside. The room was full of men, all strangers, except Rudy Little and Sheriff Thompson.

The men were talking low, but I didn't have to listen long to know this was no silly kid's mistake.

Revenuers! My heart pounded and my mouth went dry.

"Davis, you and Kelly take the left flank. Satch and Cooper will go right. Tom and I will take the middle. Fan out as you go, but be careful heading through the woods. Matthers is canny. He might have booby traps."

They were raiding Grandpa!

"You still think he's working alone tonight?" asked a tall fellow. Hatless now, he was the one, I realized, I had seen wearing the fedora.

Rudy shrugged. "I ain't seen Lucas go by this evening, but he could have when I wasn't looking."

I hunkered back down on the crate with a burning anger in my belly. Rudy Little! The snake! I had been right all along. The Feds must be giving that worm money.

The low voices kept on, but I had heard enough. I had to warn Grandpa—and Rita May! Quiet as a shadow I slipped across the open ground, heading for the woods, and then broke into a hard run.

Deeper inside the woods, it grew too dark to see. I stumbled and kept running. By the time I had gone a mile my lungs were burning. I had to slow and catch my breath before rushing on.

When I reached the hollow, dense underbrush forced me to slow and plow my way through. Briars tore my skin, leaving little bloody trails on my arms and face.

It seemed forever before the hill beside Grandpa's house loomed ahead. Quicker than going around, I went over it. Nearing the top, I grew extra cautious and hunkered to avoid being sky lighted by the pale moonlight. Dropping below the brow, I angled down toward the flat that was Grandpa's pasture. Gliding from tree to tree, I stopped for a second to peer ahead and listen. A faint stirring in the brush sent cold sweat and shivers over me. I heard it again. It was nothing but a skunk on a nightly ramble. I circled, giving him a wide berth.

There was the low hum of an engine just over the hill. For a split second I cocked my head to listen. The hair on the back of my neck rose. I got gooseflesh like someone was stepping on my grave.

As I drew near the house, the gurgle of swift water and the scent of honeysuckle drifted from the creek. I soon reached it but couldn't find a good place to ford. It was knee deep from a recent rain. The low-water bridge was a ways upstream, so I plunged in boots and all, not slowing, making a big splash with every step. Chill water washed over my boot tops and soaked my feet.

Straight ahead, the house was a dark blotch against the sky. Everything was quiet. Grandpa's windows were dark. I banged on the door breathing hard.

"Grandpa! Quick!"

In no time I heard him fumbling to unlock the door. He wore no shirt, only boots and overalls with the galluses hanging down. He held the shotgun, low but ready.

"Revenuers!" Before the word was out, he started running for the barn with me right behind. Panting, he talked as he ran.

"They may have found the still—but they ain't took it yet. I just come from there." He seemed to be thinking out loud.

"What you gonna do?"

He never slowed. "I got a plan for just such as this." He jerked Dan's halter off the wall and whistled for the mule. "The old dug well back there," he pointed behind the barn, "we'll throw all the stuff in it. They'll never find hide ner hair. With no evidence they can't prove nary thing."

"What about Rita May and Wade? Ain't they coming?"

For the first time, he looked shaken. "Done been and gone. You can still beat 'em to the main road. Cut across Roy's place and tell Wade to throw the jugs into the creek." He stopped long enough to put two fingers in his mouth and gave another shrill whistle. "Hurry up. Using the mule, I can tote everything here by myself."

I took off while he whistled again for old Dan. At first I flew over the rough ground as if it were a highway. I had to warn Rita! But going up the steep hillside, I began to tire. I had already done a powerful lot of running for one night. I topped the hill. A big rock stood in my way. I leaned against it and stopped to catch my breath for a second before taking off again. I was circling the rock when I almost collided with Delbert.

"Revenuers comin'!" I gasped out. "I'm going to warn—" He never let me finish.

Like magic, a long knife appeared in his hand. "You keep shut, boy and hug that pine yonder."

My eyes darted around. He stepped closer and held up the knife. "Don't even think it—I can hit a tree dead center at 40 yards."

Chest heaving, I put my arms around the man-sized pine while Delbert, eyes on me, stooped, untied the twine he used for laces, and tugged the string from one boot. He held the knife in one hand while he bound my wrists together, and then put it in his belt while he tied the twine and gave it a yank. I wasted no breath arguing, nor cussing him either, but hate burned in my eyes as he jerked the twine tight.

"This sea-grass string ain't stout as rope, but I reckon it'll hold you. Old Cole ain't gettin' no warning this night."

Delbert saw my look of rage and he laughed. Then his mouth turned down. He poked his dirty face right near mine, bringing the sour smell of his body and foul breath. He drew the knife again and held it only inches from my nose while he ran his thumb along the blade, testing the sharpness.

"When this is over, I jest might come back here and gut you." His mean eyes narrowed. "Oh, I all the time see you turning yore nose up at me. Think I'm worse'n dirt, don't you, boy?"

I couldn't help trembling, but I met his eyes, look for look. "Them Feds don't think too highly of murder, Delbert."

He stuck the knife against my throat. "They'd never find ya where I'd put you."

Silently I begged, "Help me, Lord!" It was another foxhole prayer. Apt as not, God wouldn't listen, for I hadn't done a thing I had promised last time. "Please!" I silently begged for another chance.

Delbert kept pressing the knife against my skin, almost but not quite hard enough to cut. I swallowed, feeling the blade right on my Adam's apple. He laughed like a lunatic. I knew he was just crazy enough to slit my throat.

"God, please," I whispered as I shut my eyes. Just then, I heard a sound and they flew open. Delbert had jerked back and his feet flew off the ground. Charlie grabbed for the knife. I heard a loud snap.

"Ya broke my finger!" Delbert screeched.

Charlie flung the knife away, lifted Delbert and shook him. "Leave Jackson alone." He slammed Delbert down with a jolt.

I didn't see what was about to happen until it was too late. Delbert grabbed at his boot. There was a flash and a bang from the derringer. Charlie crumpled into a heap, clutching his belly and rolling on the ground. Delbert pointed the derringer at Charlie again.

"Don't!" I cried.

"Ya got a point. He's more than likely done fer anyway," he looked back at Charlie, "and one shot looks more like self-defense—I'll jest say I had to pertect myself from Cole's partner who tried to kill me while I was helpin' with the raid."

Holding his right hand gingerly, Delbert pulled a shell from his pocket with his left hand and reloaded the derringer. Grimacing from pain, he stuck the gun back into his boot.

"I'm gonna kill your grandpa." He seemed to take delight in seeing my eyes widen. "Cooperatin' with them Feds will keep me out of the pen, but my life won't be worth a plug nickel long as old Cole is alive."

With all my might, I fought the twine.

"I'll tend to you later. Cole might have heared that shot and be coming to check." Delbert's wicked laugh floated back as he melted into the night.

Charlie was twitching and moaning on the ground. "Charlie! Charlie! Can you hear me?"

He finally answered. "I'm hurtin' bad! Make it stop, Jackson! Make it stop burnin'!"

"I can't get loose. You got to untie me!"

He began inching toward me, his whimpering terrible, like a suffering animal.

"That's it, Charlie," I coaxed, "just a little more." He struggled up, panting and lifting himself against the tree. With a heave, he leaned to grab the twine. It snapped in two, and I pulled free just as he collapsed onto the dirt.

He lay still. With a loud sob, I knelt. Blood had made a big wet spot over the belly of his overalls. He looked dead. My brain whirled—this wasn't real—it was all a nightmare!

Sick with dread, I used a shaking hand to feel for his heart. It was beating strong. He had just passed out. Charlie's watch lay on the ground. I picked it up and stared at the tiny gold-rimmed face and quickly stuffed it back into his pocket.

"I'll send help quick as I can, Charlie. But I got to stop Delbert!"

Shaking all over, I stood and backed away. I bumped into Charlie's shotgun. He had propped it against a tree as he came for Delbert. It would never have occurred to Charlie to shoot a man. I grabbed the gun and looked first toward the main road, then back toward Grandpa's. I didn't figure Rita's life was at stake. Grandpa's was. I bolted through the woods after Delbert, wondering all the while if I could actually pull the trigger. Somehow I knew that killing a man—even someone like Delbert—would be a far cry from killing a fox.

I figured Grandpa had just about had time to make one trip to the cave and back. Trying to go quietly, I sprinted through the trees, dodging limbs and plowing through briars. Just ahead loomed the barn. I heaved a relieved sigh. Grandpa was leading Dan away from the old well beyond the barn. But Delbert was out there somewhere. I opened my mouth to yell and then I froze. There he was squatted behind the old hay baler, and he had a shotgun aimed right at Grandpa. Heart pounding, I leveled my gun. But the end of the barrel swayed like a leaf in a breeze. I quickly dropped to a squat, took a deep breath, and willed my shaking limbs to steady. I held my breath. My heart was jumping from my chest as I put my finger on the trigger. Just that second he turned. I gasped. It was not Delbert. And the shadows behind him were alive with men. He was signaling them forward.

"Cole!"

I jerked toward the sound. Delbert stepped around the old bedsprings in the front yard, calling out to Grandpa. He must be getting closer so he could use the derringer.

"Cole! Glad I caught ya!"

Grandpa halted Dan. His shotgun barrel glittered in the moonlight.

"Cole, I seen strange rigs on the road. I think there's deviltry afoot. Maybe you best go check the still and make sure everything is all right."

Obviously Delbert had made a deal and didn't mind implicating himself. Grandpa turned away just as I put the gun sites on Delbert. I was too slow. In a flash, he had clawed at his boot and jerked out the derringer, but not before Grandpa whirled. The night was suddenly filled with gun blasts. From the darkness stabs of light showed gunfire coming from two directions. As Delbert plunged backwards, Grandpa fired again and then leaped onto Dan and kicked him in the flanks. The mule came crashing through the brush not three feet from me. Shot splattered around me like rain. I leveled my gun on the nearest agent.

"No!" bawled Grandpa. He sawed on the bit, jerking Dan to his haunches as he piled off. "Get!" he yelled at me as he lunged behind rock, but it was the mule that bolted. I was paralyzed. We were going to die! A shot grazed the leg of my overall. An instant later another struck right beside my boot.

Grandpa knelt, pulled a pistol from his pocket, and started firing. The nearest man dove under the horse trough, and the rest of them scattered in all directions like scared chickens.

"Run, I told ya!" Grandpa hissed.

Instead, I braced my shoulder against the nearest tree and raised the shotgun, aiming at a distant flash. Grandpa fired toward the man who had risen to shoot from behind the horse trough.

Another blast rocked the darkness as the man fired back. Grandpa grabbed his shoulder. His pistol hit the ground. He grabbed it with the other hand and lunged behind a tree. For a minute the firing stopped and the night was strangely quiet.

"You get, boy!" he gasped, his voice ragged with pain.

"I ain't leavin' you! You're bleeding bad!" I crawled over and jerked off my shirt and tried to wrap it around his shoulder. I wiped the warm, sticky blood off my hand onto the leaves and grass. There were voices growing closer in the darkness, and he pushed me away.

"I know he's hit. I saw him jerk. But go careful, men, he may not be down."

Grandpa scooted farther into the woods behind another tree. He was panting hard and his left arm dangled. Grimacing, he raised the pistol, propping it on his knees. He glared at me.

"I don't aim to let no stinking revenuer kill my own flesh and blood. You do like I say! Get across that creek right now!"

I backed up a bit and then hesitated.

"Get!" he ordered.

I started edging myself away. Grandpa leaned out and fired. I knew he was trying to get their attention so I could get away. I slipped on and ducked behind the next tree as more shots rent the air. I looked back.

Grandpa flew backwards, half his head gone, arms out-flung on the leafy ground. Without making a sound, I sunk to the ground, trembling all over and biting my lip to keep from crying out.

"Got him!" the yell echoed against the bluff in the creek bottom behind me.

The firing stopped. Dark blobs rose and came slowly forward. They would not be coming if they knew I was there and had a gun. I scooted back against the tree, deeper into shadow.

The man from behind the horse trough came slow and cautious. Behind and to one side came a half dozen more men with guns still pointed. The tall fellow wearing a fedora stopped and prodded Delbert with a boot. With a sour look, he stared at Delbert's body. "Delbert never was worth killing. Cousin Dora and the children will stand a better chance without him."

He came on cautiously toward Grandpa. This was no place to hide. Shaking worse than an attack of malaria, I knew I had to get out of there. My breath was ragged gasps. I was amazed they didn't hear. My legs were rubbery, and I wasn't sure I could stand—let alone run. I crawled to the next tree, heading on toward the creek. There was enough light from the moon to see silver ripples of water and the willows and long grass along the bank. I eased down the bank, sliding in the soft mud, and back into the cold water, angling away from the men in the woods. I would have made it fine except Laddie came bounding up on the far bank, barking fit to bust.

"Shut up!" I scolded loud as I dared.

He barked louder, wagging his tail. Then my heart stopped.

"Hey! Someone's over there, crossing the creek!"

When I heard the yell, I took off running, splashing water higher than my head. As I climbed out, Laddie jumped on me, licking me, but I knocked him away.

"Get! You idiot!" I snarled and tore on up the hill. Laddie whimpered, then came bounding after. Splashing and heavy footfalls let me know the men were right on my tail. I ran left and managed to pull ahead a bit while they kept going straight. I rounded the hill and kept on going, but soon the creek cut across my path again and the bluff was too steep to get down in the dark.

The men were yelling to each other. There was only one hill between us. The ridge ahead was steep and rocky. I threw away Charlie's gun and slipped, slid, and clawed my way to the top. Laddie stayed right with me. At least he was running silent now. The ridge top was just ahead. I lunged for it and then skidded to a stop. A man stood at the top and he held a shotgun. I saw the glint of the long barrel.

A sob caught in my throat. There was no getting away now.

I struggled to pull free of the iron grip. "I ain't done nothin'!"

"Ouch!" The man shook me, rattling my teeth. "Bite me again and I'll knock your head off!" He changed hands and rubbed the hurt hand on his pants leg. "You almost took my finger off. I'm a good mind to—" The man raised his beefy fist.

"Well, well, Satch, looks like you got yourself a real desperado." It was the tall fellow. When all the men laughed, Satch looked sour.

"What are you doing out here in the middle of the night?" he asked.

"I was comin' to spend the night with Grandpa." I said the first thing that popped into my head.

"He's lying," growled Satch. "He's the one that rabbited back yonder at the creek."

"You'd run too, mister, if you'd just seen your grandpa's head blown off!" I spit out.

"Lay off, Satch." The tall man searched my face. I was scared and I reckon it showed. He rubbed his jaw and spoke slow, "I don't imagine even old Matthers would have his grandkid in on bootlegging."

I swallowed.

"What's your name?" he asked.

"Jackson Loring."

"You live around here?"

"Yes, sir. Just over that rise yonder."

"Well, get on home. We'll know where to find you if we need you."

"Mister," I said, "There's a man bad hurt back there in the woods." I pointed, describing the spot. "Delbert shot him."

"Satch, Kelly, Tom—find that fellow and get him to a doctor."

Head down, I headed off. "Hey, kid." When I stopped and looked back, he called, "I'm sorry about your grandpa."

———∽———

A lamp burned at home, lighting the patch of ground outside. I hated bringing Mama the bad news. My feet dragged as I crossed the yard and climbed the steps. Laddie followed. He lay down, put his head on his paws, and fixed me with sad eyes that said he knew something was wrong.

The door flew open. "Thank God!" Mama stood in the doorway. "I been worried sick. I finally sent Roy to look for you." Her eyes grew huge seeing dark splotches splattered across the front of my overalls. "Why, Jackson! There's blood all over you. Are you hurt?"

"No," I said. "It's not mine."

"Whose?" she asked white-lipped. "Rita May's?"

"No, Mama. I haven't seen her tonight."

"I heard shooting over towards Pa's. I figured you might all be dead."

I walked into the house and looked at the brown blood dried on my hands. Grandpa was dead. That was his blood. My mind seemed numb.

There was warm water in the kettle. Scrubbing hard enough to take off hide, I washed my hands with lye soap, and then I sank down on the hearth.

"Grandpa is dead."

Mama covered her mouth with both hands and stared at me.

"Revenuer's shot him." I looked up. "Delbert tried to kill him first. Pulled a derringer out of his boot, but Grandpa got him. Then the rest of 'em cut loose."

I looked at Mama. She stood still as stone.

"Grandpa didn't suffer too much, Mama. He lay where he fell."

She surprised me by saying, "Then I don't suppose he had time to get right with God."

I shivered and looked away. "He might have," I suggested. "He knew what was coming. He could have got away, Mama, but he stopped to help me."

She grimaced and then her face softened. A slow tear trailed out the corner of one eye and ran down her cheek. She dropped into the rocking chair, her hands idle in her lap.

"I was hid in the shadows. He was running away on Dan, but he saw me and piled off to keep me from getting killed—to keep me from killing someone. I had Charlie's shotgun, and Grandpa yelled at me not to shoot." I looked at the toe of my boots. "Then they shot him."

Mama pressed trembling lips together and squeezed shut her eyes. I swallowed tears and waited a bit before going on.

"They chased me and finally caught me, but they let me come home."

I hung my head and clinched my fists. "One of them was Dora's cousin. Delbert was in with them. He caught me coming through the woods and tied me up. He might have killed me, but Charlie happened along and fought with him. Delbert shot him. I hope Charlie doesn't die!"

Suddenly I broke down sobbing. Mama came to me quickly. She knelt and pushed back hair from my forehead and kissed it. Light flashed across the wall behind her as a vehicle pulled into the yard. Uncle Roy burst through the door, face haggard, eyes scared. He looked from me to Mama before collapsing into a chair. "I was afraid you were in on this mess, Jackson."

"Roy, did you see Rita May?" quickly asked Mama.

"No, I was hoping she was here."

Mama slumped and shook her head. After a bit she looked up. "Did you hear about Pa?" she asked in a dead voice.

He nodded. "Yeah. Bob Willis, Thompson's deputy, stopped me on the road." Uncle Roy's big hands were on his knees. The right one, the one with missing fingers, trembled when he raised it to rub his chin and mouth. He drew a shaky breath. "There's law everywhere. I just now saw them searching Wade's car."

"Wade's car?" I stood. Breathless, I asked, "What about Wade's car?"

Uncle Roy minced no words. "His Lincoln is just down the road, shot all to pieces. Looks like a sieve. And it appears like most of Wade is splattered all over it."

My heart stopped. "Rita May left town with him."

I caught Mama when she crumpled. Uncle Roy jumped up and helped get her to a chair. We eased her down.

"Janie, I don't think she was in the car," said Uncle Roy, but he sounded doubtful.

Mama buried her face in her hands while Uncle Roy patted her back and tried to reassure her. His own face was a sickly gray. Finally he fidgeted, rubbed his hands along his overalls, and looked toward the door.

"I'd better try to find Buster Thompson, see if I can find out anything."

When he stepped toward the door, Mama looked up and stopped him with a hand on his arm.

"You all right, Roy?"

He bent, hugging her, and when he stood, he was crying.

When Uncle Roy left, Mama stared at the floor. Deep creases between her eyes and beside her mouth made her look a hundred years old, and when she spoke she even sounded old.

"If you and Rita May went wrong, it's my fault. I'm reaping what I sowed. I been bitter at your daddy, and that made you children mad at me."

"Mama, I'm sorry about everything—about how awful I've been," I rushed in wanting to comfort. "I know I've been wrong, but from now on, I aim to do different."

She stopped rocking and looked at me. "Maybe some good will come of this whole mess," she said with the barest hint of a smile. "At least it's got us thinking things out and talking."

We both jumped when the clock struck midnight. Goosebumps covered my body as I counted each solemn chime. White knuckled, Mama gripped the chair arm and rocked with steady rhythm, staring at the door as if by sheer will she could make Rita come walking through it. The creak of the chair was getting on my nerves.

I broke in, "I reckon the boys slept through everything?"

"Yes."

Again the creak of the chair and the tick of the clock filled the room. I looked at my hands. Although there was no blood left, I still felt it. I thought how my biggest desire yesterday had been that shiny Gibson guitar. It was odd how one evening changed everything. My eyes swam. I wanted to throw myself down on the floor and cry, but that would only make things harder on Mama.

A breeze stirred the curtains, bringing the smell of the creek through the open window and cooling the room. The noise of frogs, crickets, and jar flies drifted in. It was hard to imagine violence and death on such a peaceful summer night.

Another hour dragged by. Although I was scared stiff about Rita May, I was exhausted. Elbows on knees, I dropped my head forward, resting it on my hands as I plugged my ears with my fingers. I couldn't stand the creaking chair and the ticking clock.

Laddie barked. A second later light flickered on the back wall. I tensed. Mama stopped rocking and sat motionless. The engine stopped. Car doors slammed and there were steps on the porch.

"No, come in, Ben. She's still awake. The lamp is lit." It was Rita May! My heart leaped.

Mama gasped, but she stayed seated as the door opened.

"Mama," Rita's eyes searched the dim room, "Why are you still up?" Just then, she spied me in my bloody clothes. "Jackson! You're hurt!" She rushed toward me.

"No, I ain't." I grabbed her and hugged tight.

Puzzled, she stepped back. "What's wrong?" She wheeled around. "Mama, what's going on?"

Mama was hunched over crying. I answered for her. "We thought you were dead."

"Why on earth would you think that?" She searched my face.

"Revenuers killed Grandpa. They killed Wade too."

Rita froze. As my words sank in, she groaned, covering her colorless face with her hands. When she looked up, her eyes sought Mama. Mama held out her arms and Rita May ran into them. They held each other and cried. Ben walked over to me and slipped an arm around my shoulder.

"You all right?"

"Not really—I don't reckon I'll ever be all right again." Fresh tears streamed down my cheeks. "Grandpa got killed trying to protect me."

"Greater love hath no man," said Ben softly.

I didn't know what he meant, but his arm around my shoulder was comforting. It reminded me of Daddy.

Rita rocked back on her heels and faced Ben. "If I had stayed with Wade...." She shuddered. She looked back at Mama. "I was with him tonight."

"Jackson told me. That's what had me worried sick." Mama reached to stroke Rita's long hair. "When Roy said Wade's car was full of bullet holes, I didn't figure I'd ever see you alive again."

Rita bit her lip. "After we left Grandpa's, Wade started sayin' I had to stop seeing Ben." She hesitated. "I got real mad and we started arguing."

"What happened then?" I asked, wondering how she came to be with Ben at this time of night.

"He hit me." She glanced up at Mama. "You were right, Mama. Wade was no good." Her lip trembled. "I still hate that he's dead."

She held out a hand to Ben and he took it. It was a minute before she could speak. "I made him let me out of the car. It was three miles, but I walked straight to Ben's. I wanted to tell him what an idiot I was and to ask him to forgive me." They stared at each other and her face grew soft. "We had a lot to talk about. Pappy Tyler finally scolded us about it being late and told Ben to take me home." She let go of Ben's hand and reached for Mama's. "I said that sounded just fine to me."

Mama gathered her close and tears rolled down her cheeks.

Chapter 17

When I was tied to the pine tree, I had made God another vow to do things right from now on. He had done what I asked, spared my life and brought Rita May home safe. Now the rest of the bargain was up to me. My first test came the next day.

The sheriff came early that morning. Buster Thompson was a fine looking man, broad shoulders and a chiseled face with a firm, square jaw, just the way I figured a sheriff should look. He sat at the table with a steaming cup of coffee and looked at me with steely eyes. "Tell me what you know, son."

I wanted to lie, but I did not intend going back on my word this time. I gulped and said, "I overheard you and the revenuers talking at the store, and I went to warn Grandpa." Now I figured I was headed to jail for sure, but I went on, "He sent me to warn Wade. I was cuttin' through—"

Rita interrupted. "And to warn me, too, Sheriff. I was with Wade that night, before I got mad at him and got out of the car."

He looked at her for a minute and took a slow sip of coffee. Then he looked back at me. "Go on."

"I ran into Delbert and told him revenuers were comin'. He thought I hadn't gone to Grandpa's yet so he tied me up. Charlie came along and saw Delbert holding a knife to my throat."

When Mama gasped, I stopped for a second and looked at her. Her face had gone white. I went on, breaking out in a cold sweat from the memory.

"I think Charlie broke some of Delbert's fingers. He got the knife away, but Delbert grabbed a derringer from his boot and shot Charlie," I said with a shaky voice. "Delbert left and Charlie managed to help me get loose. Then he passed out." By now tears were running down my face and I rubbed my sleeve across them. "I ran back to help Grandpa 'cause Delbert had said he was going to kill him. I reckon you know the rest."

I was ready for handcuffs, but Sheriff Thompson finished his coffee and set the cup down. He stood.

"Thanks for the coffee, Janie. I'll come back if I need any more information."

"You aren't taking them to jail?" asked Mama, surprised but hopeful.

"No, ma'am. I think they're right where they need to be." He put on his hat and opened the screen door. Mama followed him onto the porch.

"Thank you so much, Sheriff."

He nodded. "When you write to Keith, tell him I said howdy."

In spite of the fact that I had not been dragged off to jail—at least not yet—I was still miserable. I could not eat, and that night I did not sleep at all, even though Uncle Roy had learned that Charlie was in the hospital doing fine. I especially dreaded Grandpa's funeral.

Two days later, Mama, the boys, and I crammed with Uncle Roy into the front of his pickup as we rode in shimmering heat to Grandpa's funeral. Aunt Sue and Rita May had ridden with Ben.

"The Sheriff says, as far as he's concerned, there are no loose ends," Uncle Roy told Mama. "He said in his book, you and Keith are fine folks."

Then he cut his eyes at me. "He's willing to give you and Rita May another chance because of your mama and daddy. A good name is a rare treasure. From now on, I hope you two don't do nothin' to tarnish it."

I certainly didn't intend to. I hung my head and studied my bootlaces.

The Baptist preacher spoke as many kind words as possible at the graveside. I stood beside Grandma's headstone in hot sunshine between Sammy and a red-eyed Rita May and fixed my eyes on the green hills across the valley.

At the head of Grandpa's casket, the preacher, Bible in hand, told how Grandpa had raised a family, paid his bills, and when the occasion arose, given a hand to neighbors in need.

Dry-eyed, Mama, Uncle Roy, and Aunt Sue stood near the gaping red clay waiting to receive the remains of Cole Matthers. There was a big crowd, dressed in starched dresses and ironed overalls. Some looked truly sad, but I figure some came just to gawk because of the sensational way Grandpa died. A group of Grandpa's cronies stood off to themselves looking miserable. I figure they wanted no reminders of an afterlife. I was thankful myself when the preacher made no mention of hell. I was pretty certain that was where Grandpa was right this minute, but I think it would have gone hard on Mama and Uncle Roy for the reverend to point it out.

I squirmed and looked at the toes of my dusty boots. That morning Mama had insisted they be polished. It hadn't done much good because of the dirt road. My feet were growing so fast, I realized the new boots—along with my starched, ironed, and sharply creased jeans—would soon be going to Sammy.

Although I realized now why Mama and Daddy had not encouraged family ties, I had loved Grandpa. And he must have loved me. I sorrowed for the way he died.

When shovels full of dirt thumped the wooden coffin, Mama began to cry. Uncle Roy patted her hunched shoulder and took Timmy from her hip. Aunt Sue reached into her dress pocket and pulled out a white handkerchief and handed it to her. Miss Hilda stood for a long while hugging Mama. I thought how not so long ago it had been the other way around.

We stayed until the grave was mounded over, and then we put on marigolds, red salvia, and different-colored zinnias from Mama's flowerbed mixed with some purple flowers from alongside the road. I was glad when it was time to go home. Aunt Sue hugged Mama again and climbed into the pickup with Uncle Roy. Ben offered a ride. Mama let Sammy and Timmy ride, but she said as it was only a couple of miles, she wanted to walk. I went with her. My feet lagged all the way. I was deep in thought.

For the last two days, the neighbors had brought mountains of food. We had a dinner of cold fried chicken, baked beans, and yeast bread. I still wasn't hungry. Even Miss Hilda's delicious banana pudding failed to tempt me.

Ben came the next day to take me to visit Charlie. We entered the two-story brick hospital and found him, sitting up in bed, his belly bandaged. He held his watch. A gray-haired nurse stood by the bed, holding a thermometer patiently waiting while he told her all about his mama and the watch. When he saw us, he stopped and grinned broadly. The nurse took the opportunity to slip the thermometer into his mouth and shush him when he tried to talk.

"We'll do all the talking until she's through," said Ben with a smile. "You're looking good, Charlie. The Lord must not be ready for you yet."

Charlie beamed.

We stayed for about an hour visiting. I kept thanking Charlie for what he had done. Words weren't enough, but they were all I had.

On the way home I told Ben about my vow. "I promised God I'd never do anything wrong ever again. And I aim to keep that promise."

"You can't," said Ben, keeping his eyes on the road.

My eyes widened. I was surprised that Ben of all people would say such a thing. I thought he would be glad to know I had made such a promise.

He waited until I finally asked, "What ya mean, I can't?"

He pulled over and stopped in the shade of a big gum tree. A horse grazing in the pasture just beyond came trotting and stuck his head over the fence.

"You can't be perfect, no matter how hard you try. No one can. You ever think about why Jesus died on the cross?"

I shrugged. "Something about payin' for our sins," I mumbled, remembering some of Mr. Caruthers' sermonizing.

"Yep. He ain't a bit impressed with our trying to be perfect—it never lasts but a day or two anyway."

My face grew warm. I remembered almost cussing Bossy that very morning when she kicked at the bucket. I caught myself just in time, but even then I had worried at how close I had come, so now I kept quiet and looked at my feet.

"All that impresses God is if we believe what Jesus did and trust him." Ben finally started the engine. "You think about it awhile. We'll talk more later."

That night I tossed and turned and punched my pillow, but it didn't help. It was my thoughts that were uncomfortable.

"Jackson, you asleep?"

"No," I answered Rita May's whisper from the doorway.

"I can't sleep either," she said. "Let's go outside and talk for a bit."

The hot night was full of jar flies sawing a raspy tune. A silvery moon lay soft on the yard and gleamed on the tin roof of the house. I leaned against a fencepost and chewed a piece of grass.

"You've been awful quiet since this happened," she said. "I'm worried about you."

I kicked a tuft of grass. "I just been thinkin'."

She looked at the moon. "Me too." She faced me, her face serious in the moonlight. "I've been thinking how we almost ruined our lives." She reached to touch my arm. "We both could have died the other night. Now we have a second chance."

I looked down and nodded.

She drew a deep breath. "When I got to Ben's that night, we had a long talk. I told him all about the bootlegging, about Wade, about the whole mess. I told him I hated the way things were. And I wanted a different kind of life."

I stared at the ground. I hated the way things were too. Like Rita May, I wanted a new life. Something stirred in my heart. I reckoned I would have that talk with Ben. For now I kept quiet while she went on.

"We can keep on making bad choices, Jackson, or we can get smart. Mama can be contrary—I know that, but I'm finding out she's right about lots of things." Rita shrugged. "Who knows, maybe she's even right about the money. Maybe she can save enough to buy a farm."

I took the grass from my mouth. "She and Uncle Roy will split Grandpa's place now that he's dead."

"Then maybe she can save enough to build a decent house. Whatever the case, we ought to quit pulling against her and start pulling with her."

"That's what I've been thinking," I admitted. Laddie came up, thumping his tail, wanting his head rubbed. I patted him and then idly scratched behind one ear. "With a little help from Uncle Roy, do you think me and Mama could raise a crop of cotton next spring?" I asked.

"I figure you can." She smiled a big smile. "When Daddy gets home, he'll love that." She took my arm, and together we walked to the house and went inside.

Made in the USA
Charleston, SC
25 August 2016